# *The*
# PINIONED
# BIRDS

JANET TRASK COX

# ACKNOWLEDGMENTS

I am so grateful to Peggy Larsen for helping me with the editing of the book. Also my daughter, Megan Cox Simmons, for shepherding me through the publication process. Also of great help to me were Shawn Wong, who encouraged me to go on and get an MFA in Writing at the University of Washington, and to Chalkeater Johnson, my eighth grade teacher who taught us sentence structure. Most helpful to me in times past were Hugo House in Seattle, WA, Breadloaf Writer's Conference in Middlebury, VT, and Ragdale Foundation in Lake Forest, IL.

Book I
The Prologue
The Call

January 24, 1940

Will Matthews pulled up in front of The Northern Hotel, his tire tracks the first against the fresh January snow. The bellhop opened wide the heavy door. Will walked straight through the dim empty lobby, past its Charlie Russell paintings, its worn leather upholstered chairs, its cuspidors and ashtrays lined up for the day. He gave the grand piano, snug in its quilted daytime cover, a pat on his path to the bar where Teddy Roosevelt, in town some years ago to sell war bonds, bought the house a drink, and where the dusty painting of a reclining blonde nude stretched above the polished mahogany bar.

"Morning, Sir," Will addressed Red-the-bartender as he placed his keys on the crown of his well-worn Stetson on the mahogany bar. Red was about his morning ritual— hunting typos in *The Billings Gazette* with a stub of a yellow #2 pencil. At this hour, the two men had the place to themselves.

The Northern Bar was practically Will's office.

In one seasoned gesture, Red took out a bottle and settled into a degree of solitude.

Will lit a Lucky Strike and drank the cold, pasteurized milk like a straight shot.

Today, January 24, 1940, was the day.

Will picked up the receiver, dialed the operator.

"Transfer the charges to my home phone, Naomi, if you would please," he said.

"Two-five-three-two," Naomi recited as she punched the numbers.

With the preliminaries completed, Will fortified himself with a deep breath, and placed what he considered his most critical call of the year—the long-distance call to Boston, to the Webb Wool Company, to Meldrum, the wool buyer, the purveyor of his daily bread.

"I expect he'll call back just when my breakfast comes out of the kitchen," he said to Red as he unwrapped his silk paisley scarf and shrugged off his heavy wool-lined jacket. "Or wait until I'm in the middle of lunch. To Meldrum there's only Eastern Standard Time."

Darla, the waitress who Will described as one of those women "who'd seen many a county fair," poked her hennaed head through from the coffee shop side. She gave the kitchen the go-ahead on his standing order—two poached eggs, a side of bacon, well done, a day-old biscuit if they have one. She brought in a setup, unrolled the heavy hotel silverware and red napkin, took a jar of orange marmalade from her apron pocket, put it out at the end of the bar where Will stood.

The telephone rang. Red answered.

"Good morning. Yes, he is. One minute please, Mrs. Matthews." Red could be quite formal, especially with wives: he never wanted one to hesitate to believe him when he said "No, he is not here," or "He has just left," or "I have not seen him all day." As he talked, the silver-haired bartender paced with the black telephone and long cord before he returned it to Will.

"Virginia?"

"R.T. called," Virginia said a bit out-of-breath. "No, not Meldrum—I said *your father.*"

"The Old Man?"

"Yes. He said, 'Tell Will to come and get me out of here.'" Virginia quoted verbatim as was her habit from years of taking dictation at her father's law offices. "And he went on and on—he wants in his safety deposit box, he wants his stock, he said Dixon's 'after me to sign it over.'"

If his father's first sentence, *Tell Will to come and get me out of here,* might have been welcome, dreamed of, even prayed for, at various times during the past ten years, this was not the day he would have chosen. Will had high hopes for today, and tangling with his brother and father was not one of them. But, on the matter of stock and Dixon's being *after me to sign it over,* Will thought his father exaggerated: no matter what boundaries he thought his brother capable of ignoring, he did not think Dixon would go that far.

To Virginia it had seemed to take forever to wade through the hotel operator, then Red and his nonsense, until she could talk to Will. The message from his nearly-eighty-year-old father was enough—she did not mention the surprising appearance of Graylight in the backyard.

Earlier in the morning, when she had opened the back door to set first the baby and then the hamper laden with freshly-washed diapers outside, there, on the back step, in the morning sun with his back to her sat a figure wrapped in a maroon wool blanket and a slumped black beaver felt hat. He caught her off guard. It was not that she was unused to an Indian at her back doorstep. Virginia's and Will's little stucco house was practically downtown, only a couple of blocks from the tracks. The Matthewses' home ranch bordered the reservation. The Crow knew Will lived in town now, knew where they could get a handout. Sometimes she'd say, "All I can come up with is a deviled-ham sandwich." If one would arrive with an announcement: a new baby, a daughter married, a son enlisting in the army, and if Will were home, he might give a fifty-cent piece with his congratulations. They were never a nuisance. They were polite, did not linger once they had eaten, were not like the carnival Gypsies who, when the fair came to town in August, might take clothes from the line or steal whatever was about the yard. But today, when Virginia had taken a second look, she saw it was Graylight. He had never come to the house before.

How long had he been there, she had wondered—she found it curious the Indians never knocked, never rang the bell, but waited—and why had he come? From time to time, Will would say he had run into Graylight downtown or at the stockyards or on a rare visit to the ranch, but she hadn't seen him in years. Virginia recalled some ten years ago when Will had left her, a new bride, at the ranch alone all day while he went off at daybreak to mend fences with Graylight.

She knew Will thought no one more trustworthy than Graylight, but when she had run into the house to answer the telephone and left the baby in the old Indian's care for a minute or two, she admonished herself for feeling uneasy. When she hung up the telephone in the living room, she was perspiring, and not only from her winter coat. But, once she opened the back door, she relaxed. Graylight was jiggling a clothespin puppet he had made, and the baby, propped just as she had left him in his baby buggy, was transfixed by the new toy and its maker.

"Thank you for entertaining Jack," she had said and returned to overlapping the corners of diapers to the ice-coated clothesline. Her thoughts were not of her unexpected visitor, but of the strain in R.T.'s dignified voice, his demand for Will's immediate rescue.

Then, Will's response. She was thinking of the roads, the forecast of more snow, the three Matthews men.

"Mr. Matthews?" Graylight interrupted her thoughts.

"Oh, that was Will on the telephone," she said, "he's headed down to the ranch to get his father."

"I know old father not well."

Virginia sensed Graylight's urgency. "Will should be back this afternoon."

5

Graylight disappeared as he had come, into the back alleyway through the Russian olives, without dislodging the cedar waxwings.

Will pressed the black button. He held it down for a second and offered into the silence one of the pet blasphemies he reserved for his brother, Dixon. He released the button, then clicked and signaled the hotel switchboard again.

"Naomi. Seven. Zero. Three. One. In Ballantine, if you would please." She put him through to the ranch. R.T. answered at the first ring. As Will listened to his father holler into the crackly two-party line, he reached for the car keys cradled in the crease of his hat resting on the bar.

The car was cold. The defroster sputtered. Will fidgeted. He flipped through pairs of glasses on the dash: tried one, then the next to find the right tint to cut the glare. He cracked the window open, reached out, and as he used his leather glove against the hardened waves of frost, he pulled out from the curb. He peered through the low half-moon of clearing glass and steered with his knee.

He left The Northern behind, made a wide left-hand turn at the still-dark Chapple Drug (where he had filled his share of two-dollar prescriptions for alcohol during Prohibition) onto Montana Avenue. At the next corner, lights were on in *The Gazette's* second-story newsroom. Will followed the tracks past the railroad station east into the bright cold dawn.

"Damn, I'll miss Meldrum's call—he'll think I'm nuts," he said out loud, spreading a new coating of fog across the window.

Will punched in the lighter, shook a Lucky from the crumpled pack on the dash, ignored the slick streets. His shoulders at attention, his hands like a boxer's fists on the steering wheel—he could not believe he has been rerouted to Ballantine. But, as the rows of railroad hotels and flophouses, the bars, the stockyards steaming with the breath from the nostrils of the few cows in the pens, the tarpaper shacks, and a couple of roadside dives yielded to the rubbish-blown vacant lots at the outskirts of town, the rimrocks ahead took on some sun. He coaxed his Chevy across the glassy bridge. The ice-warped Yellowstone crowded the foot of the sandstone cliffs. Will turned on KGHL and with the help of a high soprano and someone's piano sonata he settled into Highway 87 like a favorite chair. The windshield cleared, the Pryors cut into the blue sky, and as sections of snow-packed pavement disappeared beneath his tires, he fell to what he always thinks about driving home on this road: had he unwittingly made a mistake? right from the start? would Dixon try to keep him off the place when it comes time to settle? had the SOB butchered the whole goddamn ranch? and, he whispered under his breath, "what about The Old Man ranting, switching horses? calling me."

Book I

Chapter One

Cross Country

October, 1929

It was a rare stretch of Indian summer. The morning hills were every shade of gold. An early killing frost had set the cottonwoods along the Yellowstone River a ripe ginger. Will, his clear whistle following the Canada geese loud overhead, was coming home again. This time with Virginia. He sat easy. One elbow rested on the rolled-down window; his right hand loosely straddled the steering wheel. His wavy brown hair was slicked-back and held in place by his dove-gray city Stetson. Nothing checked his blue eyes from scouting the land as if it were his first time on these sandstone prairies of eastern Montana.

Will's past homecomings might have appeared more monumental. His premature returns from the cold military boarding schools in northern Wisconsin and Minnesota where his father packed him off one fall after another to master the sad lines of Thomas Hardy and a gentleman's ways of battle. Or, his return at twenty, in uniform, intact (if his lungs were somewhat scorched) and decorated for running litters behind the front line trenches at the Argonne, stacking bodies of boys his own age in rattletrap ambulances at the tail end of The Great War. He shrugged it off when the curious—the men too old or too young or for whatever reason had missed what the boys over there called "the Great Fuck-up"—asked for stories. At first, after that 1919 homecoming, all Will wanted was time to breathe without fear that the morning fog was gas, then time to dally at billiards down the concrete stairs at Benny's across the alley from The Northern. But, the war had sent him home restive and with a heightened dislike of taking orders. His impulse to escape was hard for his father or brother to appreciate. Will took off for the Boston woolen mills two winters, and then, another year, jumped a train to San Francisco and found a job as an ambulance driver, and from there, became a cowpuncher in the Sierras. But, eventually he always gave way to the tug of seasons, came back home to the stark willow, the hills in sweet clover, the quieting drifts of snow of Arrow Creek.

But to Will, today's homecoming—although he had been away from the ranch for little more than a Saturday, and only an hour down the road to Billings—seemed the most miraculous. It was 1929. Always one year ahead of the century, he had turned thirty in February. He didn't owe anyone a dime. He'd settled into his old job overseeing the livestock and herders on the place, or as range manager, if you wanted to use

Dixon's fancy college lingo. It was the work he knew, the place he kept circling back to. He'd bet anyone it was the finest sheep outfit in eastern Montana. Now he had proposed marriage to Virginia Hartwell and she, as if accustomed to high stakes, had said yes.

Coming home with Virginia, Will saw everything like numbers taken to the highest power: the low rolling hills turned Herculean; horses at fence posts, their long nonchalant necks overlapped, tails flicking off the last of summer, became wild stallions he had harnessed to haul feed to bands of winter ewes; rock strewn on distant hills by a Precambrian god became every lost lamb found. He had seen this land of auguring Easters beset by snow, swept by chinook, emerge like new velvet on the antlers of spring.

"Think anyone has an inkling?" As Virginia spoke she turned up the collar of her light wool jacket against the air and wriggled her hands deep into her pockets. There, her left thumb, like a child's tongue working where a new tooth has broken through, could finger and twist the circle of three diamonds embedded in white gold on her slender finger. She felt like a magician who might pull a white dove out of her pocket.

"You can bet they've placed their bets," he said, knowing that a wager was, in the Matthews' family's way of taking a position. "And," he glanced at her, "I bet Dixon finds himself off a couple of points."

Virginia smiled. She surmised Will would not be displeased if his younger brother were caught off guard.

10

Will's courtship of Virginia stemmed from a dare nearly a year ago. Will had tickets to the big Montana-Wyoming game for that October Saturday. "Who are you going to ask?" Dixon had baited, offered lewd suggestions. "Wish you were in my shoes?" Will had asked, rubbing in his contention that Dixon had let himself get trapped into marrying too young. Will knew Dixon assumed he would invite the nurse he had been dating, someone Dixon's wife Jeanette had too-eagerly let it be known would make a convenient addition to the ranch.

But, who knows, maybe because she had crossed his mind before, or because he'd heard she was home from Europe, or maybe simply to get a rise out of Dixon, Will said, "Virginia Hartwell."

"Christ," Dixon had said, "I bet she'd never go anywhere with you."

Virginia was a stenographer in her father's law firm in Billings. She and Will had been at some of the same outings, but he had thought she seemed shy, too highbrow for him. Off to the university, then trips abroad.

Will called.

Virginia said yes.

Will Matthews suited her just fine. When he called for her, he was ever the gentleman and brought a small box of dark chocolates, each hand-dipped and held in tiny pleated paper shells, from Burton's candy shop. As she rode off to the stadium with the rancher from Ballantine, any qualms she had faded, although she was as surprised as he that he'd called. They cheered for the Grizzlies, but as Wyoming steadily gained

11

yardage, Will found himself confessing the time at boarding school in Minnesota that he broke through the line in a heroic effort to block a drop kick. It was low and would have failed, but he got his hand on it, and deflected it through the goal posts: "Once I even helped the other team make three points to win the game in the last second."

In the months that followed, he would send a note when he was coming to town and ask her to dinner or a movie. If she knew in advance the movie might be a sad one, Virginia would go first to a matinee by herself so that if she wept she could get it out of her system and not embarrass herself in front of Will Matthews.

"In the family betting—what about your father? " Virginia asked, curious about R.T. Matthews and this family she was about to join. She shifted further in the seat, leaning against the door. Will reached behind her and made certain the lock was secure. From this position she took her time and studied his profile against the gnarled fence posts that flickered past as backdrop. They cast their own images in the long shadows of morning as Will faced straight ahead, alert to any sudden shape, a doe or a young buck, or any wild thing, that might be startled in its peaceful way to water. His jaw was closely shaved and, like his cheeks and neck and ears, tanned and weathered from the sun, winds and snow. His nose was straight and unmarred even after rounds with the boxing gloves his father had hung on a peg in the horse barn for the times Will and Dixon, as boys, required an outside opinion.

Will's mouth was generous, his lips easily turning now into a smile.

"The Old Man? He's right on the money." Will drove for a few minutes without talking, then added, "He's better at the subtleties."

"Oh?"

"He's like you in that respect—good at noticing what others miss."

"What about you?" Virginia teased. She had grown up backing her bets with kitchen matches, never pennies, in games of hearts and gin rummy. "Did you ante up?"

Will felt as if he had, with this proposal of marriage, pushed a lifetime collection of silver dollars out on an enormous green felt-topped table. "Not to any of them," he said. He changed hands on the steering wheel, and took her hand and laced his fingers with hers. Taking the advantage the highway offered, as the car swung wide like a pendulum to the south around the mounds of sun-mottled sandstone, Will drew her to him and said, "But, I have a hunch I'm the winner."

Will had half an idea Dixon would have been happier if he'd not come home. Not from France. Not from his meanderings. Least of all, not today with Virginia. Not, Will thought, as the road curved and coasted back and forth, that his brother would have wished him tossed to one of the mass graves in France. Not that the kid had any more than a black-and-white MovieTone sense of the war. No stench in his nostrils of decaying human flesh. Will felt himself jerk from such digressions. Not on this day. However, when Will had come home unannounced from Boston early in the spring of '24, Dixon, fresh from college with tight britches, cowboy heels and a hatful of theories and his taste of being the only son on the place interrupted, had muttered more than once, "Dammit—you can't play tag with the ranch." But the boys grew up with The Old Man's unspoken oath that he wouldn't beg anyone to stay: if you left you were on your own, and if you came back you'd better get to work and save the explanation. It applied to the boys as well as the sheepherders.

Will equated Dixon's frustration with his own zeal for independence. In that way, we both take after The Old Man, Will told himself. R.T. Matthews had come west on his own shortly after Custer's battle on the Little Bighorn in the late 1870s. He'd been about the same age Will was when he had gone to the war. It was not the work itself that sent him running. Not the unforgivingness of nature. A sharp wind, say, could unsettle a band of sheep, make them split up, lose their sense of direction. It would take days to gather them up, meanwhile leaving them open to predators. He was weaned on all that. No, it was the promoters—the land speculators, the bankers poking around the place, his father and brother betting against the market, the financial flux far out of their hands, which could, at any moment, undo the work of the ranch, alter the real value of the place—that made him skittish.

Coming home today with Virginia changes everything, Will told himself. The Old Man knows this means I'll stay put, give Dixon a run for his money. It'll work. We'll find a place away from the big house, away from Dixon's little blue house, away from everyone. Jesus, what am I thinking? He turned to

14

look at the shy, smart young woman sitting now quite formally next to him and realized how much he had come to count on her. He loved to see her smooth out the fresh khaki jodhpurs on her slim long legs and watch how she wound her brown hair into a soft chignon, fastened it at the nape of her neck. Will was a worrier, a dreamer. He wanted to roll out these worries of Dixon and drought and debt, these dreams of houses and happiness. He wanted her to know each victory and defeat: each lamb mothered up, each stray lost to the coyote. Let their marriage, for Chrissake, be more than the two-bit unions of geography and necessity: stoic pairs of people stranded out here and settled into silence. Am I crazy? Can I see her out making blood sausage with Mother and Jeanette? She'll go nuts out here. She's used to sidewalks and matinees and college friends who trim the crusts from cucumber sandwiches and tally up scores on monogrammed cards.

He's a million miles away, Virginia thought to herself. She was used to a family that would talk its way all the way up the Stillwater on a Sunday drive. She let herself become occupied with a pair of geese beating their dark wings in unison in flight down river and in pace with the shiny sedan finding its way east on Highway 87.

Virginia was one of the last of her crowd to marry. Most had married after one or two years of college, certainly by graduation day. She had held daisy chains, entwined stephanotis in long braids wound about her head, poured thin streams of tea from silver pots and feted friends announcing their betrothals. Virginia was now twenty-seven. Two

15

previous engagements had been interrupted by her father having found discrepancies of pedigree, not that anyone used such words to describe such delicate matters. Such analysis was geared toward things genetic, not fiscal, that might be inherited. There were facts Mr. Hartwell felt it his duty to bring to his daughter's attention; and, once she knew, Virginia, although heartbroken, could not ignore the implications. The brother of one promising young man Virginia had met on her foreign travels, her father learned, was interned in a Texas state institution for the insane, for example. It was something, no matter how brilliant the fiancé, one could not disregard.

Not marrying as early as some had allowed Virginia the leisure and impetus to complete her degree in Missoula, earn her own paycheck with the stenographic skills acquired after graduation, hike with her Girl Scouts Saturdays across the rimrocks, chaperone the YWCA working girls' basketball team on their road trips 40 miles to Belfry and travel on her own. She considered studying law like her father, but there was only one woman lawyer in Billings in the early nineteen twenties and her father had said, "I'd hate to see you turn into a Maud Reasner."

Will said, in what seemed to her out of the blue, "If you get cabin fever—even in winter—you can always jump in the car, catch the train at Corinth and get yourself to town."

"Don't worry about me. I expect we'll have more company from town for Sunday dinners at our house than I'll know what to do with. The Marshalls, the Chapmans, the Franklins, Roz and Alice and Muriel and Hap—they'll all drive out in Muriel's Packard. Bring all the gossip. We'll go skating on the creek." Virginia saw herself cutting figure-eights through Currier & Ives sketches up the willow-embroidered banks.

"Arrow Creek never freezes solid," Will said. "The big pond up by Graylight's camp, that's what you want. It freezes early. When you skate across it," he said and twirled his index finger on her palm as if tracing the rim of a goblet, "it sings like crystal. We'll go this winter in the moonlight."

Virginia was fond of moonlight. She delighted in the long-stemmed red roses Will brought when he came to town or had delivered when he could not call. She dried the roses between leaves of large volumes in the family library, filled soft linen pockets with rose petals and tucked the sachets about her bedroom, under pillows and in with her folded camisoles and undergarments. On summer evenings she gave herself the luxury of her own choices in translation as she read thick novels in French, the contents of which she assumed no one else—not her mother or father or younger sister sitting on wicker chaise or swing on the big wooden porch that wrapped itself around the three-story Hartwell house—could translate, let alone fathom.

Shortly after she began accepting invitations from Will, she found herself curious about a silly offer slipped in beneath the red silk ribbon in a new box of writing papers she'd bought at Chapple's. She'd browse in the stationary and book section during her lunch hour, when, because of weather or time or inclination, she didn't walk home for lunch. She used up several sheets of her new papers in practice. Then, she sent a sample of her handwriting to the Eaton, Crane & Pike Company in New York City, and when the reply came in a creamy, parchment envelope with no telltale return address, and the words "Personal" typed in the lower left-hand corner, Virginia read it as purposefully as she proofread the legal documents she typed. The contents were not handwritten. They were typed by the Crane graphologist who apparently wanted to divulge nothing of herself by penmanship which might detract from the insight revealed to this customer in Montana. While Virginia knew the whole scheme was nothing but a public relations gimmick, that there could be no truth in such divinations, she found herself taken with the sensitive sentences of the remote analysis from Fifth Avenue.

*This handwriting of yours is the reflection of a nature which has already passed through a good many phases of character development, although I do not believe that you are by any means old or that you are much more than past first youth.* (Perhaps there is something in the way I cross my t's—lining as many as I can at once, even inventing phrases that contain a collection of t's, then crossing them with one swift straight line—that shows at twenty-six I am of the eldest of the eligible.) *Yours is the disposition in which thought and reflection are the rulers. With all of your sensitiveness and all of your reflectiveness and with everything that you have of refinement and feeling—your mind is really what rules you.* (Is there nothing of a swooning romantic revealed in the way I loop my l's and j's?) *The caution and moderation, the reserve mingled with expansiveness, the good*

18

*sense and sweetness of disposition—all these are easily seen in even a glance at your handwriting—so well developed is your character. I'd say that you were especially affectionate but while this is sometimes a weakness, in that it causes people to be too much under the influence of those who are close to them, it is not so in your case, for you have in this, as in everything else, that queer ability to separate yourself in two—as it were—one of you to feel and the other to think. In work you are careful and orderly, doing well whatever you are willing to undertake. Mentally, you have clear thought and good sense; temperamentally, you have ardor and extreme sensitiveness and good feeling, with a strong bent to friendship and kindliness. Spiritually, you have a natural bent to the development of ideal traits. Cordially yours, A. E. Graphologist*

As the graphologist had hinted, Virginia had an ability to split herself in two. This morning, as she rode with Will—not her first visit to the ranch, but the first as Will's fiancée—she studied the wild geese out her window. Her mind skimmed along with the migrating birds, their long black necks reaching out before their downy bodies. She asked herself—what will life be like on this ranch with its rituals, its peculiar seasons, its own time tables? With this man she'd seen at some distance most of her life, but, in some ways, barely knew? And another thing: where would she and Will live? There did not seem to be an extra cottage just waiting for the newlyweds. Not even an empty bunkhouse. Dixon and his wife Jeanette lived in the little blue house down by the corrals, and even though there was room in the big house where the senior Matthewses lived, she knew Will wouldn't think of moving in with them.

"They mate for life, you know," Will said, seeing what she was seeing, "and return to their ancestral breeding grounds each spring."

"Ancestral breeding grounds?" she giggled. "Are you quoting from an unexpurgated Audubon?"

The highway unwound and lay flat out dividing the sparse land. There was not another car in view. Will was torn: he could floorboard it to the Ballantine junction, then let it out full throttle on the long gravel road, spin streamers of dust the last miles to the low ranch buildings as proclamation of their coming, lean on the horn and wave and yell out: "Everybody! Here we are! We're engaged!" or, he could take this newness at his own pace: breathe in the dry sage, let the hot sun settle.

Will Matthews shifted into low. He eased off onto the soft shoulder of the road. Loose bits of gravel scattered. He pointed the snub nose of the car at an angle to the borrow pit and took it like a rolling wave, sending tall stalks of drying cattails, the heads all mature, bursting and feathery, brushing like Palm Sunday against the fat front fenders, and, then as he reached higher ground, the low-lying sage scoured the underside of his shiny new 1929 black Ford. Before Virginia realized he had abandoned the blacktop, Will was driving up a steep pitch of uneven range. The land had never before been under the pressure of city tires. The treads crushed branches of sage, split pouches of squatty cactus onto soil, all accompanied by the purposeful strains of Will's whistled concerto. Like a hawk flying low, Will was heading off cross country. He had covered this grassy land between the Yellowstone and the Bighorns on horseback in all seasons, trailed bands of sheep across its fecund summer pastures, and spent long winters hauling tins of corned beef hash and jars of orange marmalade to herders wintering ewes in the protected coulees. But, he had never tried it in an automobile.

"You're crazy!" Virginia laughed. She ignored the deep, hollow calls of the migrating geese, and steadied herself with her hand holding to the strap just inside the door. She pressed her feet to the floor to keep herself from hitting her head on the ceiling. She looked at Will. His blue eyes danced like the meadowlarks that flew before the car. "How could I ever regret my decision to marry this man?" she thought.

Will left his whistled notes suspended as he drove down the grassy gully of fragile, thin-crusted soil. The car springs gave way to each prairie dog hole. He reclaimed his melody as they came up Squaw Creek, the wet mossy stones of spring parched white and coated with late summer's dust. His serenade reached its crescendo at the high plateau. As Will dodged the taller stands of sage, Virginia quelled her natural inclination to ask, "what about the oil pan?" "what if we get a flat?" "if the engine overheats?" Instead, she bit on the fleshy inside of her lower lip.

"From the road," she said, "it all seems like acres of velvet, but up close…"

"Wait until you try it on horseback," he answered, "with your saddle the only thing to cushion you—when we've got a

21

dozen or so lambs unaccounted for and we're riding these gullies all night."

"Only if you have an English saddle." She knew he knew she was kidding.

"You can use Mother's," he answered. Her English sidesaddle was one of the few things Clara Matthews had brought over from Edinburgh. "She'd seen pictures of cowboys in America and thought the huge saddles rude and uncomfortable and wondered how she'd keep her skirts together."

"Will!"

"You should see her ride," Will said. "She could overtake The Old Man when she set her mind to it."

Virginia's riding experience, in contrast, was in the summer Beartooths on twisty mountain trails or two-tracked roads edged in wild rosebushes. She'd tie her fishing pole to the back of her saddle, press her knees and thighs into the girth of the horse. But she had never tried the freedom of the open range. Virginia wondered if such powerful horsemanship as Clara Matthews' was required.

Will slowed to the first fence. He shifted into neutral and got out to open the gate. Virginia scooted across the seat. "I'll drive through," she called out, her voice vibrating out over the quiet. Will nodded and stretched out his arms in what seemed both release and embrace of what lay before them. He pulled the pole in towards the post and released the top loop of barbed wire. He lifted the pole from the bottom loop and dragged it as he walked in a wide arc as not to tangle or allow the barbed wire-strung gate any slack. He bowed in time with his whistling and flung his arm in an exaggeratedly gallant gesture as though he were heralding her to the Camelot of The Great Plains.

Virginia barreled through.

Will called out, "Whoa!"

She pulled up on the brake. In the rear-view mirror she watched what second-nature it was for Will to thread the skinned pine pole back in the loops and make taut the barbed wire gate. As she opened the car door for him, she made no pretense of moving over to her window.

Will was in no hurry. He eased the car on into the tall golden grasses towards the edge of the plateau. There was a quick crackle—like crumpled starched parchment. Virginia jumped. Brown and white and wild feathers flapped up. Wings slapped at the window. A pair of sage grouse clucking like chicken coop chickens fluttered up from beneath the wheels, scattered themselves in all directions.

"You can see how they feel about interlopers."

The ruffled hen and her mate set off a chain reaction and pronghorn like startled messengers darted across the range. There must have been thirty, Virginia thought as she counted the streaks like horizontal flashes of lightning. Will came to a halt. He was so close to the edge that Virginia could see nothing before her but the sapphire sky.

"There's no sneaking up on anyone out here, is there?"

"Someone always knows when you're coming home."

Chapter Two
Wind and Water

1929

The sun was climbing in a morning sky too early for clouds. Will leaned on the steering wheel, propped his chin on his arms, and, not for the first time in his life, looked across the valley wondering where he might live. The sense he'd had the first time—when he was a young boy sitting between his mother and father and behind a team of six strong horses—of protection and anticipation, came back to him this morning with Virginia. They faced the ornery Pryors ahead, the majestic Bighorns rimming the horizon south towards Wyoming, and to the east, the Little Bighorn basin fanned out before them. From this elevation it felt like Africa: hundreds and thousands of miles, boundless, untamed. Golds smudged into far purples. Distant outline of ridge, suggestion of canyon and gorge. Rivers carving their way through a land that could turn desert or ice field or sweep of spring sweetgrass.

"I wanted you to see Arrow Creek like I first saw it," Will said to Virginia.

It was in 1906. He had been seven years old. Land once part of the Crow Reservation had recently been made available to white homesteaders. R.T. Matthews had fed sheep and cattle since the turn of the century—first with two partners, then on his own—on land adjacent to the reservation and land leased from the Indians.

"The Old Man knew the country, and, like an old ewe knows her lamb in a crowded corral—by scent and sound as well as sight, he knew what section he wanted for the heart of his ranch." Will was talking to himself as much as to Virginia. "When the homesteads opened up—and he knew the day—he and Mother were at the courthouse in Billings and she filed on the 160 acres where the house and ranch buildings are. So, we were not picking out the land, he had seen to that: we were deciding on the exact place for the house. The folks had been out by themselves, of course, one time or another, I suppose, but it was the first time I had been along with such a purpose. I felt important being in on the decision. Odd what a kid remembers."

The Old Man was no dummy: he'd coaxed a raft of relatives, a sister of his and one of Mother's, a spinster cousin, a couple of nieces, one nephew and friends, into homesteading up and down the creek. That winter he built the squatters' cabins. In a year or two, he lived up to his promise to buy them out once they'd put their time in.

"The promised land," Virginia said. It reminded her of those old prophets leading their people to the new land. "Sounds so Biblical," she said, but in this case, the land was promised in another sense, and, eventually, as soon as it was legal, back it went to the old prophet. "So, no one threw a wrench in his plan? No one decided to stay and operate their own little place in the middle of his ranch?"

"That wasn't part of the deal," he said. "Most were more than happy to get their payment after sitting out their homestead. But, I suppose if anyone entertained such a romantic notion, it would be knocked out of their heads by the winter and the difficulty of trying to make a small square of dry land produce enough to live on. "

"Did you call him 'The Old Man' even as a child?" She couldn't imagine referring to her father that way. It seemed distant, even disrespectful. But it suited Will and Dixon, who both, she thought, regarded R.T. Matthews first as head of the ranch, their employer, then, secondarily, as their father.

Will didn't answer at first. He was remembering that rare day—both his father and his mother to himself. The impish little red-headed Dixon must have been left home with their grandmother, R.T.'s mother, who had lived with them in the early years.

"Well, probably not; I never called him 'The Old Man' to his face," he said abstractly, "but I can't remember when I didn't call him 'Boss,' like everyone else."

"Not your mother!"

"No," Will answered her questions in a more serious

voice than she'd expected. He continued as if unaware of her interruption.

"We had never owned our own house. It was always a place on the outfit my father was managing, or, the rented house in Billings where we stayed at least one winter that I remember—the winter I was in first grade. That year, The Old Man came back and forth from the livestock camps when he could. He was running livestock out here by then. It was the winter of the smallpox. There was a quarantine in town. One night I was sick—feverish, coughing. He came into my room, felt my forehead and took my pulse and looked at me in an odd long way. Then I could hear the talking in the other room—my mother and my father. The Old Man said, 'looks like he's caught the smallpox,' and then that night when I was half asleep, I heard him say to my mother 'we'd better get the hell out of here.' I'd heard him use rough language with the horses and around the corrals and with the men, but never in the house. Never with my mother. His tone and his saying the word 'hell' to my mother made it seem more frightening than even his naming my fever 'smallpox.' He loaded us all up and drove us out that night to his big tent at the camps, this side of the reservation here. He must have thought we'd all be safer out of the town. Eventually I came out of it. I'm not sure I had the smallpox, as I never developed the blisters. But I remember the danger and the rescue. After that, I always felt safe out here. Crazy, though, because there are a hundred ways a man could die out here."

Will let himself out of the car, his oxfords quiet on the parched soil, and walked around the hood which shimmered

with heat vapors from the overworked engine.  He opened
Virginia's door and held her hand as she stepped onto the
running board, then the ground.  She followed his footprints to
avoid the spears of spiky gray-green yucca, the white flowers
dried and scattered, the seed pods empty and hinged to the dry
stalks.  Once she'd skirted the yucca, she reached down and
picked off a head of sage and crushed it between her fingers.

She lifted her hand to Will.

"The world's best," he said. He thought it far superior to
any perfume he'd ever come across.

He led her toward a grassy hill near a trio of sandstone
towers which to Virginia seemed like something from the
corny western movies, or something stark and stoic out of the
Sunday school deserts.  A place one might starve, struggle to
find the Truth.  A miniature Stonehenge.  A place not man-
made, but eroded by ancient water and wind.  They picked
their way, at time on hands and knees, finding toeholds
Virginia hoped weren't snake holes.  She was winded by the
time she scrambled to the top of the outcrop.

"You'd be some Indian scout," he said.

"I'll toughen up, you'll see." They stood with the ranch
stretched out, a piece of the prairie below.  Will's large hands
rested on her shoulders as she took deep breaths, inhaling the
sage and sun.

Will bent down to be at eye level with Virginia and,
standing close behind her, pointed east.  A run of hills
unfolded like a bolt of soft flaxen material, looping back and
forth along the horizon. "See this side of the hills? that long
stretch—must be two, three miles—all sagebrush?" Virginia

squinted and followed the plane of his arm into the sun. "See how it runs long and narrow, then splays out into a triangle? How it shoots straight down, follows the creek? That's why the Crow named it Arrow Creek." Virginia saw the tough grayish green bushes polished silver by the sun, hammered sagittate steel lashed to hardwood. The steadiness of his arm made her shiver.

"The Old Man knew where to build—in the valley, in the most sheltered part. Back out of the wind. Towards the head of the creek. Not on a bluff like a dude might do today. Mother's concern was water. She feared Arrow Creek might dry up in summer. She was tired of the bitter water they had at the place up on the dry alkali flats of Lavina. Before they made the final decision, Mother sought out Charlie Graylight. Asked him to help her find a good spring."

"Charlie Graylight?"

"He knew how to witch water."

"I didn't know there was anything to that. Who was he?"

"Graylight has lived on this place his whole life—still does. He knows every square inch of it," Will said, reflective again. "The Old Man scoffed at any Indian voodoo, as you might imagine, but he wasn't one to argue with Mother once she had what he called her 'Scot mind set.'"

"I hope you take after your father," she said, "as regards arguing with one's wife, that is."

They sat down on the warm shelf of sandstone and pulled up their knees. Virginia snapped a stem from a yucca plant and drew curlicues in the powdery soil, flourishes absent from her handwriting sample.

Arrow Creek ranch was twenty-five miles from town, but to Virginia it seemed hundreds. Here were different civilizations, different senses of neighborliness butting up against one another. It seemed as foreign to her as the tales told by the African missionaries who visited her church. It was not that she wasn't familiar with the Crow, but the Indians in Billings for the day were peculiarly out of their element. They were stoic figures withdrawn from hot sun or bad weather under the overhang of the railroad bars on Montana Avenue, or dressed up like dolls in doeskin costumes for "Western Days" parades down Broadway and past The Northern to the fairgrounds. They were dressed up like Hollywood chiefs and warriors and princesses waving from floats rigged with city-bought tipis and campfires that blazed with crinkled red paper and Boy Scout flashlights. They did not resemble this Crow neighbor Will described.

"Where does Graylight live now?"

"Same place. He and his family. They spend the cold months on the far upper creek on the ranch, and in the summer they travel back and forth from here to the reservation. He has a government-issue house over by Crow Agency, and he owns a section of reservation land adjacent to ours that we've leased from him for years. Grazing land. But if I was looking for him, I'd try here first."

"Wasn't that odd? His staying on the ranch?"

"Well, Graylight was here before my father," he answered, thinking out how to explain to Virginia what had always been. "When the reservation land was opened to homesteading, the Indians were paid something for it—but not a hell of a lot. Even though papers were signed, I don't think it ever occurred to Graylight that it wasn't his home. Wouldn't always be. He and The Old Man came to an understanding."

"The Old Man likes the help in keeping the deer and coyote down. He pays bounty for every coyote pelt Graylight shows him, and even if he sometimes joked it was the same hide over and over, he pays. We played with the children when we were little, if we were near their camps, but they kept mostly to themselves."

"I see why Graylight never wanted to leave," Virginia said, intent on her dust drawings, "and, why you keep coming back."

Will made no reply.

Virginia traced her palm down on the crusty soil, and brought Will's hand down from his chin and placed it over her handprint.

"So, better take a good look from up here," Will said from his seat beside her on the ground, "and think about what you'd like to see from your kitchen window."

"Let's face east," she turned her head back over the land they'd driven across, "and get our share of the early sun." Or, thought Virginia, would it be good luck to ask Graylight about the placement of their dream house?

"When are they expecting us for dinner?"

"We have a while." Will showed no signs of moving more than stretching his legs out and leaning back on his

31

elbows. "I'm in no hurry, are you?"

"No, not if you're not losing your courage," Virginia said, and although she was quite satisfied to sit with Will and his stories and the sun, she found herself curious to see this family in operation, their reactions to their engagement.

"Not me," he said turned to her and kissed her. Virginia was surprised with the urgency of his kiss. "I'll take my time," he said looking across the valley. They were then only two of the living creatures on the warmed sandstone and they folded themselves in with the light winds, the day, the prairie—the jack rabbit, the cricket, the prairie dog, the crow and blackbird and raven—the unhurried things not seen from forty miles an hour down a paved road.

Chapter Three
Homecomings

1929

As if postponing dessert, Will stretched out, hands under his head on the sunlit plateau and remembered back to an earlier September. It was 1914. He stood pressed, packed, and, at fifteen, had long been forbidden tears. His duffel bag was heaved high on the depot luggage cart. He felt like a lamb singled out for market and braced himself for the vibration and screech of the Northern Pacific pulling into the Billings station. He was headed where he had never been before. He conjured up the catalog photographs of the brick barracks with cinder parade grounds and rifle ranges, the rows of boys in the windowless gymnasium, the mandatory high Episcopalian stone chapel, and the blackboards defaced with Latin declensions.

"The town girls," Dixon said as if he already knew, "will be mad for the uniform." Will winced to hear Dixon talk like that within earshot of his mother. In any event, brass buttons and city girls didn't yet seem compensation to Will for leaving home, leaving all that he knew, leaving Dixon to ride his saddle horse.

"When I was your age, Will, I was floating cattle across the Powder River," his father said, standing high above his son. Both looked east down the track. "Freezing my ass off," he continued. He shook his son's hand as if they had agreed upon something. "Work hard and make your mother proud of you."

"Yes, sir," Will said and meant it.

His mother kissed him in a public sort of way. It appealed to her that some of this Montana dust would be rinsed from her son. He would be a made a gentleman in the manner she had witnessed in her Edinburgh childhood where her brothers were sent to stiff cold public schools in the Highlands. But she would miss this eldest son, his spurts of spontaneity: the clutch of wild spring roses and new sage he stuck in a jelly jar on her kitchen windowsill, his even whistle coming up the path.

Will wasn't the only Montana rancher's child marooned by great stretches of open prairie in the years before yellow school buses gathered up children along the remote roads. After eighth grade, these boys, if they were to continue in school, had to board during the week with town families twenty-five miles away in Billings, or if their families could afford it, to go away to school. The Matthewses had decided (with no divine guidance from Graylight) Will would go east to one of the full-fledged boarding schools advertised in the backs of magazines. R.T. had the names of schools that sons of wool growers from Helena and along the Hi-line had been sent to, and Clara Matthews had written for brochures.

The Matthewses got a good price on their lambs and wool each fall. Each July during shearing Will spent smothering days tromping wool dumped in coarse burlap bags hung from rafters in the shearing shed. It was his job to tromp and pack tight at least three-hundred pounds of fleeces slick and reeking with the sweating lanolin into each bag. Then a wing-tipped Boston commission man would come examine the long staples and measure with hand and eye the cleanliness and strength and make an offer on their wool clip. With his profits, Will's father would pay down any operating loans at the banks in Billings, then buy the next small homestead claim on his list. The more sections of land on the creek in his name, the more secure his water rights. A man's wealth and standing was measured by land, water and livestock more than cash.

R.T. took pride in the fact that he could afford both the school fees and the extra hired hand to fill in the work as his son went to school. Will's father had spent his own youth worrying not about exams or the conjugation of verbs, but about day-to-day survival as a fresh immigrant, a kid on cattle drives up from Nebraska and Texas. He saw no hardship in Will's life in a school. Will had a roof over his head and hot cereal at daybreak. His only chores were marching in straight lines and copying out sweet lines of poetry.

"If President Wilson breaks down and joins up with England and France," Will's father had said that morning at the station platform, "there'll be good reason one day for you to know how to defend more than a band of sheep against a coyote or two."

"Yes, sir," Will answered.

As he left the sheltering piney draws, open plateaus, and feathered willows of Arrow Creek on the long train that stretched out like a rattler shot through the eyes, Will would have gladly traded places with the hired hands that fall. Not that the "Yes, sir" and "Yes, ma'am," the shoulders back and head erect and hat tipped, the doors opened and shut at the proper moment, the anticipated rise to his feet—all the inflicted manners of military school—wouldn't set him in good stead when it came time years later to go about winning over Virginia and Yellowstone Avenue. But, rifle practice at a canvas bull's-eye on frozen Wisconsin hay bales and the victimless "lunge" and "parry high" of bayonet would be light preparation for Will's duty in the sodden trenches of France.

Virginia, too, felt suspended that day, in between seasons—the equinox, heaven and earth intersecting. She wanted to hold herself in this time, feared any utterance might shatter it, mere word turn to the ordinary, elicit the worn response. An orange checkerspot butterfly flickered about Will's closed eyelids. She heard the friction of insects, the cured grasses shift without wind. Saturated in sun, the land circled out and around her like a weaving not in need of unraveling each night.

But the land was old. It had been mapped, claimed, deeded, fenced, sold and inherited and sold again and traded and taken back, mortgaged, leased, bartered, amortized. Put up as collateral. Promised. It had been surveyed and platted. Coulee and crevice had been flattened and squared by pen and ink into acre and section and half-section, quartered into North and South and East and West quadrant, and transferred to smooth paper and let lie in flat files in the stone courthouses of Yellowstone and Big Horn Counties.

On that day with Virginia, although Will lay back against the earth, feeling free and alive, easily and effortlessly breathing, he also had symptoms of a drowning man: his life flashed in his memory. Following fast on that first journey to St. John's Military Academy in Delafield, Wisconsin, came the cold April two years later. It was then, as he said by way of explanation, that he "came home early."

Will knew The Old Man's distaste for quitters. He knew his father would see him pick himself up off the floor of the horse barn a time or two. But Will's fear of his father's expedient discipline was superseded by his intolerance for the assistant headmaster: Rutters. Rutters was a banty rooster, all strut and puff, Will thought. Rutters might kowtow to sons of high-ranked military men or sons of wealthy school patrons, but Will was none of these. The napoleonic master would march down the hall late at night, kick doors open and storm in, to remind the boys who was in charge. When Will and his five bunk mates were the victims, the boys bolted from their metal beds, stood at attention, shivering on the bare icy floor.

"You, Matthews, wipe that smirk off your face."

"But, Sir."

"We'll whip your *butt, Sir.* Thirty laps."

"Yes, Sir."

It was not the first time Will had run the laps wearing heavy wool fatigues and carrying a heavy pack on the icy cinder track. Rutters would stand and count out each lap, yell out the number as Will passed the goal post.

Will longed for his room up under the eaves of the home ranch. He missed the braided wool rug at his bedside. His mother must have made it. The worn colors wound concentrically like the circles set from a stone skipped into water. Will longed for the window that took him forever up Arrow Creek, swelling beyond its banks with spring runoff or ripe with crisp yellow leaves of August aspen. At St. John's, Will's room was a bunker of stacked cots and homesick boys too terrified to admit it to one another. The room looked out on a tiny, crenelated courtyard where bloated leftover leaves were pasted to refrozen snow.

Will loved rigging up one of the school's iceboats and flying across nearby Nagawicka Lake faster than attainable on horseback, but the bitter regimen of the place outweighed his enthusiasm. Will ached for his Montana seasons: the blue skies, the relief a chinook could bring. Warm breezes on Arrow Creek could thaw the whole place in one bright day and set the valley alive again. He found himself longing even for Dixon, for turning their horses into the wind, and racing breakneck the length of the sage arrowhead. Will knew he was talking himself into cashing his train ticket in early.

He had been two years without an honest spring.

He couldn't miss another lambing season: old Armitage with his lantern picking his way through sagebrush to lambing pens, checking on the next ewe late into the night. Will retold himself the tales heard from that herder fortified with a nip of Scotch as he assisted in deliveries and performed a caesarean if the ewe couldn't seem to come through on her own. Will watched Armitage one starry night hold a young ewe, make a clean cut with a sharp silver pen knife across the big exhausted belly, reach in and, as if he were gathering eggs, take out the folded wet lamb. Armitage unwound a length of darning thread from a spool tucked in his baggy wool pockets. He cussed as he held the needle up to the lantern, his eyesight dulled by the blinding glare of winter snows. He gave up and handed it to Will to thread. Armitage sewed the ewe back up with the same stride Will had watched his mother take with the Thanksgiving turkey. The ewe waited, eyes not leaving Armitage, then, turned to lick and nuzzle and mother-up with her wet lamb. She nibbled at the afterbirth Armitage had set out for her. And the vocabulary! Armitage blessed each birth from a litany culled from the glens of the Highlands and the bars of Montana Avenue.

The harmony of herder with his work grew in Will's homesick mind as he plotted his escape from the barracks dormitory (out the lavatory window by rope, a distance not much more than from his room at home to the ground), and from the school and the town (a ride from one taken with his uniform, as it turned out) to the train station.

The Northern Pacific brought him west across the plains—the Badlands, the North Dakota line, Montana, Miles City, Forsyth, at last, Ballantine. Will sat in the observation car with little money for the dining car, ate dry hard rolls lifted from the mess hall. He watched the winter-worn tumbleweeds skip with the wind, then catch in the barbed wire. He thought of the quotation, about a snail that crept out of its shell. It was from his Washington Irving *Sketch Book*—the text for his literature class. He had been required to memorize it. At the time the odd words *eftsoons* and *stragleth* and *faine* sounded foreign. But, the words paraded back through his head: "...*so the traveller that stragleth from his owne country is in a short time transformed into so monstrous a shape, that he is faine to alter his mansion with his manners, and to live where he can, not where he would.*"

Armitage would think he'd smoked loco weed on his way home.

At the depot, Will ran into a foreman of a neighboring ranch who gave him a ride to the junction where the man turned off. He refused his offer to drive him the rest of the way home. He wouldn't mind the walk. But he did not head for home immediately. Will walked overland towards Grapevine Coulee. He took his time through brush alive with new shoots of green sage until he saw wisps of smoke rise from Armitage's wagon. He knew Armitage would open an extra tin of corned beef, welcome an extra hand with the cranky ewes and spring lambs.

Will wandered into camp.

"How'd you smell the sweetgrass way off in that frozen school of yours?" Armitage asked.

Will squatted down by Armitage's black border collie and the dog flopped his white-tipped tail back and forth like some first year man on the semaphore signal squad. Will rubbed the white ring of fur around the neck of the sheep dog.

The dog did more than half of Armitage's work, and in repaying Will's affection, the dog kept butting his nose under the crook of Will's elbow. Will had no choice but to continue petting the dog as he looked up at Armitage.

"I thought you'd fallen for some blonde Scandahoovian and were fishing through a hole in the ice and would never look back—but, here you are, earlier than Easter!" The sheepherder was out of hash, but handed Will a battered enameled tin pie plate of stone cold baking powder biscuits and thick orange marmalade. He poured him a cup of stiff black coffee cut with a shot of Scotch. "Looks like you could use this, boy," he said as they settled under the wide night sky to manufacture truths and predict tomorrow's weather and what it all might mean to Will's future and to all mankind.

Will finessed over a week of freedom out among the downy pasque flowers uncurling their penitent heads and the budding willows until the morning Armitage looked up from rinsing the week's dishes in a bucket of rainwater and said, "Well, things are getting might fancy out here." Both he and Will looked to see R.T. Matthews ride over the ridge with the spring wagon load of supplies for Armitage.

"What's The Old Man doing bringing out the provisions?" Will asked, but he knew it was his father's way of letting him know it was time to own up to his truancy.

Will's father had learned his son was home, but not from Armitage. Armitage respected privacy. "Better come down and say hello to your mother," was his father's welcome.

"Hey," Virginia said as she nudged her dozing fiancé. "Are you going to sleep?" She did not anticipate Will's reaction. It was like a horse shying from a coiled rattlesnake. It was the most spectacular leap from slumber to military attention Virginia had ever seen. He shook his head until he realized where he was—in the sunshine, on Arrow Creek, with Virginia.

"You'll learn to stand back when you wake me, I'm afraid. Armitage says it's nasty, that I'm apt to throw whatever's nearby."

"I see. So, this is something you're famous for?" Virginia was ready to make light of a childish trait, but when Will had answered, "Since France," she left it at that.

"Let's get on down to the ranch," she said and extended her left hand like some prima donna. She watched her finger perform little pirouettes to catch the sun. "I do have this ring to flaunt about, don't forget."

Will was as pleased with the ring as Virginia. On trips to town in past months he had examined diamonds poured from silky pouches onto velvet trays by Mr. Abrahamson. Will had clamped Abrahamson's magnifying glass on his own head, and held the individual stones between tiny jewelers' instruments and studied the cut of each facet.

Will gave some short taps on the horn.

"They won't think to look for us coming from the spring pasture," Will said as he headed down the long two-tracked road from the plateau, straight for the dots of the orchard and the fringe of cottonwoods along the creek. He gave the horn three more taps.

"Now, see, there's The Old Man come out on the porch," Will said. "It'll take him a minute to look up this way."

"You have better eyes than I do," Virginia said.

Will leaned on the horn. "Now, they're all out there craning their necks," he said, not hiding his satisfaction.

"They'll think we're crazy."

"Well, we are a bit," Will said.

"At least I don't have to ask your parents' permission," she said, "or, do I?"

"Not formally, I suppose."

As they drew closer, Virginia saw Dixon and Jeanette on the corner of the porch. Jeanette balanced the baby on her hip with one arm and sheltered her eyes against the glare with the other so she might follow the dust clouds from the spring pasture. Virginia could see Will's mother waving her handkerchief back and forth in wide arcs.

Chapter Four
Place Settings

1929

The crushed gravel sounded its own processional. Will
drove at no reduced speed the long length of it and nothing,
not the shade from the leafy latched arching elms, nor the
stillness that had come over them both, could hush the
crescendo. Sharp rock bits pinged, shot against and ricocheted
off the underbelly of the car until Will and Virginia passed
through the black knobbed iron gateposts, past white pickets
and pruned hedges and drove across the quieting clipped grass
to the porch. It fanned around the front of the big house like a
run of ivory piano keys. Here were great terra-cotta pots of
geraniums, thickened red clusters thriving on late summer days
rid of aphid and cutworm by the first hard frost, covered like
infants each night. Clara Matthews could not yet bear to let
them go. Each evening she brought out the washed-thin
blankets and called the chore boy to hold the other ends like a

soldier casing the flag. First she, then he, like gust and gale one after the other, waved corners until the flannel billowed like April. They let it settle like a silk parachute over the plants to ward off the glaze of tiny ice crystals that would kill if the night dew condensed at a temperature below freezing. Any night from now on could bring it all to an end, Clara Matthews reasoned: there was such a short season.

Virginia could not imagine the level of anticipation in the house before their arrival. How can a young woman know what her fiancé's mother would already know.

Will had said nothing about a ring, but the lineup of Matthewses and Sunday company waiting on the porch to greet the couple was ready to query and chime in with best wishes and with remembrances of their own courtships. All were eager still for what it was about the eye and edgy touch of expectant lovers that recalled in themselves memories of loves not lessened though they might lie dormant.

When he called his mother at daybreak that morning from The Northern Hotel (where the Matthewses and most of the ranchers in the county stayed when they came to town to make offers of all kinds: for love, for money, for sheep, wool, saddle horses, a cook, a hired man, for bets for better/for worse at the August fair), Will said nothing about an offer boldly made and as boldly accepted. He said nothing about an engagement, nothing about a spring wedding. He had called to ask that his mother set an extra place next to his: he was bringing Virginia Hartwell out for Sunday dinner. But his mother, being his mother these thirty years, sensed on the telephone the whole triumphant story from the pitch, the inflection—the absence of his hesitant pauses, the presence, instead, of a confidence as he presented the situation: the guest, the immediacy. His mother was a woman who had listened to men talk, listened to sons and fathers talk, and had waited out their silences. She herself, who in R.T.'s words, could be so 'closed mouthed,' could not suppress some nuance, some lilt in her own voice that morning. It was a voice pleased in knowing her eldest who had come through wars and retreats and preemptory returns had come now to a reciprocal love with a young woman she thought a good complement to Will, one who would prize his wit, his gentleness—one who might survive his stubbornness.

So, when Clara Matthews told R.T. when he came down the staircase smelling of shaving soap in anticipation of Mrs. Lochwood's Sunday gossip from town, and then Dixon when he came through the swinging door from the kitchen for breakfast with his father and then Jeanette later when she came up from the blue house with the proper placement of the salad fork and the dessert fork in relation to the dinner fork predominant on her mind and then the Lochwoods when they drove down after church in Billings (taking the perfunctory highway route rather than loping dumb struck cross-country) and lastly the Treets fresh from the wooden steps of the Ballantine Congregational Church who came out as a matter of habit after shaking dozens of callused hands, each knew what Clara Matthews knew but what none had been told.

The lineup on the Matthewses' porch that Indian summer day in October of 1929 had but faint hint of the plain

Grant Wood stoics one expected to find on an American homestead. The first stakes were twenty-five years behind them. Land had been leased. Contested claims bought up. Post holes dug. Wire strung. Fields cultivated. Roads built. Dams made. Ditches dug. The Crow bribed. Churches started. Ministers called. Children horsewhipped. The school built. Normal School girls contracted to teach—but not to marry, smoke or drink. Bankers wooed. Lawyers retained. Trainloads of wool sent to Boston. And now, collars dipped in starch and pressed smooth by heavy irons held high the heads of the men. They were dressed as they always dressed on Sundays. Clothes an outsider might expect to see in town rather than on a sheep ranch surrounded by what an outsider might consider a vast nothingness.

Clara Matthews wore a soft navy wool and at her thin throat a heart-shaped pin of tiny opals her husband had given her on their anniversary the year Will was born. Jeanette was in a washable navy blue, amorphous enough to accommodate her nursing state. Mrs. Lochwood was all russet, head-to-toe in tweed things the well-heeled who shopped at Mrs. Gregory's in town thought smart for the country. And, Mrs. Treet, her well-tended serge fastened about her, looked more practical than she was. No gay splashes of silk. No skin visible below the neck or above the wrist.

They had watched the couple descend from the plateau, wind down the spring road, flash in and out of view like sun in aspen, then send sparks from the gravel drive.

Virginia had a moment of feeling too sporty in her corduroys and jodhpurs. At least she had not bobbed her hair like her sister. I hope this won't be too embarrassing, Virginia said to herself. She knew from Will what they went through buying a new broodmare, and wondered if they'd want a close look at her teeth.

Neither Will nor Virginia would have heard Dixon's response. "Son of a bitch," was what came to his mind when he saw his triumphant brother, then, "Jesus Christ!" But because he was too well-drilled to utter blasphemies in mixed company on the Sunday porch in such circumstances, he only allowed himself "Well, I'll be damned," which went unnoticed.

"When's the date?" they all shouted before the car came to a full stop.

"I told Virginia—any time," Will said as he jumped out and ran to open the door for Virginia. "Any time," he clarified with the Matthews refrain "—as long as it's after lambing and before shearing." Real boundaries that appealed to Virginia.

"The Tenth of May!" Virginia amazed herself at how loudly she shouted out the window. The fifth month. The tenth day. The thirtieth year of the twentieth century. It sat well with Virginia's preference for multiples of fives and tens. She liked the contrast of the odd Five doubled into the even Ten, the combination of the independent One, the mysterious Zero. Her birthday was on the 25th (of the sixth month, however, and she wished Will's birthday was on the 10th, not the 12th, of the second month). Dates of birth could not be arranged exactly, dates of death should not be, she believed, but a wedding, yes. The tenth of May would be a good beginning: it came naturally, and, fit neatly between lambing and shearing. It was a Saturday. Her mother's flower beds on Yellowstone Avenue would be in bloom, and, if they were lucky, she thought, there would be no late last snow to weigh down the first burst of mock orange.

Virginia would wait to announce her engagement to her friends with the traditional brunch or luncheon, perhaps, she thought, until New Year's Day—the very first day of the new decade! That would be a proper length of time for an engagement, allow time to get used to the idea herself, allow time for all the parties given in her honor in Billings, and time, as well, for arrangements on the ranch for a home for the newlyweds.

"The tenth of May… The tenth of May," R.T. repeated, then sang out *"…the darling buds of May!"* and led the others down the steps and out on the lawn. Pairs of his pet sharp-tailed grouse scuttled ahead of him, coo-ooing and pecking at bits of seed. Everyone surrounded Will and Virginia. R.T. was the first to shake Will's hand. He offered his "Congratulations, my boy!" in a firm tone as if he were conferring degrees, administering oaths of office. Will had anticipated the man's approval. "Well," R.T. said to Virginia taking her hand, "you *are* as adventurous as Will's led us to believe!" He gestured grandly toward the others. "Do you think you want to take all this on?"

"I do, Mr. Matthews."

With his courtly old-world manners, his blue eyes and crisp, trim mustache, his precise buttoned-up vest and Sunday suit, he seemed to her at least one step removed from the autocrat Will described. He appeared younger than his seventy years. He must have been forty when Will was born, Virginia estimated. A man who got his financial footing before getting married and starting a family.

"You must not call me Mr. Matthews," he said, still with her hand in his,

"—call me R.T. or, call me Dad…like Jeanette does."

Could he see her reluctance? She hoped not; regardless of any precedent set by her sister-in-law-to-be, she could imagine calling him neither. Only her own father was "Dad." "Father Matthews?" Never. To make him sound like he was a member of the clergy? "R.T.?" She couldn't think of anyone of her parents' generation with whom she was on a first name basis. Nor could she refer to him as "The Old Man" as Will and Dixon did. (Although, to his face they called him "Sir," a habit Will said as little boys they had picked up from the ranch hands and which was reinforced at military schools.) She worried she'd never call him by any name at all.

Dixon broke into the knot of R.T. and Virginia and Will.

"Well done!" he said. He pounded his brother on his back. Then he repeated the pounding as if calling a meeting to order. He not only dismantled the conversation, but made some ceremony of wedging himself between his father and his brother and squarely across from Virginia to whom he turned his full attentions.

Virginia could see it in the set of Will's mouth, the slightest adjustment in the line of his jaw, while he waited out this performance of Dixon's in front of his fiancee. This was how they looked like brothers: the fine lines about the eyes and mouths when about to laugh, or about to say (or had just thought) something amusing, a crack. The other saw it coming. Each reacted, exposed himself, at least to the other, by the look that took over the tiny muscles in his face, at the edge of his eyes, at the corners of his mouth. Neither, however, could pass up the moment. Each took great glee in nailing the other. Although, Virginia thought, and she knew she was biased, Dixon pushed beyond the bounds of sport.

A look between the two could relay gradations of approval or disapproval. Such glances had become the bulk of their vocabulary. But the bully-bully-for-you back-pounding was new. It spoke of Dixon's just-joined Masonic Temple where he and the young heirs apparent traded in secret grips, pledged fraternal allegiances on Bible, flag and flask. Will dodged such camaraderie. Felt it short-lived like that of barracks and cold childhood dormitories. And having "the SOB pour it on," as he said later to Virginia, irked him. If Dixon had tried such a gesture when the two were alone (which was unlikely since he required an audience), Will would have cut it short: cursed, turned, left.

To Virginia, Dixon first gave a very formal "Best wishes," and added with a grin, "but, Virginia, sometime you'll have to tell me how you ever let him talk you into this?"

Dixon was a good head shorter than she, Virginia thought, but maybe it was her shoes with their heels stacked-up, or the slope of the lawn. His wiry hair had a dark reddish cast, but, unlike Will, he had none of his mother's natural curls. He was stocky, built like a wrestler, which made him seem not as short as he was.

51

"Don't tell me he did this on a bet?" she said and smiled at Will.

"No, not this time," Dixon said, "he didn't even stoop to consult his more experienced brother. He won't admit—will you, Will?—what wisdom I offer on the intricacies of matrimony." There was something of a paradox about him—an odd mix of bravado (Will would have a stronger word for it) and a manner she didn't trust, but, all the same an appealing boyishness.

"Maybe his gambling days…" she said and shrugged rather than finish her sentence, wondering if she was going too far.

"But the jackpot? " He looked off as if delivering lines off stage. "How? It escapes me." If he meant it as a compliment to one, he meant it as a rebuke to the other.

"That may well be," Will said.

Virginia blushed. She wasn't used to being the center of attention of three men whom she began to suspect might be vying for something quite apart from herself.

Jeanette stood back while her husband spoke. It was not that she was shy. She was still in awe of her husband and vicariously relished what she considered his smooth skill in all situations, taking the upper hand with his older brother and this refined girlfriend, whose accent derived from books and the luxury of second-generation parents. Jeanette could only wonder why God was sending her this sister-in-law. She thought a person like Virginia might make a fine neighbor, but found the idea of Virginia as sister-in-law disconcerting. Jeanette was satisfied biding her time until she might ascend to mistress of the big house as Dixon had assured her she would, but she didn't know now what would be required of her to secure the position. It was one thing to have a brother-in-law who whistled to himself out in the sheep camps, but all together another to have one with intentions of bringing an additional household to the place. And, with a wife so self-assured, Jeanette thought, who might expect the eldest son would naturally expect nothing less than first dibs on the big house.

Jeanette had come as a young girl from the Dakotas when her father won by lottery the opportunity to prove-up on 40 acres of tough, greasewood land in a government irrigation development opened up to optimistic hard-working German farmers. Jeanette had worked hard on her father's gumbo fields of sugar beets and had worked hard to rid herself of her German accent. To that end and to the dismay of her parents she discarded their German-speaking Lutheran church because, she said, she thought people backward who hid inside a language from a place they'd never see again. Jeanette had aspirations, but one wasn't vacationing on the Rhine. She joined, instead, the Ballantine Congregational Church.

She had eyed Dixon sitting in the pew between his parents, and season after season getting on and off the train in his military school uniform, and then driving fast through town, coming home from the ag' college in Bozeman with schemes from fattening rations for slaughter lambs to mechanized shearing. Jeanette quit high school when it became necessary for her to take a job in town as well as work on the farm—seeding, irrigating, weeding, then topping the beets—rather than spend her hours with books. College wasn't a consideration for her brother, let alone herself. She was satisfied with the bank job—its carpets and oak desks and polished glass, its safes and locks and precautions and its handling of all the town's money. Also, it gave her access to the vital statistics of the young men in the county. Not that you needed bank balances to judge a family's worth. You could gauge that from the size of a ranch, the number of sheep or cattle and, in the case of the Matthewses, by the number of wagons heavy with wool pulled by teams of horses to the train station each fall. Jeanette worked hard not only at the bank but also with the responsibility of not letting herself fall in the trap of many pretty girls her age. She kept herself from getting pregnant by one of the gangly farm boys whose sexual imagination was fueled by little more than watching the buck rams turned in with a band of ewes.

Aware of Jeanette's distance, Virginia stepped aside to open up the circle. While Jeanette accepted the gesture, she moved between R.T. and Virginia. Dixon and Jeanette flanked The Old Man, Virginia thought, like acolytes. When Dixon was finished with his pounding and his slick talk, Jeanette cleared her throat and said, "May I offer my congratulations?" as perfunctorily as she might have addressed someone opening a new account at the bank and Virginia deflected the talk away from Dixon's professed expertise on matrimony.

Virginia turned then toward Clara Matthews. Will's mother looked genuinely pleased, Virginia thought, and that put her at ease more than any words of welcome. Their eyes met, and as if that broke the spell, she walked down the steps and joined the group and said: "Look how happy you've made Will." The two women together looked admiringly at Will. Virginia felt, more than with the other members of the family, as if she'd been granted a form of joint-tenancy.

"I've not seen him so…" and her future mother-in-law hesitated in search of the right word, "so light-hearted in a long time." Aware of these two admirers he shifted around so he could put his other arm around his mother. Clara Matthews leaned forward and said to Virginia, "I hope you'll have many years of happiness with Will—and, with all of us." Virginia bent down to hear her and when Clara Matthews lifted her head slightly, she realized the older woman intended to kiss her on the cheek. It was the most demonstrative she had seen Will's mother. It wasn't a family that went about kissing each other.

"Promise to bring your mother and father out soon for a Sunday," Clara Matthews said as Virginia straightened up, "before the weather turns." Then added, "of course, we'll call on them in town as well."

Virginia looked at Clara Matthews.

Clara Matthews was a woman of formal bearing. She had left Edinburgh only in the geographical sense. Though she had unearthed bullets and arrowheads in her garden beds, she set her mind to ordering a civilized household, overseen by the ghost of Calvin rather than Custer. This dictated that all accouterments—the rough language, the off-color stories, the manure-splattered clothes—required to run 8,500 head of sheep and any number of men in this new place must be left in the back storm porch when entering her tall white-frame house that at dusk resembled a landlocked lighthouse.

She required no center stage like R.T. and Dixon. Yet, she expected to be heard. What has it been like, Virginia wondered, out here with these men? Someday she'd ask her to tell her own story of leaving her home in Scotland. Whenever Virginia left home, whenever she even thought about it, or thought about other people leaving home, she felt homesick. She could be overcome as she waved goodbye to her mother and father at the train station even knowing—the pass in her wallet—she could come home anytime she pleased. It occurred to her that she would miss them terribly. She felt lonely then as she stood enveloped by welcoming wishes from people she knew only second hand. Some had made her nervous, and she realized she made some of them nervous. She was not used to having such an effect on others. But, as quickly as the possibility of homesickness had arisen, it disappeared. The thought of waking up here—every morning with Will—replaced it. It would be strange: a husband who would likely leave before daybreak, a man with no hours etched on the beveled glass of an office door, a man not walking home along elm-lined walks precisely at noon. No telephone call explaining any delay. A million miles from Yellowstone Avenue.

"Come inside. Come inside," R.T. said. "We must have a toast," he insisted merrily, in a tone of a man used to having his will be done at Sunday dinners and when his first born son had made such a first rate decision, "even though it is Sunday—and, the ladies must join us."

Chapter Five

A Sunday Toast

1929

At R.T.'s invitation, everyone followed Will and Virginia through the opened front door, into the foyer. The door reminded Virginia of hers at home: there was a thick pane of glass set into polished wood, and on the inside, a gauzy lace curtain. She imagined in winter there would be a velvet drape to thwart the cold. Dixon moved into position putting coats and hats in the hall closet. A full-length beveled mirror hung at a slant to the ivory papered walls. Facing it, a threadbare oriental rug hung from brass rings. A short hallway branched off to R.T.'s office. The dining room was in the middle of the house, and was reached on such occasions from the living room. Although Will and Virginia were the first into the dining room, they moved to one side until Clara directed the guests to their seats. Virginia looked north out the spotless plate glass windows to the front porch and beyond to the way they had come.  On the east side of the room, a heavy door swung to the pantry and kitchen and the narrow stairway to the maids' rooms.  On the south wall, double oak doors slid like eavesdroppers in smooth wooden grooves between the walls. One could choose between privacy, she mused, or warmth from the maroon brick fireplace in the living room.

Will held Virginia's hand lightly in his.  They stood by the starchy linen-covered oval table.  She wondered if, when Will was a boy, they had left the leaves in, giving the four of the family big pastures of mahogany stretched out between them, barely allowing knobby arms of little boys to reach the distance to pass the cold, salted butter, then the bread, to one parent or the other.  She could not yet know all she wanted to about this family.  She tried to picture the dailiness of the Matthewses.  Did they eat every meal at the big table?  Or did they take their January bowls of soup in the steamy kitchen?

"Every day. Right here," Will said as if reading her mind. "Unless The Old Man was out—off to the sheep camps or in town," Will leaned forward slightly, both hands on the back of a chair, "then Mother let us eat on trays in front of the fireplace."

"But not when your father was home?"

"No. It reminded him, he said, of days when he had no choice but a tin pie plate on his knee." Will shifted his weight, and rested his hands lightly on Virginia's shoulders. "Mother would turn it into a winter picnic: she'd spread her wide tartan wool blanket on the rug.  She'd let us toast marshmallows, drop them in our hot chocolate."

My kind of toast, she thought, but wondered what to do about the one R.T. was proposing.

They weren't alone long. The others came into the dining room in pairs, talking more than listening.

"Heard Simms ended up at thirty-one?"

Lochwood and R.T. stood at the doorway, letting the ladies go in first.

"You must know," R.T. answered, "the man's on your board."

"I wouldn't hear it from him," Lochwood said. "You wouldn't expect much talk from Simms about a drop like that. Must be down six, seven cents from last year?"

"Seven," R.T. said. "It wasn't the year to hold out."

There was no laughter at the other man's loss. The wool market rarely played favorites. But Will knew his father silently congratulated himself at beating Simms even a quarter of a cent. The two had long been competitors. He knew such a drop in the market didn't bode well for anyone.

"Doubt that will stop Simms for long," Dixon said as he came into the room after Jeanette.

Clara Matthews stood at the east end of the room to direct the seating. It looked as if she were deciding then and there whom she would pair up, but she had, of course, decided much earlier.

Lochwood raised his bushy eyebrows at Dixon. "You're right," he said and lowered his voice, "I heard he turned around and picked up that bottom land this side of Lodge Grass. The Whitebird place."

Lochwood wasn't telling R.T. anything new, Will surmised.

"Well, let's see—Mrs. Lochwood," Clara said, "you'll be at R.T.'s right."

Fanny Lochwood beamed at R.T. "Delighted. Delighted," she said. His right hand was on the back of her chair, holding it for her. Once Clara made official the designation, Mrs. Lochwood stepped over to the place she had come to expect, and the woman in all her russety tweeds raised her skirts slightly as if it were a ball gown, and lowered herself into place. R.T. gently moved the chair as she put her hands at the side to guide it along. "There. Just right," she said brightly as if she had accomplished a great deal.

Dixon said what had crossed R.T.'s mind: "That's prime. Down on the Little Horn. I'd like to get my hands on it one day."

"It's a rattlin' good time to buy," Will said, "if a man had cash."

"That's what bankers are for," Dixon said, as he slapped Lochwood on the shoulder.

The men laughed.

Virginia was used to running into Fanny Lochwood at church or at any number of teas. Mrs. Lochwood was a new member of Virginia's mother's art club, a group of older wool crepe women given to self-education by means of laborious winter afternoon book reports on Michelangelo's sculpture, *per esempio*. They were not yet set on their response to the 1913 Armory Show in New York City, which Mrs. Lochwood claimed as one of her favorite moments in art history. She had not seen it for herself, but relied on clippings and a scrawled note from a dotty Central Park aunt: "Darling, what a fuss over nothing!" But, from then on, Mrs. Lochwood was apt to compare any nude to Duchamp's startlingly mechanical one that was the talk of the show. She prided herself on knowing the latest rage, the latest person to move to town. She was always throwing a tea for one of Mr. Lochwood's list of debts or debtors. Virginia was intrigued that R.T. paid attention to her chatter on form and function.

"Exquisite!" Mrs. Lochwood's eyes settled on the bowl of cut asters, "It's a Rachel Ruysch painting. Isn't it?" She turned to R.T. as if she expected him to be familiar with eighteenth century women painters. "Clara!" she continued, not waiting for any response, "I covet that English garden of yours!"

"Scottish." Clara Matthews did not allow the proper nouns "Scotland" and "England" used interchangeably. "It's a *Scottish* garden." Virginia wondered what distinguished it from an English garden besides the pink heather borders grown fat as hedgehogs. Did its nationality spring from the gardener or the garden? In any event, Virginia could see that Clara Matthews and Fanny took the other's presence quite matter-of-factly. Side by side, Clara Matthews looked the more practical one.

"Do you garden, Mrs. Lochwood?" Virginia asked from the sideboard where she and Will had moved.

"Only bulbs, dear," Fanny Lochwood laughed. "I love to order them in the winter, can't resist when the catalog comes, then practically forget to plant them when they arrive in the fall."

"Your eyes, my dear, are greener than your thumbs," Mr. Lochwood said from the opposite side of the room.

"Usually Mr. Lochwood is the one to spade up the frozen ground. It's dreadful."

"I order sticks of dynamite like the gravediggers use in January," Mr. Lochwood added in a lowered voice. Only Virginia heard him.

"But, irises in spring! It's worth it, don't you think, Clara?"

"If you're not gaining on them, you're losing ground," Dixon said to Lochwood, easily keeping his mind on real estate, not art and gardening, as he restated one of R.T.'s favorite maxims.

"Nothing's ever big enough for Dixon," Will leaned closer and said for Virginia to hear. To the men who were standing until the women were seated, he said, "Depends on the price they stab you with."

Virginia saw that Will and Dixon didn't speak directly to one another, but aimed their comments at R.T., Lochwood, or both.

"Simms came out okay on that one, I can assure you," Lochwood said. "He's a pro at buying land on the reservation."

"And, Mrs. Treet, you'll be at R.T.'s left," Clara continued.

Will helped his former Sunday school teacher, one of his mother's most devoted disciples, with her chair. R.T. began to open and close doors on the buffet. He interrupted his wife.

"Clara, excuse me, but where have you hidden my wine glasses?" And muttered good-naturedly, "My very own Carry Nation at work." Then to Dixon he said, "Would you please go down to the cellar and secure a bottle of my fine plum wine?" Will was pleased to see his father ask his brother on his behalf. R.T. was known for never giving a flat order. The ranch hands in particular respected him for this. They knew he'd been a ranch hand, a cowpuncher himself. His polite requests, as his family knew, carried the same expectation as any command.

"And, Mr. Lochwood you'll be here." Clara indicated the chair to her right. The jovial, slightly pearish banker bowed slightly in acknowledgment.

"He's all soft soap," Will whispered to Virginia, "until someone can't pay."

Mr. Lochwood had been R.T.'s banker since the earliest day, granted him a line of credit against the land to buy the first bands of sheep. Virginia's father knew Hugo Lochwood to be shrewd in real estate along with his position at First National: the two— foreclosure, then acquisition—often went hand-in-glove. She supposed that both R.T. and Dixon saw him at Masonic meetings.

"Mr. Treet," Clara Matthews said and patted the chair to her left. The Treets were seated at the Matthewses' dining table as they were most Sundays after church.

The Matthewses were of the democratic persuasion that referred to ministers as ministers, not pastor or father. They called them "Mister," rather than "Reverend." But, in writing or addressing an envelope or wedding invitation, they followed the proper "The Reverend." Whenever R.T. wrote "The

Reverend Treet" in his bold handwriting, it pleased him that the three words relied on "e" for the solitary vowel. He liked the sound and he was apt to call him "The Reverend Treet," especially when the matters were scholarly.

R.T. took communion the few times it was offered in the Congregational Church, paid his yearly pledge and then some, but abstained from voting at the meetings. The Reverend Treet never questioned R.T. on why he'd never chosen to become a sign-on-the-dotted line member of the church, as Clara Matthews had when the church was first built.

As long as Will could remember, the family had attended church at the white, wooden frame Ballantine church. They sat on the aisle, three-quarters of the way back, on solid oak pews that circled the podium like a half-moon. R.T. and Clara Matthews, the boys between them, sang "When morning gilds the skies…" and recited in unison "The Lord is my shepherd…" with all its green pastures and still waters, and listened to Treet's sermons salted with sheep and pilgrims. But during responsive readings, R.T. kept quiet. He disliked predetermined answers to questions. He thought it leaning toward Catholicism with all answers coming down from "some Goddamn Pope," he would say, if one of the boys asked why he was silent while the congregation boomed out the answers printed in the program.

But R.T. relished his philosophical dialogues with Treet late into a Sunday over a dram or two of cognac. "He's my Virgil," he said to Virginia by way of explanation, and nodded toward the bookish man who was standing across the table from her. Treet was a man who might struggle to make payments on his land, but not with his interpretations of the Bible or Dante.

"Not that I'd need a guide through the underworld," R.T. added. "Hell, I'll know ninety-nine percent of them."

The Reverend Treet was quick to quote (and this was a routine they performed as often as they could work it in)— *There were ninety and nine that safely lay / In the shelter of the fold, / But one was out on the hills away, / Far off from the gates of gold— / Away on the mountains wild and bare, Away from the tender Shepherd's care..."* But once started on the possibility of purgatory, R.T. charged on regardless and took an opportunity to rib Clara Matthews: "But the Scots don't have the luxury of limbo: the Scots go straight to hell, or John Knox was just pulling your leg!"

"R.T.!" Clara said, to register disdain at his language, not his theology.

"Sounds like I missed grace," Dixon said as he returned. He held out the bottle of wine for R.T.'s approval.

R.T. held the bottle to the window admiring its clarity. Virginia had not expected wine would be a part of Sunday dinner.

The minister held Clara's chair.

"Virginia you'll be next to Will, of course," his mother stated. She gestured towards the chair next to Mr. Lochwood. "If it wasn't your big announcement day, I'd mix you young people up more."

Virginia could see her future mother-in-law was as at home with Emily Post as she was with giving a quick twist of a plump hen's neck. Both were required for the proper care of Sunday company.

"He's mixed up enough," Dixon said.

Jeanette gave a look Virginia could not quite read: disapproving or conspiratorial? She wasn't sure others at the table had caught the remark.

No clemency, Will asked himself, even on this day? He's jealous, Will thought. He puts Jeanette up against Virginia. That sharpens his tongue. Dixon, not one to be bested, had never recovered from his bad timing—born a couple of years too late: missing the war. Will felt his brother overestimated the heroic acts he might have attained if it had been he, rather than Will, who'd managed to get himself in uniform and shipped out to France. Will's approach to Dixon, when Dixon alluded to the toll the war and the gas might have had on Will's ways, swung from silence to tossing his kid brother the gloves. But he didn't imagine excusing themselves from this table, rolling up their white cuff-linked sleeves and stalking off to bloody each other's noses. Today he settled for silence.

"Jeanette," Clara beckoned Jeanette to take her place to the left of The Reverend Treet.

"Now, my dear, you must be seated at last," said Mr. Lochwood as he assisted The Reverend Treet in seating Clara.

Jeanette was sitting between The Reverend Treet and Dixon. Will thought this put his sister-in-law, at least geographically, in limbo. Virginia sat directly across the crystal bowl of cut asters from Jeanette. That's just fine, she thought, I'll have a better chance to get acquainted this way.

"Let's hope Little Andrew sleeps through the first course," Jeanette said more to the cut asters than to Virginia. The baby had been nestled away within earshot in the living

66

room. Dixon and Jeanette had named their baby boy for his great grandfather Matthews.

"If he wakes, you can always hand him to me, although I'm not much experienced," Virginia said. "This past winter in Helena I rented a room from a couple who had a darling baby, and I'd spell them for an hour or two when they decided to go out at the last minute. I got pretty good at rocking both of us to sleep."

"You wouldn't like him spitting up on your new jacket."

"Oh—it's not new, and it's quite washable," Virginia said, surprised at what a quick liar she could become, but doubted if Jeanette would take her up on her offer, regardless of credentials or clothing.

"He'd be hungry, like as not."

The glasses clustered like wild crocuses on the silver tray. R.T., at the sideboard like a smooth sommelier from a men's club in London, uncorked his private vintage wine. He had the fruit picked and pressed. It aged to his specifications in the low stone room where spring water ran beneath the house. This cooler kept the wine a constant temperature, and the cream, milk and eggs fresh. R.T. offered a glass to each one at the long table. He held the tray first for Clara. Next, Virginia. She accepted. Everyone held a glass.

R.T. gave a toast to his wife: *"Sweethearts forever… O these forty years!"* Clara took a sip. Virginia followed her example. Virginia found the lines of poetry flowery and romantic, but noticed how Mrs. Lochwood tugged at her russety lapels and shifted in her perfectly-placed chair. R.T. turned to Will and Virginia and raised his glass. "May you be as blessed."

Toasts as short as the glasses were given up in a chorus from Dixon's "May the best man win," assuming, presumptuously, that he would be the best man at the wedding, and ending with Will's *But never doubt I love.* Virginia took a tiny sip with each toast. Whether affected by the drops of wine or not, she felt flush: five words of Shakespeare from this man she was now engaged to had her in a flutter. When her glass was empty she was relieved to return to the big glass of cold, clear spring water that one of the hired girls kept filled from a silver pitcher.

After the last sip everyone sat content with the warming wine until Jeanette cleared her throat. She looked out over the golden asters and said, "Well, that must have been a surprise." Virginia realized it was she Jeanette was addressing. She looked nonplussed. Jeanette confided, "I had understood you were one who never took a drink."

"A toast is not a *drink*," R.T. said mimicking the tone of the anti-saloon league and then with the laughter returning, he said: "A toast is a toast."

How awkward it would have been to decline, Virginia thought. It would have brought too much attention to her, and made too much of her old Sunday School pledge, of which, in truth, she seldom thought. But, it was a pledge she never had revoked. She'd never drunk liquor of any kind. The Congregational Church deemed Christ's blood best represented by Welch's grape juice, not communion wine. The Reverend Treet must approve of her pledge, she assumed. However, he seemed to find no sin in drink. Virginia found abstinence quite natural in her own home headed by an expatriate Philadelphian

Quaker (her mother) and son of the Nebraska Bible belt (her father). Not that her father didn't take a drink, but not now, during prohibition. Her mother carried a small vial of bourbon in her purse in case her heart faltered. But here, although she knew the drinking was usually men only in R.T.'s study with shots of Scotch before dinner and sips of cognac, cigarettes and cigars afterward, it seemed today's occasion called for whatever ceremony this parched land could offer.

There was a silence. Clara Matthews took her napkin from the table and let it unfold across her lap. Everyone followed her lead.

The Reverend Treet told a string of mishaps at weddings where he'd presided: licenses forgotten, rings rolling under pews, a fainting bridegroom. Surely no one's thinking he should preside at our wedding, Virginia thought. It had never occurred to her that anyone but kindly Mr. Sloan be considered, but she was grateful for Treet turning what might have slipped into dreary temperance talk.

Everyone was in the mood to indulge in love stories. R.T. started, but Clara Matthews interrupted him. "Oh, R.T.," she said, "let's not dredge up my old hesitations."

"Hesitation? My dear, saying 'no' is no hesitation." He turned to Virginia. "When I asked Clara to marry me, she didn't hesitate, she said 'No.'"

"She must not have had the last word," said Virginia.

"You're right," he said. "She looked at me and said, 'No, it's not me you want, it's May.'" He paused, "Her younger sister, Mayelle, you know." Virginia nodded. Will had never told her this story. She wondered if he had heard it himself.

"And, he said…" Clara Matthews interrupted him again, "he said, 'I guess I know who and what I want.' So," she said almost blushing, "I said yes."

"It's the last time she let me change her answer," R.T. Matthews insisted.

Years later Virginia came across pictures of the two sisters, both smaller, their bones shrunk with osteoporosis, their white hair looped on top of their heads, white ironed dresses with long sleeves to keep off the summer mosquitoes. She thought that although you couldn't see much difference between the two, R.T. was wise to choose the one who would be remembered as the one who laughed until she cried at the dinner table. Not May, the sister who was remembered as the one obsessed with washing her hands, the one who sat inside her house in Billings while the town built up around her, hidden behind heavy ecru lace curtains, not answering the front bell when it rang, and approving that her spinster daughter did likewise, even if it were members of the family paying a call.

Chapter Six
The Wild Brook

1929

Platters of golden chicken, peaks of mashed potatoes and circles of yellow squash were hurried hot through the swinging door from the kitchen to the sideboard. Then a silver tureen of light gravy, hot Sunday biscuits enveloped in white linen, compote of transparent currant jelly. Squares of iced salted butter.

"The biscuits," Will said and nodded at his mother.

"I hope it's not a secret recipe," Virginia said.

"No secret to it. All it takes is a little flour, milk, butter, salt, baking powder…"

Will broke in—"and a jelly glass."

"Yes," she said, "to cut them with. Well, that's the family secret."

"Speaking of secrets," Virginia said, "I'll have to ask you, Mrs. Lochwood, to keep our engagement under your hat; Will and I have decided to save our announcement until the first of the year."

"Of course, my dear. Secrets are my forte! We'll have to work on Mr. Lochwood, though. He's less reliable."

Virginia was mildly curious about the studied emphasis of pronunciation Mrs. Lochwood gave *forte*—"fort" without the "tay" at the end as so many Americans thought proper. She was curious as well as to what secrets Fanny Lochwood might hold.

"Not so. Not so," Mr. Lochwood boomed out. "Right, R.T.?"

"You're the one man I can't afford not to agree with," R.T. answered.

"Not so, you old devil!"

"Tell us about the wedding plans," Mrs. Treet asked.

"There aren't any yet," Virginia said. "Only the date."

But there had been many family weddings before the fireplace in the Yellowstone Avenue living room as her mother's younger sisters moved out from Philadelphia and found husbands. She could see herself coming down the staircase, taking her father's arm and walking into the room filled with fresh flowers and old friends.

"I imagine your father's upset?" Mr. Lochwood asked, "losing a daughter, *and* a good legal stenographer?"

"Well," Virginia laughed, "he's had to get along without me before. And, I work mainly for his partner."

"Of course. You must have taken a leave of absence to work at the legislature last winter," Mrs. Lochwood said. "Tell us what *does* go on in those cloakrooms." Mrs. Lochwood was adept with questions that suggested their answers.

"Arm twisting." Virginia laughed. Before she and Will had started seeing one another with any kind of serious intentions, Virginia had decided to work at the sixty-day session at the capitol. It broke up the long winter. She liked politics. She'd grown up with dinner debates between her mother, a Republican, and her father, a William Jennings Bryan Democrat. A freshman legislator from her father's law office and his wife let the guest room to Virginia in the house they were renting for the session.

"I don't suppose it was hard for W.M. Hartwell's daughter to find a job in Helena," Mr. Lochwood said. Virginia supposed he thought it a compliment.

"Well, a Republican looking for a job in that legislature should not have had a Democrat for a father," Virginia said, "but I finally found a job in the Senate steno pool." Her shorthand improved as she recorded long-winded debates at her committee assignments—Livestock & Public Ranges, Banks & Banking, Federal Relations. She liked the symbols— their grasp of speed and secrecy, was pleased that no one could read over her shoulder, or get the essence of her notes from a sideways glance.

"The belle of the ball," Dixon broke in.

Will cleared his throat, cocked his head to his brother as if saying, *and how would you know?*

"Well, if the Woolgrowers' was any measure," Dixon replied. "There, don't forget," he reminded his brother, "it was Virginia who knew all the bigwigs: even old Senator White sent over a round of drinks in her name." It was the sort of thing

Will knew impressed Dixon. The Democrat Senator was one opposed to the wool tariffs the Matthewses and all the sheep ranchers favored.

"He had to be polite," Virginia said, "or fear I'd misquote him. On purpose!" Everyone laughed. "To quote verbatim can be the most punishing. I found the time a senator might object to the minutes of a meeting, clear his throat and say 'to set the record straight' and then point out what he thought misquoted, was, in fact, where I'd been the most diligent reporter. What the good senator said or didn't say often wasn't what he wanted on the record."

"Sounds like you'd better put your new daughter-in-law to work lobbying the Senator," Lochwood said to R.T.

"You bet. Put a crimp in that foreign wool market," R.T. said as he cut a sliver of jelly to put on his bite of white meat. He caught Virginia's eye. "Gilding the lily." He winked.

Virginia credited her winter in Helena with the speed with which her romance with Will advanced. Both were shy in expressing their feelings in person, Virginia more than Will. But imaginations left alone on cold winter nights in rented room or camp shack heightened what they wrote. In January of 1929, Will sent this note:

> *Dear Virginia—*
> *Your letter found me here on the desert today—*
> *and I certainly was pleased to have you remember your*
> *sheepherder friend—*

*I certainly hope that your law makers voted right*
*and that you are coming down to the wool growers—*
*I'm just plain selfish I know but I want you with me*
*at the banquet—*
    *Always, Will Matthews*

The next day, Virginia sent a postcard to her parents:

*The legislature voted to adjourn on Thursday to*
*convene again on Monday, so that some of them can go*
*to Billings for the Woolgrowers. Will Matthews wants*
*me to go to the banquet, so I hope I can get home.*

"I bet there's over five-hundred packed in here," Will
had said to Virginia as they looked around The Northern
ballroom. "I'd say 560." He was used to estimating numbers of
sheep crowded in a loading pen or covering a river bank. What
she remembered of that evening was too much liquor. There
were thick layers of smoke, rounds of drinks sent back and
forth from table to table, political protocol drenched in trays of
"bourbon & ditch." There were "bum lamb cocktails" to start
off with; Virginia decided not to ask the contents. There were
legislators—many of them ranchers themselves, competitors
and partners, bankers and merchants, one or two wool buyers
from Boston. They argued grazing fees, railroad rates, tariffs.
With each round, there'd be another seltzer with a twist for
Virginia. She ended up with a platoon of full weeping glasses
before her.

"Who can blame 'em—they're snowed in all winter long," was Will's explanation. He was attentive, and, she imagined, toned down from previous years. "It's our Mardi Gras—especially when the legislature is in session. Everyone loves out-talking the boys in Helena."

R.T. sat at the head table next to Bishop R.R. Smith. His eloquent Episcopalian invocation, reminiscent to Will of mandatory chapel matins and vespers, was absorbed into the shushed smoky hall.

Looking back on that night, what Virginia saw was Will and Dixon.

Dixon, there without Jeanette, was a little drunk. Virginia had watched him tease the cocktail waitress, then listen sycophantically to the homely mink-coated spinster sisters whose father was the biggest sheepman in the state. He had the sisters giggling. Too smooth, she'd thought. At dinner, it was Dixon who jumped to his feet to introduce her to whomever was passing. It made Virginia uneasy. Between courses, he'd trot across to Hugo Lochwood's table and scratch columns of figures on the white tablecloth. He'd signal for drinks. He accompanied Fanny Lochwood out on the dance floor whenever she crooked her finger.

"He's everyone's pal, tonight," Will had said, not unkindly. Although Will stayed close by Virginia, he got himself into debates on the matter of grazing fees. At one point when a loud red-nosed, pot-bellied sheepman who'd had too much to drink picked up on the words "reservation" and "lease," he slurred, "Why the hell aren't the warhoops here

76

buying us a drink? They've tied up the best grazing land in the goddamn state thanks to our goddamn socialist government."

It got a nervous laugh from a few at the table, but Will walked the man out into the lobby, and tipped a bellman to get him to his room.

"You were wise to stay home with the baby," Virginia said across the table to Jeanette. She saw that Jeanette had that left out look. Virginia often felt so herself, but she wondered if she'd sounded condescending. Jeanette might be in awe of her job in Helena, but, Virginia thought, if she had the choice between a life in the hubbub of the legislature and a life working with Dixon on the ranch and caring for Little Andrew, she would pick the latter and everything it entailed.

"Where we need arm-twisting," said Mr. Lochwood, "is back in Washington. I fear where this inflation, all this high priced speculation, is going to take us."

"That's not how I like to hear my banker talk," R.T. said.

"The country's talking itself into this depression," Will said.

"There's more to it, Will," Mr. Lochwood said. "A man without a job is a sad sight—we don't see it so much out here, but, I fear there are too many such men in the country today."

"If a man wants work, he'll find a job," Dixon chimed in.

Dixon spoke rather grandly Will thought, but refrained from asking when Dixon had looked for a job outside the ranch.

"That may be," his mother answered. "I well remember

before coming over—" and everyone knew she was talking about Scotland, "a decent job, no matter your education, was as scarce as hen's teeth. But," she stopped herself, "this is a celebration. This isn't Sunday talk."

On the topic of where Will and Virginia would live, there was no mention. No jokes about sheep tenders' wagons, haystacks, the lambing shed. Even Mrs. Lochwood hadn't brought it up, and Virginia thought it was her sort of question. No one gave a hint that such a matter might be prime on the minds of the newly affianced couple. She wondered if it was not Sunday talk either.

The apple pie was eaten and dessert plates cleared away. Clara Matthews drew the big linen napkin from her lap and placed it where her dessert plate had been: "Let's take our coffee in the living room. It's almost chilly enough for a fire."

The baby stirred when they walked in. Jeanette whisked the warm sleepy wad of blankets up and handed him directly to Virginia. "Here you go," she said to Virginia, and added in a confidential tone: "Sundays, I always do the silverware for Mother Matthews. It can so easily get scratched or, worse yet, a piece lost." Jeanette said. "I worry the girls might scrape a spoon into the garbage."

"Little Andrew and I'll keep you company."

They pushed through the swinging doors into the pantry, then into the kitchen. Both of them surprised the cook and the helpers. There was barely room for two more in the narrow kitchen, but Jeanette seemed at home and the kitchen girls, used to this ritual, relinquished their places at the one deep sink by the drain board on the tin-covered counter. Virginia polished her share of silver at home, quite liked smearing the cream over the metal, rubbing it to a shine, seeing the tarnish vanish from one's own effort. Jeanette slipped on a little pair of cotton gloves she'd stuck in a corner below the sink. She handled each knife, fork and spoon as if it were from the Last Supper.

"Let me give the baby to Will," Virginia said, "then I can help."

"There's just room for one at this sink."

Virginia stood swaying with the baby. She liked the warmth and small kicks and tugs of the little body next to hers in the steamy kitchen. She watched Jeanette. She doused each piece in the sudsy bath, poured scalding water over the silverware, then set each hot piece on a clean towel. Then, she peeled off the wet gloves, slipped her reddened hands into a dry pair, like the white ones Virginia wore to church. With a soft flour-sack towel, Jeanette dried each tine, each shallow bowl of spoon, each blade and, as she slipped each like a puzzle-piece into its fitted padded case, under her breath she counted as a bank teller might at close of day.

"Might one have slipped accidentally into Mr. Lochwood's jacket pocket," Virginia asked in jest. If Jeanette heard, she didn't look up: there was no allowance for humor here.

Clara Matthews appeared through the swinging door: "Oh, here you two are."

"Don't mind me," Jeanette said to her mother-in-law, "it's my odd habit."

When the baby started to fuss, Virginia welcomed a reason to leave the counting. She walked with Little Andrew into the living room, and browsed through books in the bookshelves. It was nosy, she knew. Some women judged others by the status of their stoves or the arrangement of their red spice tins but Virginia favored books: fiction? non-fiction? poetry? which were handy, which out of reach? She started out in the biographies —Pele the Conqueror, Bonnie Prince Charles, Arctic explorers; then the poets Robert Service and Robert Burns in gold stamped leather. She came upon a slim, white volume, quite worn, with thick deckle-edged pages: a book of love poems. She opened it feeling as if she were looking into someone's diary. She scanned the table of contents: her favorites: good old Anonymous… then, Elizabeth Barrett Browing… *Browing*? Virginia couldn't believe it—a typo—it was printed *Browing*, even though above in Robert Browning's listing, it was correctly spelled. George Eliot. Shakespeare. On and on. There were faint pencil marks at three on the list. Like dipping further into the private papers, Virginia turned to each marked poem to see what might be revealed.

"I wonder who made these little marks, don't you?" she whispered to the baby. "Maybe your Grandmother Clara," Virginia said and flipped to the frontispiece and its pastel drawing of a romantic hand-holding Victorian pair. There Virginia saw an inscription. The penmanship had open letters and plump capital *A*s, long dashes crossing *T*s nearly half way

across the page—from t-to-t in the words "truest" and
"sweetheart." Virginia read: "*Clara darling, you are the truest and
best of all of God's good women, and we will be sweethearts always. R.T.*"
"*Sweethearts, always,*" Virginia repeated to herself. The baby was
gurgling and Virginia suspected he was hungry, but she
thumbed to the first of the three marked poems with the guilty
feeling one had when reading the last page of the novel first.
Or a postcard from the stack of letters in the hall corridor. She
read aloud softly…

> *It was Maytime,*
> *And I was walking with the man I loved,—*
> *I loved him, but I thought I was not loved;*
> *And both were silent, letting the wild brook*
> *Speak for us…*

"I have a feeling," Virginia continued in her one-sided
conversation with the sturdy little pink face and pale blue eyes
that looked up at her, "that there's much too much of relying
on '*letting the wild brook speak for us*' out here, don't you think?
Since we're both new here, we can say what we want, can't we?
Okay, I'll finish the reading. This is bound to have a happy
ending."

> *till he stoop'd and gathered one*
> *From out a bed of thick forget-me-nots,*
> *Look'd hard and sweet at me and gave it me.*
> *I took it, tho' I did not know I took it,*

*And put it in my bosom, and all at once*
*I felt his arm about me, and his lips.*

"So, you favor the rhymed couplet?" It was Dixon, at her elbow.

Virginia hadn't noticed anyone approach. She snapped the book shut. It is as if I'm ashamed to be found reading Tennyson, she chided herself. She slid it back between Burns and Stevenson.

## Chapter Seven
## No Mention Made

### 1929

When each spoon, fork and knife was returned to its fitted flannel slot in the crested chest, Virginia turned the hungry baby over to Jeanette and ducked out the back door. Will was waiting. He took her hand. Virginia was glad to be off center stage. The romantic notions of engagement, all that delicious waiting, and then the wedding were one thing. This finding your way into a new family, the two-way scrutiny with imminent in-laws, was another altogether.

Virginia tugged at his arm, pulled him and they practically ran down the road.

Will was bursting with pride. "You were the best: you had them eating out of your hand."

Were we at the same table? she asked herself.

Virginia, who was apt to take things too literally, envisioned a flock of pine siskins descend upon the linen table, hop about the platters, teeter at rim of goblet, tug at bit of biscuit. One fluttered in where another seemed lord of a choice crumb, forcing the other bird to preen and flap. Virginia saw the birds flit and peck and tap, tap at her ring until Clara Matthews swooped down and swept them into the silver butler's helper.

"Your mother…" she said with three-times the volume of her sedate voice at the dinner table, "she saved me! Could you believe Jeanette and the toast!" I could have died, she thought. Must sisters-in-law be natural enemies, she wondered?

"You two will be good friends."

What? It took her a minute to realize he was talking about Clara.

"Mother deserves such a companion as you out here."

An ally, she thought, yes. When Clara had appeared at the swinging kitchen door and said in a not unkind voice, "Jeanette, no need to be so finicky. Silver can take quite a bit, you know. The Queen's has lasted all these centuries." Virginia was surprised how relieved she was. What if Will's mother had been the instigator of all that polishing?

I could imagine talking to Clara without couching my words, Virginia thought as she sorted through the women at the table. She hoped Will's mother might feel the same.

"Jeanette has some distorted view of me," Virginia started in. Her own life had seemed quite ordinary until she'd fallen in love and Will had proposed. But Jeanette—well, she's got an odd idea of how I live—she doesn't see me day after day typing carbon copies of long legal contracts. Taking the Girl

Scouts on hikes across the Rims. But Virginia knew inside that she was by-passing the Yellowstone Avenue part of it.

Will and Virginia escaped across the wide driveway, slowed by the sprawling garages. The big sliding doors of the blacksmith shed were shut for Sunday. It was here that things were fired and shaped, welded and realigned: a horseshoe, a tiller ripped by unseen stone, the gear and shaft of the thresher. Here was a hold of wrench and vice, socket and drill, oil and paint, the tools to keep the line up of tractor and combine and cultivator, hayrack and wagon and truck in repair. Work here could not be long put off for fractured piston or crank shaft. The gasoline tank stood on stilts at a remove from the shop sparks and friction.

Virginia arched her neck to take in the crown of the woodpile.

"The Old Man's a pruner," Will said, pointing as they continued. "He'll whittle away at a dead tree until each piece fits his fireplace. When he's out chopping and stacking or," Will paused, "finding someone to do it—he's his happiest. No idle hands. No dead branches. The woodpeckers can't keep ahead of him. Dixon and I worked off our sins on this wood pile. He's nuts about keeping the creek cleaned up."

If my future father-in-law equates reading novels with idle hands, Virginia thought, I'm in trouble. She split her share of kindling at the lake, but didn't think she'd offer her services to his woodpile.

"Now," Will said as he squeezed her hand, "let's do a little window shopping."

"What are our choices?"

"It's up to us," he said, but he wondered if that were so: no one else seemed to be giving their future accommodations any thought.

They walked on, assessing the possibilities: a little place of their own by the creek, or on the edge of the Indian meadows, as Will preferred, although that would put Virginia further from the home ranch buildings and the companionship of the other women.

"What about the little cabin?" Virginia asked.

"When The Old Man wants to get a rise out of Mother, he talks of taking one of the tractors to it."

"I bet she'd never stand for it."

"She can be pretty practical."

The little cabin was first built to meet the homestead requirements. The four Matthewses had camped there and in wagons and heavy canvas army surplus tents set on plank flooring from early in the spring of 1907 until Thanksgiving while their house was being built. Clara Matthews, by then in her early forties, had put her heart into the big house. The cabin had neither electricity nor plumbing, a great sagging roof now, no running water. In the past it had been put to order for the lambing or shearing crews if the weather was intolerable. Otherwise the men, if they slept at all, used tarps and tents near the pens. It had become a place to stow odd bits of machinery Clara Matthews insisted be out of sight so that her ranch wouldn't become a place where a broken thing—like plow or wagon tongue let lie where it gave way—were overgrown with rust, hollyhock and Russian thistle in the far corners of fields.

The homestead cabin was at the junction of the ranch roads. The main road came in from Ballantine and one fork veered east and separated the cabin from the barns and corrals and kept on going—right through the shallow creek—to the upper pastures. The other fork split again: one continued on the everyday way to the shop and the back porch of the big house—the way Will and Virginia had driven in—and, the other led the Sunday way through the apple orchard and arch of elms to the front porch. In the opposite direction, south of the corrals, was the little blue house.

Thirty yards away was the ice house. It was made out of rock upturned from the plowed fields and rough-cut timbers and insulated with sawdust and straw and stacked with backbreaking blocks of clear ice cut free with saw and crowbar once the deep pond froze solid. "You'll freeze your bum," Will said. He unlatched the door, lighted one of the kerosene lanterns and stepped into the dark, cold room, "but cut whatever you want."

"How?" Virginia stood her distance from the carcasses.

Will patted a wooden box of knives on the chopping block. "Watch your fingers."

Goose bumps popped up on Virginia's warm forearms. It seemed so much more complicated than Mr. Spear, his spotless white apron tied around his middle, at the 10th Avenue meat market in Billings. Virginia wondered how she would overcome her city ways: snap an old hen's neck in a twist of her wrist, hack two flank steaks from the dangling carcass.

Sausage wrapped in waxy white butcher paper was stacked in the ice house for the taking, but the sides of beef and pork and mutton and choice leg of lamb hung intact from hooks bolted to ceiling beams. At home, Virginia's father might be given a half a side of beef by a client who couldn't pay otherwise. They'd keep it at a commercial meat locker. Once, as a child, she'd stepped inside out of curiosity and when the heavy metal door shut, she felt the solid locked-in cold of the place and she saw the meat as cadavers from her father's thin green volumes of Edgar Allen Poe. She grew to dread her father trading his services for anything but cash. Here there was no electricity, and no lock on the door. Light came only from the opened door. Since it couldn't be left open long, Virginia thought Alma or the cookhouse cook or Jeanette or whoever came, lit a lamp, made their selection and did their butchering with little indecision.

On the opposite corner of the ranch crossroads was the burnt-red barn—a sampler, in its way, of the twenty-five years the Matthewses had been on the place. Its square-cut homestead logs were chinked with cement, its rafters twice raised to double each time to hold the hay in the loft. Its length had been extended, once with timbers from the railroad line that ran through the ranch on its way from Toluca to Cody, to merge cow barn with horse barn. And, a second time, to add the tack room now strung with oiled harnesses, bridles, working ropes and everyone's saddle. All of it was linked to the maze of corrals and watering troughs.

Then, looking beyond the corrals and the horse barn, Virginia asked "Wouldn't you think they would want to fix it up?"

Will knew she was talking about Dixon's little blue house. Two tiny bedrooms made from a shed had been spliced on the back. Even at a distance it looked ill-kempt. But, other than the big house, it was the only real house on the place. Virginia found little there to covet. It reminded her of the "beet house" she and her sister had painted that fall on a tract of irrigated land their father rented out to sugar beet farmers east of town—a summer house used for itinerant workers.

"At least a coat of paint? "

"Dixon's only marking time until he moves into the big house."

Virginia saw he wasn't kidding.

"Not that he hides it," Will said, "but, I say it only to you."

Past the corrals were the cookhouse and the bunkhouse. The chore boy and the cookhouse cook and—depending on the season—what hired hands there were lived there. Alma and the girls—usually there were two—who worked in the main kitchen and did the housework, lived in two small rooms above the kitchen that were reached by a door and stairway that came and went from the pantry.

Such self-sufficiency, Virginia thought.

"And your grocery store—" Will said, as they walked west from the homestead cabin. Virginia pushed the heavy commissary door open: there were two fat cats on duty, and case after case of store-bought canned goods and burlap sacks of dry foods: its flour and sugar and salt, tins of tobacco for the sheepherders, jars of chokecherry and plum jellies and marmalades, bottles of thick garden catsup made from bushels of ripe tomatoes forced through sieves into sweet pulp in early September, jars of dill pickles and sweet and sours and preserves of all kinds put-up in hot sterilized glass jars each fall. "You just have to share with the herders."

"Alma must have raided the ice house and commissary for the dinner today," Virginia said. "I've never seen such a feast."

The seasons had defined where Will lived. His headquarters was his childhood room under the eaves in the big house: he kept clothes in the big chests of drawers, but, since boarding school, he'd rarely slept in his wide birds-eye maple bed. If his parents were gone, then he'd stay to keep the place company. He liked having the place to himself. If he couldn't sleep, he'd put a Jeanette MacDonald record on with the volume turned up loudly, walk barefoot from room to room. He'd put in a call to Virginia. If it was fair weather, he'd end up with his bedroll, out on the porch.

"I'm a vagabond, you know," Will told Virginia.

He spent nights off a ways across the creek in one of the rattletrap lean-tos a herder might use on a rare night at the home ranch. Will never stayed in the bunk house because he felt the men deserved what privacy they could get. To some it was their only home. Most often Will was out with tarp and bedroll or bunking in a sheepherder's wagon, himself out on the range. Sometimes he was on the road visiting ranches on the Musselshell or over at Ingomar or Ismay where he'd be looking at yearling ewes for spring replacements. The ranchers welcomed the company, put him up. He'd drive to Miles City for the ram sale, curl up in the backseat of the Ford if he didn't want to pay for a room. Another night, he'd have reason to be in town at The Northern. He liked being on the road as much as being out on the range. The variety of accommodations suited him.

"Not for much longer," she answered, turning to him.

Will stopped. He touched his hands to the crown of her head as if in a blessing and her head encircled by his large fingers and thumbs on either side felt as light as a shell. They kissed in the stillness of the full sun. "Now, that's how I know I'm home."

# Chapter Eight
## Second Generation Sons

### 1929

In the first weeks following the engagement dinner, Will broached the subject lightly. "A place by the creek," he'd say as they walked down to the corrals, "but a half mile at least up from the big house?" His father would look like he had it under consideration.

Will was patient. Initially, he relied on his father to say "let's fix you and Virginia up with a little house" in much the same manner in which years ago he had said to the young Reverend Treet "you're going to need a horse," when the man straight from seminary had come with his young wife to start the church. Treet hadn't had to anguish over having to ask the prominent, older man if he were going to make good on the bay mare. Yet, when the horse and buggy were together and carting the minister around on his calls, The Old Man got a kick out of growling to the earnest young fellow "too fancy a setup for a preacher."

But Will came to think he was a fool to think that newlywed story was kin to his.

He was not one to beg. But, eventually, he said, "Where do you suppose Virginia and I will be on the Eleventh of May?"

His father was president of The Matthews Sheep Company, which owned everything to do with the ranch. Will felt it was his father's place to make the offer of housing, as he would to any foreman. He knew his father to be a practical, not a stingy man. But Will's assumptions thinned like the winter air. He didn't raise the subject with his mother—he wasn't sure why. Although he sensed it must be on her mind as well. Perhaps he hadn't wanted her to feel torn, in the middle of things. Once he'd had that thought—*the middle of things*—he questioned the silence circling the subject of where he was to live.

Then, as winter burrowed its way in for the numb months of January and February and into March, there was little chance to talk about housing. R.T. and Clara, as they had in recent years, had taken themselves off by upholstered Pullman car to Santa Monica.

It had become popular to present oneself not only at the warm ocean side verandahs and at the dressing rooms of Bullock's but at the doors of a California clinic for a thorough physical examination and observation of any infirmities that one might have accumulated when there was neither time nor inclination to drive across drifted dirt roads for less than emergencies. Clara nursed the slightest tremor in her right hand and, when necessary, she held it firm in her lap in a gesture that recalled the tiny curved and shaky shape of her grandmother. Although she didn't mention it to R.T., she welcomed a doctor's opinion. R.T. was encumbered with painful inflammations in his feet which he himself diagnosed as gout. No doctor had yet concurred. Lochwood kidded him with "ailment of kings" jokes, but the banker didn't have to fit his sore swollen feet into a pair of R.T.'s tightly laced oxfords.

So, in the incubating months when nothing was born, bought, sheared, slaughtered or sold, R.T. left the cares and feedings of the ranch to his grown sons. If the two of them were on the peck, R.T. had no quarrel with the stratagem of divide and conquer. He granted that 'that fool Custer,' in his imposition of ill-fated division of his troops, 'had played into the Indians' hand' and had given a negative, ricocheted twist to the military theory. R.T., however, figured the boys would work out their way with only the two of them on the place. The matter of permanent living quarters on the ranch—other than the implausible idea of Will and Virginia just moving into his bedroom up under the eaves—seemed neatly avoided.

But there was little precedent for these second generation sons. The arid land bred rivalry between brothers: each felt the pinch of more than one family expecting to live well off the land, the prospect of inheriting the place himself remote, the expectation of any sort of cash payout unrealistic. A ranch might have tens of thousands of acres of land, of livestock, of crops, but what it would not have was cash. The value of an outfit on paper might barely outweigh its debt.

Any fluctuation could be devastating. If, for example, the wool market or the lamb market dropped suddenly, and a man's credit had been pegged to the higher number, this could diminish his ability to borrow to buy new stock, ordinary supplies, pay his lease fees. At worst, it put his loan in jeopardy.

When two brothers lived year after year on the same piece of land, one brother or the other might take the notion to cut loose and run his own sheep, to get a section of land in his own name. He might start off with a lease some distance from the ranch. Eventually he might go so far as to take over leases once held by the family corporation. The business of the brothers might not be out in the open. One brother might pick up leases on his own, and the father would know that. He might know that one son or the other was out borrowing money to buy land of his own, or borrowing for the lease money or borrowing to buy a hundred-head of sheep. The father might be inclined towards the son who had the itch to go ahead: it was one way for the ranch to grow. The father might be inclined towards the son who had a head for dealing with the Indians as he had, rather than the one content in trading stories with the "longhairs." The later son might be considered the less ambitious—the one who accepted the work and the place, the one preoccupied not with the stock market or fraternal rites, but with a city bride and a little house.

## Chapter Nine
## Always One Indian

### 1930

With R.T. on the promenade at Santa Monica watching the wool market slide and the winter waves erode into the Nova Scotia shores of his childhood, Dixon and Will were left to look after tiers of frozen hills, the expectant ewes, the cranky sheepherders and one another. It kept Will out on the winter range, and not in town evenings on Yellowstone Avenue with Virginia concocting a wedding, a honeymoon, a little dream house, not sitting on the petit point couch in the living room planning their future before the burned-low fire with just one light on: the green glass lamp, set on the paisley shawl, its neck craning over the much fingered upright Steinway in the alcove. This separation let letters drift back and forth like the winter snows, and allowed Will to put into writing things he might not have said face to face.

One January night in 1930 Will wrote Virginia:

> *Dear Virginia—We are not snowed in (if I was
> I would not complain if you were here too)—but one
> has to use so much profanity to get out, we make as
> few trips to the post office as possible. Had a letter
> from the Old Folks written after they landed in
> California. The Boss writes
> that he had been figuring on extending his holdings
> again about 20,000 head—it's wonderful the pipe
> dreams one gets when the sun shines—but this year
> he's decided to hold tight where we are. He's listened to
> too many old pessimists sitting around counting the
> waves. Would be more to my liking if he was
> calculating where we'd live come the Tenth of May.
> Tomorrow I'll head out to check on Armitage and his
> pals so I'm afraid you can't expect much news from
> me, but don't let it stop you from writing me.*
> *My love always, Will.*

Below Armitage's winter camp there was a bare cabin
with one cot, no stove. It was a place Will knew was so cold
that after he had spent the day hauling hay—forking it to the
wagon, hitching a team of horses to the top-heavy load and
breaking trail through new knee-deep snow, and pitching side-
by-side with Armitage the same hay from the wagon to the
carpet of obeisant Old Testament mouths—he welcomed
Armitage's dinner invitation. It came in the gesture of the
herder's head as it emerged from his self-sewn buffalo poncho,

beckoning like a horse resisting the rein, towards his sheep wagon. Will accepted: he tipped his hat with a finger of stiff leather glove. Will knocked the snow from his overshoes as he took the last step up into the wagon. The wagon smelled of old man and dog, of lanolin and sweat, grease, coffee and tobacco and smoldering coal. Heavy pieces of coal that R.T. bought by the carload for the hard winter. Will's head barely cleared the cross beam.

Armitage set two fry pans on top of the cook stove. He got out two tins of corned beef hash and two spoons. Each man opened his own can with a gadget too small for his thumbs. Will wiped the rust from his spoon and scooped out the contents which, when they hit the hot pan, sizzled and spat. Armitage knocked a spoonful of bacon grease on the rim of Will's pan. The men stood up to the stove, their padded bodies close to each other, each concentrating on the frying and turning of their hash, the smell of the food, the ping of hot grease on their skin, the warmth coming from the coal stove. They didn't talk.

Armitage took two big brown eggs from his rations and cracked one on top of Will's browned hash.

"You spoil me," Will said.

"That bride of yours will take care of any spoiling." Armitage cracked the other one into his own pan, lifted the lid of the stove and dropped the flecked shells sputtering into the coals. He covered each pan with an ill-fitting lid.

Will took his flask from inside his coat. He helped himself to a jelly jar from Armitage's crammed pantry which felt more like a glove compartment than a china closet. He poured a shot more generous than you'd get at the Ballantine Bar and handed it to Armitage. "I'll drink to some spoiling," Will said. He raised the flask to his lips. They took the drink in one swallow.

"You ever get married?"

"I tell you: I get married every summer, but..."

Will waited. He poured the herder a second shot.

"But, well...me and them don't winter so well."

The two peppered their hash with each turn and filled crevices with salt. They mopped up the hot, runny yolk from the bubbling greasy edges with stale crusts of bread. When the hash was gone, each took a last thick slice of bread and fried it in his pan with the leftover grease, then spread it with curls of cold butter and mounds of Clara's golden marmalade. Will folded his like a jelly roll and finished dinner standing now with his back to the stove.

"I thank you, sir," Will said and nodded.

"Yes sir." Armitage returned the nod.

Will drove the horses down to his camp. He unharnessed them, pulled the curry comb down their sides, threw dry heavy saddle blankets across their backs, forked in new hay and freshened their water. He took his overshoes off as he stepped inside the hut. He sat on the cot. He peeled the newspaper wrappings from his shoes and unlaced them. He took off his belt. Then, fully clothed in long underwear, silk scarf around his neck, a pair of wool shirts and wool pants— the clothes he had been wearing since he left home—he climbed into the very middle of his bedroll. He kept half of the covers beneath him since the cot had no mattress, and, with the warmth from one last swig of Scotch, he stayed there for a good ten hours until just before daybreak, sometimes sleeping, sometimes waking to a coyote singing across the prairie and he'd mutter "stay on your side of the coulee, you sonofabitch" as he might have acknowledged the unseen but familiar Fritz across No Man's Land. He would prop himself up in the bedroll and light a cigarette and smoke it down to the last twist and imagine Virginia between her white sheets. Was she asleep now? Did she have the light on, a pink quilted sateen bed jacket over her shoulders, lost in one of her thick novels? If she were to take as much pleasure in the real thing as she did the elucidating French paragraphs, Will thought how well one might winter with Virginia.

At dawn, he worked the last load down to Armitage's band. He drank coffee so strong and good he ignored the burning metal rim of the mug on his frostbit lip and spat out the grounds when the other man wasn't looking. He took the long-handled ax from Armitage's wagon and worked on the water tank until he broke the ice and the water ran free again. When he finished, he headed home. He had been ten days out on his line. He hoped he'd be in time for a hot lunch on a clean plate.

There was always one Indian in the cookhouse. Will was used to Graylight. But as he rode in with his string of horses, ice balls caught on their fetlocks, he saw there was more than one pony breathing steam into the ten below day, more than one pair of reins wrapped at the corral. Not Graylight's sorrel. Will didn't credit Emmet—the chore boy turned cook during the winter when Clara Matthews was gone from the big house—with asking uninvited visitors to stay for a meal: Emmet was as stingy as a pack rat. Will looked at his watch. He hoped Emmet hadn't dished it all out: Emmet wasn't the sort you wanted to ask to fire up the cook stove once it'd been damped down.

Dixon stood as Will opened the door.

"Back early?" Dixon said. The two Indians next to him got to their feet. One pocketed what sounded to Will like a short stack of coins. Maybe half-dollars. Dixon was folding a paper away into his vest pocket, back of his fat pack of Lucky Strikes. He clipped in his fountain pen. He shook the first man's hand and dismissed the pair.

"Not particularly," Will said as he walked back to the kitchen. "Finished up at Armitage's about noon. Colder than Christ out there."

Will recognized Two Legs. Will didn't credit Dixon with much more philanthropic tendencies than Emmet, but Will was more intent on his own food than Dixon and the two Indians. Dixon hired men from Crow Agency to do odd jobs on the place. Dixon could just as well have hired Two Legs and his companion to haul hay, clean out stalls, plow the road. Usually Will and Dixon discussed any labor, any cash outlay, regardless how small, but Will had been out.

"Good deal," Dixon said. "I'm going in for the mail. Need anything?"

"Not that you could provide."

"You underestimate your own brother."

That evening, Will fired up the metal stove in The Old Man's office and sorted through the stack of mail Dixon had left. There were three notes from Virginia. Will flipped through the ledger to cash disbursements to see what penny ante transactions had occurred in his 10-day absence. R.T. was meticulous in recording to whom each cent was paid and for what job. So were Will and Dixon in his absence. There was no new entry.

In those next weeks while R.T. was away, Will ran into Two Legs and a couple of other Crow at the cookhouse. He wished he could have attributed the Indians being around the kitchen to someone's generosity. He knew the depression had hit the reservation as well—that they were getting less for their hay, probably more hard pressed for cash and a clean bite than anyone.

"These fellows blackmailing you," Will asked only half-kidding the next time he came upon Dixon and his entourage.

"These boys have been doing some work for me."

Will had kept his eye on the books. After the two Crow left, Will said, "Put it in the ledger so we come out even when The Boss comes back."

"It's between me and Two Legs, not the ranch."

"Greasing wheels? You suddenly some rich bastard? Our own fledgling *entrepreneur?*" Will said extending the syllables of one of Virginia's French words.

"My big brother, back checking how I squander my two-bit allowance?"

What was Dixon up to? Will asked himself. How could
he one minute pull one of his pranks, and still be in some way a
likable son of a bitch? Will could hear the voice of his mother
reading from her childhood bookshelves in Scotland: *The
Strange Case of Dr. Jekyll and Mr. Hyde.* He could imagine even
now in himself or in anyone splitting in two like that. As kids,
he'd wring Dixon's neck one day. Another day, the two might
conspire against the city sons of The Old Man's friends by
making it look easy to rope a calf. They'd give the dude the
dull-looking but skittish horse and give their guests a turn. Will
and Dixon were that kind of brother: reading each other
without words. They had ridden one horse to school in
Ballantine in the years after R.T. stopped hiring an elementary
teacher to teach on the place. When Will was sent off to
boarding school, Dixon complained about riding alone. Will's
broad back had warded off the snow that cut at a slant into
their faces. Will was strong, bigger than Dixon, and ready to
block his little brother's nose from foreign punches. But when
it came to talking their way out of a bind, then it was Dixon
who did it. Even if he protested Dixon's bullying or wooing,
Will admired him. This was the way it was when it was the two
boys against the world. But, when it came to chores at the big
house, then each boy was rewarded not for a good job, but for
the better job. They'd have it out when one saw the other go
beyond fair play. But Will took some delight in a brother who,
for example, when tight from too much whiskey in town might
make a fool of himself, but could drive ass backwards fast up
the gravel road home and miss culvert, corner and ditch. Once

he even missed the Reverend Treet in his horse-drawn rig
coming home late from a neighbor bereaved.

They were called competent leases. The word
competent referred to the Indian, one deemed by an arbitrary,
often lax, administrative authority at the agency, competent to
lease his land to anyone upon terms and conditions he
negotiated. After 1920, a sheepman, say, could negotiate these
leases directly with the Indian. No going through the agency.
No lawyer to complicate matters. These were five-year grazing
leases, but, annually, on sign-up day, the Indian and the
sheepman could agree to cancel the lease and renegotiate it for
the next five years. The sheepman would pay new lease money
to the Indian. In this canceling and renewing, the Indian
would have drawn down all of the lease money: he would be in
perpetual lease to the rancher. The rancher made it easy for
the Indian to take an advance on a future lease, as well. The
Indian rarely could extricate himself from this circle. Gradually
the whole reservation was leased up in pre-paid leases. The
benevolent rancher who loaned the Indian a dollar when he
needed it, who bought hay from the Indian when he had hay to
sell, held the Indian in bondage. The Indian could be paid up
to twenty-five cents an acre on an average, but seven cents was
more likely. The only way the lease might change hands, from
one rancher to another, was if someone got between the
rancher and "his Indian" by means of a better offer. In such a
case, the man after the lease might be advancing sums to the
Indian, in an agreement that he get the lease when it was due
from the other rancher.

The sheepman used his reservation leases as collateral at the bank. He borrowed the maximum against his land and his leases in order to buy a band of ewes, more land, more leases. The more he borrowed and bought—as long as each year the crops came in, the livestock brought a good price—the more he could borrow and buy. The Indian, on the other hand, was less likely to use the lease money for the purchase of land or livestock.

In 1930, the reservation was leased-up and the ranchers were borrowed-up and after the market crashed on "Black Thursday" on October 24, 1929, the bankers had depositors and bank examiners to satisfy. No one was free from pressure from the man one rung up.

Virginia put in a call to Ballantine. "Fanny Lochwood called. She's such a dear. She and Mr. Lochwood want to have a dinner—for us. Could you come in? if the roads are passable? Fanny thought Valentine's Day would be fun. That's next Friday." Will could hear her enthusiasm. "It's to be quite an affair at the Hilands Club."

"I see," Will said. "How can one say no to one's banker."

"One can't," Virginia said. "And, one ought not say no to one's fiancée."

"That's my line."

"Will!" she said not minding at all, but knowing how little privacy there was on country lines. She suspected that Juanita, who had put the call in from the phone company, and even Mrs. Treet, the minister's wife, were likely listening in.

She found herself relieved to remember that Jeanette did not have a phone in the little blue house. "It has been over two weeks since you've been to town."

"I guess it is Dixon's turn to ride herd on this place for a day and a night," he said. They were used to spelling each other. Winter, when anyone could go stir crazy, was the one time Will found there were advantages to being in business with one's brother.

I'll wear my black lace, Virginia thought. She was only half-listening to Will's detailed weather report and predictions. She didn't expect Will to come in to town for all the parties, and she was well primed for weather and crises on the ranch claiming first rights to his time, but she did like anticipating her handsome fiancé coming to town. She imagined him changing at the Northern into his dark blue worsted wool suit and his starchy white shirt and his cufflinks. And, she bet, the paisley tie she had made him for Christmas. On his way through the lobby he would stop and let the bootblack take polish and fast rag to his Florsheims.

As Virginia speculated about who would be invited and who would not, it passed through Will's mind that sign-up day with Graylight was near. It was one of many leases the ranch held, and as routine as any harvest. For the last 10 years Graylight came by the ranch and signed a new lease. Will knew there was no guarantee the Indian wouldn't come in a day or two early, a day or two late. The weather, the position of the moon, were all factors.

"Even the ocean tides," Will said, thinking out loud.

"What?" said Virginia.

"Oh, I got sidetracked."

One day you would ride in, see Graylight's sorrel at the corral, see Graylight at the back table in the cookhouse taking his time with Emmet's mulligan stew. If R.T. were at the ranch, he would be the one to come out and walk down from the big house and invite the Indian back to his office, offer him a seat in the straight-back leather chair at his desk. Graylight would wait until R.T. or one of the boys brought up the subject of the lease: would he like to renew? Graylight would nod. The proceedings, in exact repeat of the previous year, would begin. In the end Graylight would sign the same lease, enjoy the attention, the lengthy explanation of the clauses of the agreement, receive the check and a bonus of a silver dollar for the lease and a handshake from R.T. and a handshake from each of the boys. In return the Matthews Sheep Company was free to let a band of, say, 200 ruminating sheep each with their thirty-two teeth nip and pull at the grass and fill their four stomachs day after day—pawing through the snow, or in summer take the sweetgrass from the high hills on the fertile reservation land of the Crow. The sheep were good tenants, leaving the land often better than they found it.

If Graylight comes in while I'm gone, Will had thought, there's no reason to think Dixon can't handle it: Dixon can write the company check as well as I.


"Only a fool would head into a storm like that," Dixon said. Will stopped at the cookhouse to bid his brother farewell for the weekend. The Ford was idling. Dark blue clouds were heavy and low along the western slopes of hills.

"Hell, I bet I beat it into town." He followed his brother's gaze where midday the sky was like steel, the sun itself "darkly circled" like Whittier's *Snowbound*.

"I thought you'd given up your train-racing days."

"A man must go to town now and then," Will said. They grinned: they could agree on that. Dixon let his hand rest on his shoulder in a manner unlike his newer, showier back-slapping Masonic pats.

Will was bowled over by Virginia in her black-lace dress. It eased long over her hips, down about her ankles, sleeves narrowing at her wrists. Her eyes seemed a deeper brown than he'd remembered. Gone were any traces of the stenographer, the shy woman in jodhpurs. Will was on his feet the minute she walked into the library where he was talking water rights with Mr. Hartwell. "You look beautiful," he said and he gave her a kiss on the cheek. He felt himself blush, knowing both that he'd never kissed her before in the presence of her father and that the quick polite kiss belied his feelings. He almost forgot to hand her the roses.

Virginia had fussed with the front of the dress. She was not used to such a décolletage. She had thought the thick straps of her undergarment unsightly: the tiny silk corded straps of the under slip were all that she wanted to show. In the end she discarded the brassiere and had her Aunt Ella take a few stitches to the very front once she was in the dress. "I'll worry about getting out of it when I get home," she said. At the last minute she thought it all looked a little "too-too," so she pinned on a floppy velvet camellia at the lowest point of the V. She'd seen it done in *Vogue*, and thought it worked quite well. The look in Will's eyes, even more than his kiss, said her efforts had been worth it. Virginia's parents were guests at the party, as well, but Virginia had thought to have them ride with the Marshalls next door, so she and Will could have the car to themselves.

He held her arm as they made their way down the slippery porch steps and the silvery sidewalk. Will had left the motor running, so, even though it was below zero, the car was warm when she stepped in. Will got in and adjusted his coat and he put his arm around her and said, "I can do better than that pantywaist kiss in the parlor, don't you think?" Virginia didn't say "don't crush this" or "what about my lipstick" or "not now."

She wondered how they could wait until May.

"Stay over," Virginia coaxed the next afternoon after the party. "Give the roads a chance to thaw." They were sitting on the parlor couch. Virginia had her feet tucked underneath her and was leaning against him. The radio was on, and Will flickered the dial up and down, hoping to catch a high-powered station from Butte or Denver.

"Dixon can't get us into too much trouble in forty-eight hours, but I hate to press my luck." He started to tell Virginia of the misgivings he was having about Dixon. He wanted to get her ideas on it, but it had been a perfect weekend, and he didn't want to worry her. Maybe Dixon's designs were all in his imagination.

Will started back towards dusk on Sunday. There would be drifted roads once he left the highway. The highway itself promised to be slick. When Will drove late into the home place there was only the stockyard light at the junction by the barn. No lights on at the little blue house.

The big house felt deserted after the weekend in town with Virginia. It had been hard to leave her. Will walked from room to room alone. The chairs seemed rigid, straight and empty, the halls silent. The chandelier over the dining room table needed dusting. Frost threatened the big window behind R.T.'s cracked leather chair in the living room. Static nipped at Will's oxfords on the worn Oriental rug R.T. had brought back from the Chicago World's Fair. He poured a jigger of his father's good Scotch, sat down in The Old Man's oak chair, riffled through what little mail there was. He picked up last Sunday's paper: Babe Ruth had signed a two-year contract for $160,000. He fanned the thin gold-edged pages of Bobbie Burns, twirled the combination on the safe and reached for the ledger.

There was one new entry.

"Dixon T. Matthews."

It was written in his brother's precise print. The notation read: "1930-1935 sublease payment for C. Graylight, Crow Allottee No. 2209 lease of grazing land, Lots 6 and 7 and N/2 SW/4 Sec. 36, Twp. 8S, E. 32E." It was a straight five percent of the amount that would have been paid to Graylight. There was no record of a Matthews Sheep Company check to Graylight. Instead there was this.

110

Sublease? You bastard. Will threw back the Scotch as if shoulder to shoulder with Armitage. "You've developed a taste for the clabbered," he said under his breath as if to spare any eavesdropper in the cold empty night office, "you son of a bitch." This is it, he thought. It explained the presence of Two Legs and the others. You've turned into a goddamn coyote: taking out a lamb just for its full rich tender stomach, leaving the rest of the carcass to the magpies. You can mimic your lawyer and your goddamn accountant friends with papers and signatures and figures and you think you can give me the bum's rush. No. Well, The Old Man will be livid.

Will did what he never did: he went down to the little blue house. He rode a horse down because the snow was deep and the wind sharp. He was no fool in winter. It was quiet. The waning moon gave off an ice blue shadow. The house was dark. He stood on the front cement slab. He knocked on the storm door. He's liable to blow my head off, he thought. But, instead, when Dixon came to the door, it was his calm midnight face that caught Will's breath.

"What in hell? do you think? you're doing?" Will broke his question out like three short questions.

"Okay. Okay, Will." He glanced back to the bedroom where Jeanette and the baby would be, "I'll meet you back up at the house."

Graylight's sorrel had been at the corral when Dixon came down from cleaning out the spring after Will left for Virginia's party in town. Dixon's hands were icy cold. He walked into the cookhouse, went over to the cook stove and poured himself a mug of hot coffee. Held it tight between both hands. Then he walked over to greet the Indian.

"Wise to come before the storm," Dixon said, indicating the dark blue horizon. "On my father's calendar he has written that your lease comes due soon. Would you like to take care of that now?"

Graylight nodded. "When you and Will are ready."

"Left for town. Cupid's tug, you know. Stronger than the barometric warnings. The combination could hold him up a day or two."

Graylight trained his eyes on the sandstone ridges of the hills with no change of expression.

They walked to the big house. Dixon opened the front door for Graylight. He turned on lights in the hallways and in the office he switched on the big globe that hung from heavy brass links. The sun had sunk into the horizon.

The lease was ready. Jeanette had typed it with two sets of carbon copies.

Graylight could write his name. He could read the names of the Matthewses. He looked at Dixon and said: "Name changed."

In the beginning, when Graylight first leased this land, it was in the name of R.T. Matthews. Then, it was the Matthews Sheep Company. Now it read Dixon T. Matthews.

"Yes. You are right. Please allow me to explain. With the market fluctuations—" Dixon used a string of his smoothest Wall Street jargon, then in an assuring voice, as if he had traded his for the all-knowing voice of the Reverend Treet, he said, "I have taken on the responsibility of your lease.

Nothing will change. You have my word. You will be doing business with my father as always and with Will, of course, and with the Matthews Sheep Company; the only change is that I sign your yearly check. You will come to me for any financial advances in the interim."

Graylight showed the slightest hesitation. Dixon handed him a certified bank check in anticipation of his signature. Graylight would not have insulted Dixon, nor any of the Matthewses. The family had been his business partner since R.T. and Clara came on the place. He trusted them as much as he trusted any white. And, he needed the money. He signed his name. Dixon shook his hand. Graylight folded the check away. He cashed it that afternoon as the snow whipped in against the tiny sandstone bank at Crow Agency. He was reassured: the money was forthcoming whether the signature was on a Matthews Sheep Company check or on a check with Dixon's name in boldface.

Will and Dixon stood, coats on, in the office. Neither bothered with the stove.

. Will said nothing. He figured the one who spoke first lost.

"Hold on," Dixon said evenly, "you will see the merit in it." He sounded as if he were reciting Masonic lines.

"You've turned into a two-bit horse thief. Using Charlie Graylight, for Godssake."

"The opposite," Dixon continued as if talking to a recalcitrant child. "I am taking the burden of a cash payment from the ranch: you may not be aware of what tight straits we, the ranch—the company—are in. What I am saying is this: we have no cash, very little cash to pay our leases. I have stuck my neck out for the company, and taken out a loan in my name. I am the one taking the risks here." Dixon kept his own voice measured.

"You lied. But, you did not fool him. Graylight is not stupid. What could he say? He needs the money, you know that. He can't question you without fear of not getting the payment. He trusted us."

Dixon ignored Will's use of the past tense.

"You think you can steal this place for a few filthy bucks? And as for your great sacrifice? You are paying yourself interest. We are paying you interest. What about a finder's fee? I'll stop payment on that check Monday morning."

Both Will and Dixon knew Graylight would have gone immediately to the bank. It would be too late. Both knew the check with Dixon's signature was good.

"It's business, Will. I expect the interest any lending institution would."

"Who asked you to turn into our goddamn lending institution. Who asked you to be Christ Almighty and save our neck?"

"I've taken the responsibility of the lease. A fee is reasonable."

One day, Will thought, you'll have me coming to you, like Graylight, hat in hand, nodding and agreeing and signing. And you'll throw in a stack of silver dollars for my signature!

"There is nothing illegal. You have a simplistic view of the economy. You don't see the goddamn stock market crash has any effect out here. You'd better wake up. But until you do, and while you fuss around with your Yellowstone Avenue people and all that hoopla in town, I am the one working to hold this ranch together!"

"How was Lochwood involved in this?"

"He made the loan available to me."

So Lochwood knew, Will thought, as he stood shaking my hand and congratulating me and ingratiating himself with Virginia and her father and mother that he was aiding and abetting Dixon. It may not be illegal, but it's dirty. I will never trust that sonofabitch again. He's better at secrets than his flouncy wife Fanny thinks.

"And what did you use as collateral?" Will continued. "Your interest in the ranch? Or the lease? Or both? Yes. So, if anyone forecloses on you they foreclose on me."

"Wait a minute—no one is foreclosing on anyone. That's why I'm doing this. Don't run off and get nutty on me again…you'll end up in the loony bin—a free trip to Warm Springs—if you start seeing that Fritz of yours jumping out of every coulee at you like before…"

"Stop," Will said in a cold even voice. Dixon had gone too far. The old nightmares Will endured after his return from the war were not his brother's prerogative. "You are so goddamn good at the cheap shot."

"I have gathered a group of leases, Will. That is a fact."

Jesus, Will thought. My brother has taken elocution lessons while I've been sitting on that stiff couch at Virginia's.

He sounds like a goddamn Bible salesman.

"I plan to sublease it to the corporation," Dixon continued. "It is a way for the ranch to avoid foreclosure. It's a way, in fact, for the ranch to take advantage of the depression, maybe expand while others can't. It's merely a change of the legal papers. All I intend is to sublease it to the corporation."

"Expand? What do you mean? The Graylight land has always been land we have leased and suddenly you end up with it—in your name."

"You don't understand, Will."

"I do understand."

"It's a way of leveraging the place."

"This is going a bad way, Dixon. Get out. Get out of this house. Go back down to your goddamn fucking chicken shit blue house."

Ten

No Inquest


March 1930


With the first issue of spring lambs in early March, R.T. and Clara were expected back from Santa Monica. Will stopped for coffee at The Northern before the train was due. Red had the newspaper spread before him, his pencil to one side. "Poor son-of-a-bitch," he said, and started reading out loud to Will:

> "...the body was discovered in the granary by his wife where she sought him when she discovered that he had not fed the stock on the farm in accordance with his usual custom. From the evidence gathered by the coroner, it is apparent that Hatch had secreted a shotgun in the granary a day or two before he killed hmiself," (Red reached for the pencil

and circled the typo without hesitating in his oration.) "He had placed the butt of the gun against the floor and the muzzle against his forehead and then pushed the trigger with a stick. The top of his head was completely blown away. Ill health and losses at ranching are attributed as the cause of the deed. No inquest will be held according to the Coroner."

"Jesus," Will said. "Written like an instruction manual."

Red poured the coffee. After a couple of sips, Will took the paper, read it for himself. "Call for a inquest if you hear shots out on Arrow Creek," he said.

"Hey, don't talk like that," Red said.

"We're going to have a full house out there with The Old Man coming back."

As the winter of prenuptial teas and bridge luncheons, hostess prizes and centerpieces swelled the society columns of *The Billings Gazette*, the livestock market turned sour. Ranchers on the remote western plains might have thought themselves safe from the nation's mercurial stock market, but the crash starting the fall of 1929 was devastating. Loans were called. Mortgages foreclosed. Banks, especially small rural banks, themselves were closed. Drought compounded by a tough winter hounded The Matthews Sheep Company as it moved through 1930. Everyone had the jitters. The affianced couple might have felt their timing poor. However, ultimately, Will would see The Great Depression primarily as camouflage and accomplice for Dixon.

The brothers had only known expansion. Nothing topped the early years up to 1913 when the range was open and R.T. ran 20,000 head of sheep. In the winter of 1930 they were at 10,000 head. In the past, R.T. would buy an adjacent homestead when a neighbor allowed he might sell, and at times, he might preempt the decision. He'd buy up leases on good grazing land on the reservation. He talked Lochwood into loosening up his credit, but, he expanded with prudence. The man was no spendthrift. Clara Matthews ran with an inherent parsimonious gait.

Dixon and Will met the train.

"You two boys keep the place in one piece?" R.T. asked. He was jovial in his Hollywood mood, brown as a bean and dapper in his tweed topcoat. Under his arm were a half-dozen boxes of See's Candies, powdery nougats and pastel Jordan Almonds. "Here's a box for you to take to Virginia and the Hartwells and one for you to give Jeanette," he said. In supervising Clara down the slushy steps to the platform and in bumping into friends at the depot and in giving his extensive report as to the weather and the condition of the land seen on their return trip up the coast of California, across the Cascades and down through the Rockies—what had been overgrazed and what had not, the depth of snow in the passes, the flood threat of rivers and stream—from ocean to the mountains to the plains, the fact that neither of his two intractable, silent sons answered the father's question went unnoticed by the returning titular head of The Matthews Sheep Company.

Will expected his father would bellow the minute he discovered the Graylight lease in the records. But there was only silence. It puzzled Will. The longer the silence, the more he avoided it. Instead, he worried. It wasn't like his father, he thought, to allow one brother such a duplicitous advantage.

Will went to town.

He and Virginia drove up the airport road to a spot they favored on the rimrocks, the lover's lane that overlooked the Yellowstone valley like an Indian scout. But their usual amorous tendencies were quelled by the dilemma at the ranch. They sat in silence.

"I can't make peace with whatever's going on," he said. "Dixon's headed the wrong way for me—he has The Old Man buffaloed, or I'm reading it wrong. There's more to it than a place for us to live." He gave Virginia a short version of his Graylight-lease encounter with Dixon after Lochwood's Valentine's party.

"Take your time figuring it out," is about all she could say, but to herself she thought, I can't believe I'm marrying into a family fight.

The next week, in a letter, Will expressed more specific plans.

> *Dear Virginia—All that we've talked about*
> *goes unchanged—I may not leave the outfit, but that*
> *is a fair possibility—at any rate I wish to leave my*

*work in order if I do leave. And, as it's just little more than a month's time left—I think we might as well see about an apartment. I haven't had time to talk over things with the Boss—But I'll have everything straight when I come in about this time next week—so until then—*

*Love Always, Will.*

Finally, with May near, Will had little choice but to make his move. It was their custom for the three men to meet in R.T.'s office before dinner. Will walked in. Dixon and R.T. were at the ledgers, Dixon with his projections—long scratchy columns of figures, working things one way, then another.

"You'll wear those numbers out," Will said.

"Thirty-two cents on the wool last fall," R.T. said.

"But this year we'll do well to get twenty-one, twenty-two cents," Dixon said.

"Think so?" Will said.

"Even Simms says it could fall below twenty," R.T. said.

"Don't you think he's just needling you?" Will broke in.

"Don't bet on it," Dixon answered.

Will spread out the day's newspaper. He looked through the futures market listing for himself, but his mind was on other things. The market will come back, he thought. "It'll stabilize," he said. "Hoover can't watch the stockmen go to hell."

"I hope you're right," R.T. said. "The prices haven't dropped that low—down below twenty cents—since before the war. Back to 1907." He could recite the wool prices, the price of lambs, ewes, rams, hay, coal—you name it—for every year of the century as rapidly as the Reverend Treet could chant the books of the Bible.

"That's what we need," Dixon said, "another war. Boys in uniform. Wool uniforms. Keep our boys warm in wool. I saw where it takes thirty-six and a quarter pounds of wool to outfit one soldier. Blankets. Overcoat. The works."

He's serious, Will thought.

"The fleeces of ten sheep, I'd say," added R.T.

So was The Old Man.

"Jesus Christ, slaughter a hundred thousand boys and keep the goddamn wool prices up." He felt like he was reaching for the gloves, but that this time The Old Man had his back turned, ignoring the bloody noses. It was time to change the subject.

"The wedding's not a month away, you know," Will said. He saw that there was not going to be a right time to bring up the subject of housing.

The Old Man nodded. "And how is our Virginia getting along with it all?" he asked. Will could tell he was still manipulating pounds and cents in his head.

Dixon let a minute or two pass. Then, breaking the silence, he asked his father, "What do you figure the wool clip for?"

"Jesus, boy, not a hell of a lot, not a hell of a lot. We have to cut where we can."

"The 'herders. Could cut them back, say...?"

"There's talk around the state of cutting herders back to $60 a month," R.T. answered.

"Careful with my herders," said Will. "If one of the good ones goes, we'll be up to our ears in problems." It was Will's job to look after the herders; it had become Dixon's to look after the bankers. Neither had much empathy with the other's constituents.

"They drink it up in one day," Dixon said, sounding as if he'd taken up with the WCTU ladies, "no matter what they get."

Will thought he might as well be speaking of his bankers.

"Where will they go for a job? In this market, they'll thank us for feeding them."

"Christ. You'd turn them into indentured servants."

"Cut where you can," R.T. said, mostly to Dixon.

"Look," Will said evenly, suddenly feeling determined, "we have to talk about where Virginia and I will live."

"It maybe not honeymoon fare," R.T. said, "but the whole upstairs is as empty as a bear's den in summer."

He couldn't believe that his father thought this could be a solution.

No one said anything.

"But how can we get the replacement ewes we need?" Dixon continued his conversation with R.T.

"That's a question for the bankers," R.T. said.

Will wadded up the financial page. Worked it into a tight ball. Tossed it into the ashcan. He stood up. Shoved his chair into the kneehole of the desk.

"Well, son," R.T. was addressing Will, "in this down market building's out of the question. There's damn little cash."

Dixon couldn't resist. "We can barely pay the longhairs on sign-up day."

"There seem to be loans for such business expenses."

R.T. said nothing.

"It's going to be a hell of a meeting with the boys at Security Bank as it is," Dixon said to his father. He shifted in his swivel chair and folded the spent adding machine tape methodically back and forth.

"You can handle it," R.T. said.

"Right," Will said. "Our new landlord here knows how to handle the bankers." He walked up to the window and looked down the long gravel road from the house: "He can handle everything."

R.T. ignored Will's reference.

"Jesus, they've covered everything and the bastards have left me out."

It wasn't Will's game. It didn't set straight with him. The Old Man would have looked in the ledger. He knew. Christ, he probably knew before he left for California. He was doing nothing about it. Will had a vision of Rutters booming down the cold hall of St. John's kicking doors open at midnight for no reason. He saw the sheep riled by wind, drift into the fence, the carcasses pile up.

"Christ, the wool market will be up," Will said. "It will be down. It will even out. We'll be here another fifty years if we keep a level head. This damn depression can't close us down. We've got the hills packed with fat ewes and a good hay crop coming. The silos are full. We could tighten up so far we'll strangle ourselves. I'm not asking for a mansion." And no matter what, he thought to himself, you two seem to find ways to add to the ranch.

There was no answer. He felt he was begging. He looked at the intransigent pair: Dixon refiguring his figures, The Old Man engrossed in the numbers that floated up and down the pages. To hell with them, Will thought. He stood up. The Old Man wouldn't stay if he were in my shoes.

"I think it's about my time to quit."

Dixon kept his pencil going, his head down.

Will looked at his father. R.T. squared off his jaw until it looked like the butt-end of a two-by-four. He looked at Will. He looked back at the column of figures lined up like windrows on the green-tinted spreadsheets.

"What the hell is going on?" Will said. "Whatever you two have cooked up, it has nothing to do with the wool market." He walked over to one of the windows and pressed his big hands against the grooves in the oak sashes on either side of the cold window pane. He focused on a lozenge-shaped flaw in the glass. He moved his head slightly from side to side as the bubble distorted with ripple and bulge and diminished the twisty branches of the squat plum trees outside in the winter yard. Either The Old Man's thrown in his lot with Dixon, or, Dixon's outfoxed him.

"I'll leave after shearing."

It was late when he got home from the Ballantine Bar and quiet upstairs. The lights were low. The fire was out. He sat down at his chair at the dining room table. His mail was stacked where his bread-and-butter plate would be at dinner.

A man in his right mind, Will thought, wouldn't quit his job, cut himself off the month before he marries. He'd stay put, ride it out. He saw the consequences of leaving. But, he feared more the repercussions of staying—Dixon and The Old Man teamed up, ignoring Will's quandary of where to live, and more unsettling, ignorant to Will's way of seeing the place. Will saw Arrow Creek as home. He felt R.T. saw it now as his life's achievement, one the sons must perpetuate. He felt Dixon saw the place as a commodity.

He read his mail. He answered Virginia's letter.

People would not understand his reasons. It was like falling in love. Something unexpected, unexplainable. Like asking Virginia Hartwell to marry him; it was without strategy, without a logic to it. But the right thing. He hoped by God it was the right thing. Virginia's parents would not understand. They'd given their consent based on what seemed a dependable financial future, "the joining of two pioneer Montana families," as the engagement announcement had read in *The Gazette*. Now they'd see Virginia looking for studio apartments in town, a husband ricocheting between city and ranch, like some sugar beet worker. "Jesus Christ," he whispered, ran his fingers through his hair.

# Book II

Book II

Chapter Eleven

The Apartment

May, 1930

They took an apartment in town. If Virginia had known where she would be living, she might have chosen a bedspread less at odds with the worn floral wallpaper. Nevertheless, at night, with the Murphy bed pulled down, the room became a meadow of the long-stemmed art deco roses appliquéd on Virginia's trousseau quilt. She had not sewn the quilt herself, but had ordered directly from Marshall Fields. The stems reached from the silvered radiators to the fresh-painted kitchen table. Its skinny leaves dropped, its knobbed legs were flush against the wall. The view from this artfully covered but flimsy mattress began with the horizon the room's one windowsill imposed on the world. The patchy tarpaper rooftops of the slightly lower buildings across the street were erased. All Will and Virginia could see was a glow from the arc of red neon—

often a-buzz with static—that jutted out over the five-cent hamburger shop below. Will forced the window wide in hopes of a breeze before morning.

He did not mention to Virginia that the nightly mirage of hot sunsets mixed with the backfire of motorbike boys with their Maybelline girls astride and the smell of gas, grease and hot rubber tires below on these warm May nights fixed a surreal backdrop of shell-shocked skies to dreams that still, ten years later, would roll out across the Eastern Montana plain from the riddled Argonne Forest to the ranch at Arrow Creek or to wherever Will happened to be spending the night.

It was the first week after their honeymoon high in the Beartooths. There they had seemed barely able to budge from the snug one-room cabin. The granite fireplace threw enough heat to remove any reminder of winter, although the night outside went well below freezing. It left a frozen coat of morning dew on the matted brown grasses. Will had leaned over on the bed, in the midst of the second afternoon, and wrestled Virginia's pen as she wrote in her diary. He wrote on the faintly lined, onion-skin page, 'We tried to take a walk and promise to do more tomorrow, but this is a honeymoon, you know.' Then they escaped again beneath the winter wool blankets.

Beyond the red neon glow and above the tops of the elms and city-pruned cottonwoods, Will could see the pink tiptop of the grandest house in Billings—fringed with its wrought-iron parapet marching around the edge of the red tile roof. "Someday," he said to Virginia, "we'll order up flatcars of

Georgian marble and have our own mansion." In his mind he saw boulevards leading up to the place lined not with hedges severe and leaves perpendicular to each other, but the arching sky high, branchy and blossomy linden. "That's what we'll have."

"Do I deserve such a dreamer?" Virginia whispered almost to herself. She gave way and slipped to the intimate concave center of the mattress and fitted her knees into the zigzag shape of her husband lying on his side, pillow knotted under his head. I'd settle for our own bungalow in the meantime, she thought. After a while Virginia slipped off to sleep in sanctioned satiety. She dreamt of penciling-in white clapboard and green louvered shutters and a sunny front porch and pointy pairs of dormer windows on the sheaves of blue-grid paper floating like errant pages.

Will was up, no alarm set, the hour before daybreak. After dousing himself with water in the postage-stamp bath, he took his carefully-folded trousers from the kitchen chair and stepped into them, buttoned his shirt. In the neon shadow, he sat on the chair as he tied the silky grosgrain ties of his oxfords while Virginia watched him drowsily from the still-warm covers. The petals resembled now more potpourri than bouquet. She did not recite to Will her "if onlys." She did not say, "If only you didn't have to leave before dawn, If only you hadn't felt duty bound to quit, If only your father would take notice, If only your mother would get her Scot back up, If only you could talk one to another, If only Dixon…" But she could not put into words what she wished of Dixon. And, she didn't say, "If only I…" because she could not see what difference she might make in these matrices long in the making.

"A more dutiful wife would get you something to eat," is what she said.

"A couple of your oatmeal cookies will do me," he said, his wide hand barely fitting through the top of the yellow Dutch girl cookie jar, "until I get to the ranch." He took the milk bottle and poured himself a glassful.

"When do you think you'll be back?"

"I'll telephone tonight. But, what if you take the afternoon train out tomorrow?" Like his father, Will had adopted the mannerly way of putting his request in the form of a question. "I'll pick you up at Corinth. We'll do something cosmopolitan—like go on my rounds of the camps. You can meet Armitage and the fellows first hand."

"How can I resist?"

"And what's on your docket today?" There was a teasing tone in his question.

"Don't rub it in," Virginia said.

In town Will and Virginia spent evenings snuggled in the balcony loges of the Babcock Theater where golden muses leapt bare breasted, framing the stage and screen against the rough gray walls. Virginia would lean against Will's shoulder as they watched Ronald Coleman woo Vivien Leigh. Or a foursome would meet at the apartment and play rubbers of bridge for pennies. Or they'd meet Muriel and Hap at The Northern for a club sandwich. It was much like the year of their engagement. They spent the rare evening alone now at the apartment interrupting each other's reading. They read out loud to the other or upped their bets in the marathon gin rummy game they'd started on their honeymoon. Virginia, who was apt to hold on to an Ace/Queen waiting for the King, say, while Will would go down fast, catch her with a handful of points, did not sense his propensity for the fleet discard. She misread his poker face time and again. At the end of two weeks she owed Will practically the cost of one carload of Georgian marble, as well as several silly favors. Will was clever at making little side bets, so that who ever won that night's round, for example, would be the one to do the night's dishes teetering and forgotten in the sink.

"And, then?"

"Laundry," she smiled. "A tea with The Gillygouch. Oh, unless Orpha calls."

Virginia's days were filled with invitations. A new bride was a treasured guest, but the possibility of a call from Orpha at her father's law office took precedence. A call to substitute for an absent stenographer once meant money for clothes and travels, but, with Will's work tenuous and the economy making any paying job prized, it now meant everyday money. Virginia accounted for each penny. She was cataloguing the wedding presents, and had packed the unwieldy, elaborate gifts—such as the magnificent porcelain punch bowl from the Lochwoods— away in trunks and crates stacked in the damp cellar at home on Yellowstone Avenue. "Until we move into our mansion," she said.

He leaned down and kissed her goodbye and said "talk to you tonight" before Virginia could—not that she would— ask, "But, where will we stay?"

For years, Will and Dixon had started the day at dawn across from each other at the polished mahogany dining room table. Will faced out the picture window to the front yard where he could see pruned fruit trees and lilacs and peony bushes and the rope of willows shadowing the creek downstream. Dixon faced the tall grandfather's clock with its medallions depicting the seasons, its thin-serifed Roman numerals attending with the two sons their own "stand-to" with their father. R.T. Matthews sat ramrod straight, dressed in white-collared shirt, at the head of the table, ready to advance on the day. Like a colonel and his lieutenants, they went over each pasture, referring to each by name—Biddie Pasture, the Charlotte Place, Crow Meadow. Or Arcadia, where the silver-lined leaves of the cottonwoods and willows fanned out from the reservoir R.T. had engineered. It held rainwater, runoff and ground water that seeped pure though crevices in the cochineal sandstone outcrop. The place reminded him of the harsh lushness of Nova Scotia where he'd spent his cut-short childhood. They inventoried each spring, each creek. They noted if any of the spring casings or adjacent water troughs of pine logs bound with steel bands required cleaning out or shoring up. They went over each draw and ravine and grassy plateau and run of fence and each hay field now newly green with alfalfa or timothy or red clover and eventually ripe for haying—if the sun stayed hot, if the rains came at the right time, if the darkened afternoon tapioca clouds held off until the Bull Mountains. They surveyed the fields lying fallow but always needing to be turned. The big disk would plow the weeds under and free the roots from choking the soil. These cultivated fields were Dixon's responsibility, as Will's was the livestock on the place, although both worked at what the season and their father demanded. Nothing of this was written down. They culled each band of sheep: the ewes, the lambs, the bucks, the dry band. They second-guessed the wool buyers who might bid that year, the bank notes and bankers, the invoices for seed and supplies. All this while they split baking powder biscuits with butter, helped themselves to black pudding and golden eggs sunny side up, drank unstrained glassfuls of fresh-squeezed orange juice and read the funnies and the futures market. The papers were folded in thin thirds to accommodate the breakfast things but not their elbows which were not allowed to rest on the table.

Sometimes Clara Matthews would join them at the table though she'd had her bowl of hot oatmeal with chunks of brown sugar and fresh cream even earlier. It didn't seem to Will his mother had her old energy, but she was back and forth through the swinging kitchen door. She set out plans with Alma for the day's meals and the provisions due herders, and mapped out for Emmet, the chore boy, now in his late fifties, the work of the house and the gardens.

This morning, as Will drove east in the dark from Billings, mile after mile, his was the only car on the road. At dawn, light outlined the Bighorn Mountains as if they were the first edges of the world with the sun leaving its fingerprints on the foothills. He felt the cockcrow, and, as he drew closer to the ranch, he felt sheltered, even under the circumstances. He would admit this to no one, least of all himself. He would spend this day and the next two or three at work on the ranch as if he'd never left, then return to Billings for a late afternoon and evening with Virginia. He would split himself like this for the next month and a half. He had quit, but had said he would stay through shearing. This was a courtesy you would expect from any hand on the place. He would be damned if he would shirk his job—or let anyone suggest how he do it—while it was still his.

Virginia counted Will's twenty descending steps and heard the gentle closing of the outside door, then spent a few luxurious moments in bed, assessing her work on their first apartment.

She had pounded thin nails in the wallpapered walls and said to herself that in *her* mansion, there would be no strips of spent lilies of the valley glued to the walls. She would have fresh, creamy white paint cover smooth new plaster. She had hung her lithographs. One was of a dark old narrow courtyard in Vienna where, she had been told by the owner of a small shop where she had drunk a miniature cup of black coffee, Schubert once composed his romantic, unfinished symphony. The other was a pair of Japanese women walking arm-in-arm, one carrying a collapsed parasol, the other, a lowered paper lantern. For good luck, and to wash the room in color, she tacked up a long width of red Indian Madras studded with tiny hexagons of mirror framed in bright embroidery threads. She had hurriedly hemmed lengths of fabric cut from drapes her mother had discarded which she first bleached, then tinted in laundry tubs of hot tea, and finally fed through the scorching rollers—one exposed hot metal, one padded with old sheeting—of her mother's mangle in the laundry room.

Unlike some husbands of Virginia's friends, Will liked to shop for the apartment. He'd taken out a small loan. Virginia didn't believe in spending money they didn't have, but Will assured her he'd be paid well after shearing. It was she who jotted down each item and price in a tiny leather-flapped notebook that fit in her coin purse. They spent thirty-five dollars at Billings Hardware on a good straight-back chair, its seat and back upholstered in dark nubby green, its legs and curved arms of wood; seven dollars for a kitchen stool, twenty-four dollars for a set of everyday dishes.

"Better than the hand-me-downs we'd get at the ranch," he'd said. "I've no love of old things."

They paid fifty-one dollars for two-months' rent. Will sanded and she shellacked an old bookcase, and they set out their books. His were Arctic explorers. "Penguins and icebergs?" Virginia teased. Hers were French novels and dime mysteries. She preferred the body dead and discarded before the story began with the bulk of the book intent on solving the mystery, and a little romance between the survivors. The apartment was quite gay, and if not her dream house, at least their own place.

She called it "the apartment." "Home" was still the big house on Yellowstone Avenue where she would go, as she did this morning three hours after Will left for the ranch. She'd packed her laundry bag full of things washed and hung to dry yesterday on the clothesline stretched above a bed of bleeding hearts and sweet alyssum in the backyard. She would fold and iron while she talked with her mother in the sun-flooded room off the kitchen.

Virginia crossed to the maple and elm-shaded residential blocks at Division Street. Early on the city fathers had changed the layout of the streets from lining up with the railroad tracks, and set them on a north/south, east/west grid. As she turned up the wide sidewalk to the house, her mother called from the flower garden alongside the big screened porch. The roses and heavy peonies had not yet opened fully. The pink petals overlapped and were covered in dew. As Virginia tiptoed down the dewy grass path towards her mother, she brushed against the blossoms, and they spilled off onto her cotton dress.

"What a glorious morning," her mother said. "It'd be a good time to put on your wedding dress and we could take your photograph out here before this light escapes." Mrs. Hartwell had her pruning clippers in hand and snipped a yellow rosebud. "Agnes Pepperling has been after me. She wants the write-up for next week's society pages."

Her father rapped out "hello" in Morse code on the breakfast room window.

"Pretty good for a Nebraskan," Virginia called back. "Any coffee?"

"Enough for one cup," Mr. Hartwell said out the window.

"Go along—have a visit before your father leaves. I'll join you after I cut one or two more roses for the table."

After coffee and a triangle of toast, Virginia ran up the polished stairs to her old bedroom. At the window, thick flaps of maple leaves blocked her view of the rimrocks that circled the north and east sides of the valley like an ancient city wall. She stood in the roomy closet and she wished she could tack it onto their tiny apartment. Her ivory lace dress hung from a padded velvet hanger. She stepped out of her cotton dress and into the creamy silk slip. It felt cool against her morning skin. She fingered her way into the long thin lace sleeves of the dress and let the delicate web of bodice and skirt skim down the slip. The lace was heavier than it looked. She liked the weighted drape of it, its tea gown length. Virginia had slender ankles and didn't mind showing them. Now where are the shoes? she asked herself. Then she saw them, fitted with arched quilted shoe trees, balanced on their hourglass heels on the shelf. She had felt quite ritzy trying on all the fanciest slippers and settled on these alabaster moiré mostly because of the delicate rhinestone pavé straps and silver clasps. À la Marlene Dietrich. Quite transformed from the Monday laundress, she came down the stairs and gave one twirl in front of her admiring parents.

It had been a morning wedding. The tenth of May. The ceremony was in the living room and the French doors to the adjoining sun porch were folded back to allow for rows of wooden folding chairs borrowed from the church. There was room only for aunts (one bosomy, hatted Christian Scientist aunt from Los Angeles; wiry twin aunts from Beaver City, Nebraska), a watch-fobbed and much-mustached uncle, one Psalm-saying grandfather, beautiful cousins and close friends.

But there were at least a hundred guests immediately
afterwards. The reception began outside with a receiving line
on the porch, then circled into the dining room where sunlight
slanted through the leaded glass windows. The linened table
held open-faced sandwiches, white wedding cake and sugar-
flowered mints and salted almonds and cashews and hot coffee
and tea and icy fruit punch. Cousins and Theta roommates
took turns cutting and pouring and ladling. The surprise had
been Virginia's Aunt Edith traveling all the way from
Philadelphia with tins of homemade fruitcake packed in her
train case for the groom's cake.

From the table in the vestibule, Virginia's mother picked
up the black square Kodak. She cleaned the lens with an edge
of her dress. "Watch that the shutter's open," her father said.
Then he was off down the street to his office, and Virginia and
her mother went into the garden to select the perfect backdrop.

Chapter Twelve

The Northern

May, 1930

Virginia walked back to the apartment shortly before noon carrying the folded clothes and towels, the sheets fresh from the mangle. She shifted the laundry to get the key out of her pocket.

She opened the apartment door, arms full and warmed. There was Will. He sat at the kitchen table with *The Gazette* spread out before him. The smoke from his cigarette curled out the big open window. She could tell he was in low spirits. Quite the opposite of the man who had left before dawn. Virginia was glad she had declined her mother's offer to stay for an egg salad sandwich.

"You should have called."

"I'll stake you to lunch at The Northern," he said as if to preempt any question she might voice about his coming home early.

Virginia put on a pair of hose and changed her dress. No matter what the circumstances, she wanted to look her best for a walk down the three long city blocks to the hotel with her handsome husband. They took the two flights of narrow stairs in a little race they had developed. Virginia's fingers skimmed the blue and white tiles of *putti* embedded in the stucco walls, as her heels clicked across the chipped tiled entrance, the remnants of the original owner's not recovering from a grand tour of Tuscany. Once out the frosted-glass door, down the three steps to the sidewalk, they slowed. Will reached for her hand. They didn't talk. She didn't inquire as to his drive before dawn or the health of his mother or the level of animosity between the minority shareholders in The Matthews Sheep Company.

They walked past the empty, well-lighted Christian Science reading room next to the grooved cement pillars of the Masonic Temple. Its glass doors were cloaked in maroon velvet swags. At the corner, Lindemood's window display of sheet music, French horns and violins was modest since the economy was down. They passed Mrs. Gregory's shop where Virginia had purchased her wedding dress. They didn't linger in front of the Hart-Albin department store windows, but Virginia did run her fingers over the 1902 on the cornerstone. It was her birth year. On Sunday afternoons they would window-shop here and not be tempted by what they could not afford since the doors were religiously locked until Monday morning.

Billings in 1930 was a town with 16,332 people, and covered four square miles. Seventy-two percent of the population was "native born," as were both Virginia and Will. Clara Matthews had come from Lavina by sleigh on the coldest day on record to give birth to her first born. There were three banks, 4350 telephones, 21 churches and an untabulated number of bars, speakeasies, houses of ill repute. The Northern Pacific, the Great Northern and the Chicago, Burlington & Quincy (CB&Q) pulled into the downtown railroad station. It was the third largest city in the state, after Great Falls and Butte, and on Friday nights you could listen to organ recitals on KGHL radio.

Will checked his wristwatch against the ornate clock balanced atop the black Ionic column standing free at the curb. It was the one fancy thing in this utilitarian downtown. But he ignored the islands of emeralds catching the light in the velvet windows of Abrahamson's Fine Jewelry, and did not stop as he usually did to admire the precious stones and say, "Someday, I'll buy you…" He adjusted his hat and tie and the collar of his shirt and looked ahead the half-a-block to the stately four-story brick hotel. The striped canvas awnings gave it an air of carnival.

"Dixon is being a son of a bitch," was what he said. Then, "Excuse my language."

Virginia's upbringing in a family of reticent Quakers and Puritans hadn't prepared her for such internecine struggles.

"Maybe he feels guilty," she said of Dixon, then wished she'd sided outright with Will.

"Guilt? Bullheadedness."

You are both capable of that, she thought, but replied, "What brought all this on?"

But they were at the door of the hotel.

"Mr. Matthews, sir," the bellman said as he swung open the door. He tipped his cap to Virginia. Will removed his hat He thought that only ill-bred dudes kept their big cowboy hats on in the lobby. No matter that they might be wealthy remittance men sent out here by their families to ranches across the state line in Wyoming. Will held his hat by the crease in the crown and didn't let the hat check girl put it on the top rack in the cloak room. Too often someone had walked off with his hat and these were not days he wanted to put out cash for replacements. Will stopped at the tiny newsstand on one side of the lobby. A boxy middle-aged woman sat on a stool inside the booth, her mouth working one Chiclet after another. Her red fingernails penciled in her best crossword guess as she rang up his pack of Lucky Strikes and counted out his change. She told him who was in the bar ("Just Red"), who had just left, and who he missed yesterday and where had he been? and, "Oh, yes, my best wishes to you, Mrs. Matthews."

It was the crossroads for ranchers from the southeastern part of the state and the northern part of Wyoming—Sheridan and Cody. Most conducted a big share of their business in the lobby and at the bar. When times were good—the right price on their calves, their lambs, their winter wheat—their wives could buy a new dress from Mrs. Gregory or Hart-Albin & Company, spread things puréed on corners of toast at the hotel tearoom, have their hair waved, see their friends at matinees at the Lyric, fill up their cards with new novels from the Parmly Billings Library. All within a few blocks of the hotel.

The marble lobby was on the scale of the great room of the Masonic Temple. Will prided himself on never having joined, even though his father had gone to some length to gain membership there. He had sent a leather desk chair to a rancher who'd sponsored him and more recently Dixon.

"You'd find it beneficial to join," his father had once suggested, but didn't insist.

It reminded Will—with all the inflated purposes and regimen of rank and secrecy and duty—too much of what he didn't like in the military. It was the camaraderie of privates, not the elbowing of officers, that had saved his neck. He didn't tell his father his opinion of grown men in sashes and badges, with secret grips and oaths and loyalty pledges and secret passwords. All in the name of God and country. But, in 1930 in Billings, Montana, Will was in the minority on this.

The grand piano, cloaked this early in the day in its green quilted cover, was rolled towards one side of the hotel lobby. Around the large square of dusty rose carpet were rows of overstuffed leather chairs and couches and spittoons. There were elaborate standing ashtrays with pearl buttons to release hinged-dishes to hide cigarette butts and snips of cigars and ashes and matches.

If Will had come to The Northern alone, he would have first paid his respects around the dusty rose square, seats filled with "a bunch of damn kibitzers" second-guessing Hoover's mismanagement of The Depression he had gotten them into, then turned left into the bar. Before Prohibition, the Dewars and Johnny Walker Red and Old Granddad would have been out in the open above the shot glasses and tumblers and Old Fashioneds where Red the Bartender, who, like a man with a new Cadillac, washed and polished. As he held each glass to the light from the chandelier, Red nodded. So often was he in agreement with his patrons, his head bobbed up and down like the Sunday bell high in the Congregational Church bell tower. If, however, the news or opinion being relayed called for it, his head swung solemnly from side to side like a winter bison foraging for grass. In 1930, however, the bar looked to be only seltzers and sodas. The men, all treading lightly until they might see the Volstad Act repealed, all cursing their fellow Republicans who blocked it, stood with one foot on the brass railing of the bar trading their stories in limbo. Who was to say that if some times, later in the day, this was not a place where Scotch was poured not entirely out of sight of the law, where if one tipped the bell man, a five-dollar bottle of bootleg whiskey could be made available for twice the price?

The other route from the lobby, which was the direction Will and Virginia took, went straight into the white linen dining room where one could order fresh Rainbow trout, Maine lobster, Rocky Mountain oysters in season. The luncheon favorite was The Northern Club: a number of preferences of patrons of long standing were printed in italics and indented under the sandwich list in the menu. The Woolgrowers, for example, when in town, might insist the usual layer of beef be replaced with wafer-thin slices of roast spring lamb dotted with clear mint jelly.

The dining room was busy. Alfred, who had spent his younger days at the Brown Palace honoring requests with discretion, gave Virginia and Will a corner booth where they might be alone. Will slid in on the smooth leather seat. Alfred set the napkins like parachutes on their laps. While Virginia opened the menu, Will helped himself to a spoonful of the colored crystals from the pressed glass sugar bowl. He had a sweet tooth.

"This morning I rode out to the shearing shed," he started. Virginia glanced up over the menu. "The place had been shut since winter. I jacked-up five or six of the big shutters. Let the light in. Time to remind the swallows whose shed it is." He took another spoonful of sugar. "There are always busted gates, a whole hatful of things that need repair before the crew shows up. I was seeing what's what, then I'd go back and get a couple of the boys to come help me get it into shape. So who shows up but Dixon on that pet saddle horse of his, you know, and he leans with his arms balanced on the saddle horn, and he says to me in this new slick tone he has adopted, 'By the way, you don't have to worry, I signed up Harry Evens to come over and give us a hand.' I didn't say anything."

Virginia smoothed the gold ribbon that fell down the center of the menu.

"He kept talking, filling in the air," Will continued. " 'You know,' he said, 'troubleshoot the shearing.' What could he be thinking? Troubleshoot? I said. 'You keep out of it and there won't be any trouble.' And to be sure he understood, I said: 'Cancel Evens.'"

"He knows I'm not leaving until after shearing," Will continued. "Not fast enough for him apparently. What I can't figure is, why Evens?" He ran his hand through his hair. "I've never trusted him. If we need help, we'd need a man who knows the work. Evens—he'd only bollix things up."

Evens was a 'lease-wrangler' friend of Dixon's from over by Pompey's Pillar. Once Will had seen him palm a card at the poker table in the back room at The Stockman's in Ballantine. Will knew Evens knew. Will never said anything about it. If Dixon couldn't see his pal was a cheater, what good would it do to tell him. Will believed a man who'd cheat at cards would cheat at anything.

"There are a hundred things that could go wrong," he said to Virginia. "You've got the outside crew—over a dozen shearers, in addition to the men who tie the fleeces, men who throw them up to the tromper. He tromps thousands of pounds of wool a day into the big, hot and smelly greasy wool sacks. Wranglers who run the sheep in and out of the pens, and then there's the tallier—the accountant—who keeps track of the fleeces per shearer. Wranglers who brand the sheep once they're shorn." He drank the hot coffee Alfred poured. "Cooks. Water boys. Great choreography." Time and weather were the unknowns, he thought to himself. Rain or even a freak late snow could bring costly delays. "Tempers can flare. This year, maybe more so. With the market down, every ounce of wool matters more. Even in a good year, The Old Man expects the highest count."

Virginia listened. She felt lucky to be the one Will was confiding in. How lucky to have a husband who would come home and take her to lunch rather than go to the bar alone. She expected some of that. But, still, even under the circumstances, this was good.

"Did Dixon mention," Virginia asked as she twisted the corner of the belt of her navy faille dress, "anything about this Evens at breakfast this morning with your father?" If not, Virginia thought, he's going around both you and your father.

"No," Will shook his head, "and I hadn't thought of that." But he thought Dixon seemed to be sparing R.T. many particulars in recent months. "I'm counting the days until I have no part of Dixon's way of operating."

Virginia must have looked to him as if she were waiting for a more disturbing rationale for his storming back to Billings.

Will said, "Well, that wasn't all that we said, but it's all that can be repeated in polite company." I don't know what the hell I am doing, he thought to himself. "I know it would kill me to rot out there," he said. The odd man out, he added to himself. Virginia will understand. If she doesn't, at least she won't tell me right away. And if not staying was the most important thing he might ever do in his life, he didn't recognize it in the moment of its happening.

Does she think I've not only relinquished my job, but my mind as well? He looked at Virginia. "So, I decided I'd best come to town and cool off, and besides," he said and finally grinned, "I thought maybe I shouldn't leave my new wife too long."

"Oh, Will," she said and felt herself blush. "You just left this morning," and reached her hand over to his. "But, I was going to take the train out tomorrow."

"Well, now you won't have to—I'll give you a ride." She was relieved to know that he planned to go back to work as usual in the morning.

Chapter Thirteen
Crow Meadow

May, 1930

Perhaps because they were newlyweds or because of the unspoken, "but where will we stay?" Will did not to stop at the big house. He bypassed Dixon's little blue house, turned west at the junction, past the log barn and horse corrals. He sped through the rain-swelled Arrow Creek and on up past the neat lineup of harvesting machinery until the core ranch buildings were out of view. Alfalfa brushed against the belly of the car on the two-track road as he reached Crow Meadow. He stopped three-quarters of a mile down from the low red shearing shed, a building more than four times the size of the Northern lobby. And there, barely decipherable from the mottled cottonwoods by the creek, was the old tipi.

"The Ritz Carleton," Will said.

"Can we really camp here?" Virginia jumped out of the car. Her arms spread out in a wide stretch. The morning was filled with yellow arrowleaf balsam root. The hills echoed with the calls of meadowlarks, the syncopated creek.

Will set to work. He swept out the tipi. He made a ceremony of fitting it with a plump clean wool sack filled with fresh straw—"it's of finer stuff than that mattress that came with the apartment!" he called to Virginia who was poking around in the meadow—and on top of it all he spread his bedroll, made it big enough for the both of them.

Virginia turned with a start when she heard the clanking coming up the road. "It better not be Dixon," she said to herself. An old open-topped war-surplus truck made the turn.

It was Clara Matthews. Will offered her a hand. She stepped from the beat-up truck she'd had R.T. buy at auction for its high clearance.

"You two do take your stubborn streak in style," she said.

Will took it as a compliment, reached down to pat Argus, Clara's border collie. The dog had trotted ahead, taking short cuts, anticipating Clara's destination.

Virginia finished picking an armful of the just-opened yellow flowers. The large gray leaves sighed in shock over their relocation and drooped over the speckled edge of their gray enamel coffee pot vase. Will had pumped up a pair of kerosene lanterns ready for nightfall.

Clara had seen, from her kitchen window, the black Ford come up the gravel road, then turn at the barn. She gave them time, followed a hunch and brought a goose down quilt from Will's room under the eaves, a jar of freshly-squeezed lemonade, a tin of her butter cookies. She leaned against the truck and smiled at Virginia.

"I remember when R.T. and I made camp out here before we had the homestead," she said as she took a deep breath. "It can be lovely."

"Was it on the reservation then?" Virginia asked.

"Yes. In those days R.T. was running sheep with two partners here, as well as in Lavina—where we lived when Will was a baby. We'd come out here daydreaming. R.T. was on good terms with the Crow and Graylight offered the tipi to us." She sat on the platform of the tipi.

Virginia loved hearing Clara roll her r's, especially when she said R.T.

"No one went on holiday in those days, but we were in paradise. No fences then." She looked across the meadow. "It has the wideness of the Highlands."

Virginia wondered if she was acknowledging Will's leaving. Could she see an advantage in it? She knew about seeking a place of one's own. Was she weighing the price of it, recognizing in her son the impulse for independence? Virginia thought she saw it in the woman's full blue eyes.

When Will walked down to the creek to fill the water buckets, Clara said, "I wish he could find a way to stay." And to herself Clara Matthews thought, it breaks my heart, these three obstinate men.

It was her, Virginia realized, not her son Clara was addressing. Am I the only one she can tell? Virginia had no answer, but wished she could put her arms around the strong woman and ask all her own questions. Instead, they stood, quietly and each with her own thoughts. The only sound was the spring-fed creek.

Late that May night Will monkeyed with the tall poles to adjust the round opening at the peak of the tipi to bring in what breezes slipped over the hills. They lay together and Will was his most tender in his lovemaking. It saddened Virginia and she could not hold the tears from flowing down her cheek. Afterwards she and Will fell silent and they looked out the big triangle where he had tied back the canvas flaps so they could decipher planet from star over the leafing willows.

Will slept and Virginia dozed until the mice started in. After timing the pair of mice running up one of the poles and down the other, she asked herself, why do they go back and forth and back and forth? until it seemed like dawn. The mice and lack of sleep may have accounted for her not hearing Will rise, even on the creaky plank floor, before dawn.

Long before she was awake, he rode off with Charlie Graylight. When Will had walked from the big house after breakfast, he saw the still silhouette of Graylight watering his horse at the corral.

"Morning, Will."

"Good morning, Sir."

"We ride the fence together."

Will recognized the invitation. He walked past Graylight into the tack room. He picked his bridle off a high peg and walked slowly, dangling the bit from his right hand, the reins in his left, beckoning the brown bay who stood in the midst of a half-dozen horses in the corral. Will whistled through his teeth. The mare's ears twitched. She tossed her black mane and flicked her long black tail. She stood still. Will slipped the bridle over her alert ears. He led her across to the open wide door of the tack room. He dropped the reins, took his blanket with one hand, lifted his saddle down with the other and fitted both to his big-boned bay. Will tied a fifty-foot length of tightly-rolled barbed wire to the back of his saddle, packed the tool pouch with pliers and a sack of staples. He handed Graylight a shovel, and the Indian lashed it to his saddle.

"That should do it," he said.

The men on their horses took leave of the corrals and horse barn. Will left a note for Virginia without waking her. Graylight's sorrel shone redder than raw sienna in the early sun. His lean back, covered in a dark purple cloth shirt and doeskin vest with only frayed remnant of ornamentation, was hunched slightly and splayed out from taking some seventy winters. Will was straight and tall and easy in his well-soaped, working saddle. They rode east, then south. They rode toward the ridge that separated one section of the Matthewses' ranch from the reservation land. As the trail narrowed along the sandstone spine, Will reined in his bay and Charlie Graylight took the lead. They fell in two abreast as they came alongside the line of knotted and gnarled pine posts that stood their inspection like weary soldiers. Many of the post holes had been dug and set by Will and Dixon in their boyhood. Three strands of barbed wire were strung horizontally from post to hand-split pine or cedar post. The neat lower section of barbless wide-wire squares made the fence "sheep tight."

They rode in silence. The fence was a joint responsibility of the two landowners. Both looked at the fence for places sprung by the migrating winter elk or for wire sagging from weight of snows and ice, or a length of fence merely given in to time or a greedy ewe. Graylight stopped at a stretch of the sheep-tight squares come loose at three posts, lying flat on the ground. They got off their horses and lifted the whole section. It had been down all spring and where the wire had been, the new grass was colorless. When the wire was lifted, the thin path of land along the fence looked like a checkerboard brand sizzled into the land. Graylight crouched down. He held the strip of fencing as Will stapled it to the front of each post.

Two or three miles out, Charlie Graylight reined his horse away from the fence line and forced Will's horse to sidestep. Will's first thought was "Armitage," until he followed Graylight's line of vision and saw a pair of new born fawns in the wild sweet grass. The sunlit brown-white striped twin coats through the shifting grasses gave gentle camouflage.

The men gave the newborns a wide berth.

They heard the flutey notes of a meadowlark. The voice came straight up its black-bibbed yellow throat, out its arched-open beak to mislead the men and the horses from its nest, which, like that of the fawns, was in the near tussocks of grass. When Will turned toward the song and saw the bird on the barbed wire, he saw the doe. She hung limp, her forelegs outreached as if halted mid-flight, her eyes forever opened, her throat cut fresh and jagged by the ruthless garland. *That horror of harsh wire...* Chased as well, Will thought. She must have caught her hind foot on the second strand as she went over the top and so, as it came up, it brought the lower strand up and the upper wire became the bottom of the snare and it twisted itself and snapped her leg. As she struggled to free herself, the weight of her body must have snapped the bottom wire, and it sprung back like concertina wire. Will and Charlie Graylight stopped.

"What spooked her?" Will asked as he dismounted. A coyote picking up the scent of afterbirth?

The Indian put his hands on the wire and, pulling against the tension in the fence, forced the barb wire strands to separate enough for Will to pull the leg out. The still-warm animal slumped to the ground. The two men disentangled the body from the bottom wire and pulled it from the fence line. Will stooped down and took a handful of the dry dirt and rubbed it between his bloody hands. Graylight took his knife from his belt and skinned the carcass out. Will stood a moment before he went to his saddle bag. He took out a handful of staples and his pliers.

The top two wires had been ripped from the posts. With the hammer-face of his pliers, Will stapled the loose wire into each post. Will straightened out the two unraveled strands so he could get at the ends, then tightened a loop at the end of both wires. He took his lariat out and made three half-hitches around the long end of the break. Graylight brought Will's horse around by the fence, back away from the break. Will took his lariat, which was fastened to the wire, over to the horse and made a couple of turns on the pommel. Graylight would have the horse step backwards, keep the rope taut, as if it were holding a roped calf. Then, Will cut a short length of new wire from his pack and looped and twisted it to the short end and then to the one held taut. It would never be as strong as the original, but it would hold. Once Will had the wire spliced, he stapled the wire low at each post. He broke a sweat now. He picked up a good-sized rock and he pounded the post into the ground with twice the force required.

When he was finished, he leaned his big dusty blood-smeared hands on the post. He thought of spectral young bodies: the once-strong boys caught in the spiral of barbed wire set out by either army, great rolls unwound by night, creating the cruel boundaries: No Man's Land paved by mud and the day's dead. He saw himself with the other ambulance boys at the Argonne forest, come in only when shells had ceased and most of the gas drifted off, it nearly safe and maybe days after the slaughter—they always were behind, never caught up with their work—and he turned his head from Graylight. The words *and I remember things I'd best forget* boiled in his head.

Graylight looked straight up into the sun. He remembered Will both as he had seen him when he had first returned: all heavy wool uniform and ribbons and brave stories told about town by his father, and as he had been out on the range, riding his horse too hard initially, then walking out alone to Ten Mile, then sitting off by himself. The boy took the camp tender job in the numb winter months—October into April. Holed up in the dark sheep camp shacks, jockeying horses and provisions for the lousy herders, hauling winter hay by bobsled to the bands of sheep. And, Graylight had seen

Will, with no more notice than a shooting star, take his leave—upsetting the father, who had little regard for change, counted on the boys to work the ranch—once to drive ambulances in San Francisco, once to work the Boston wool mills. But, always to return in the spring.

Now, at the fence with the deer, Graylight knew. He tied the deerskin to his saddle. He gave his shoulder a shrug in the direction of the fawns, and he and Will doubled back with their horses. Each scooped up one downy wet one and tucked it as they would any motherless lamb, secure between themselves and the curve of the saddle.

"We'd better take our offering over to Armitage," Will said, "before the bastard comes back." Graylight looked at his young friend. They turned east again and rode in silence until they saw apostrophes of smoke lifting from the far wind-ridden plateau.

"Christ Almighty," Armitage hollered when he saw what the two men were bringing, "You two make the sweetest goddamned Red Cross nurses." He reached up and took one fawn, then the other, and walked back to his herder's wagon feigning great burdens and admonishing his two new charges, but folded the pair in the soft rumpled crevices of his bedroll. "Now," he turned, "I suppose you two wise men have already laid bets as to whether I can get these orphans to suckle up to my nasty old ewes."

"Tell me tomorrow," Will said. "I'll be back with another visitor and…" He had promised Virginia a trip out to meet the sheepherders.

"…extra snoose and extra marmalade for these Girl

Scout efforts," Armitage said, as if he were used to finishing Will's sentences for him.

Will and Graylight continued working almost wordlessly. Graylight would stop at a snapped or snarled wire. Will would dismount. If the break required one to steady the post or hold the wire, Graylight would descend and hold it in place while Will hammered the staple over wires.

They came upon a fence post swinging in the wind. The pine post had long been rotting: ants with transparent wings laying their eggs and hatching generation after generation had eaten their way into the little decaying fissures. But the stub of the rotted post held fast in the ground. They must cut another fence post, dig a new hole. That would be faster, even with the unseen rocks, than trying to dig the knotted post out. Trees were scarce. But it would save time, Will knew, if he could find one the right size nearby. He and Graylight rode to a stand of scraggy, wind-stunted cedar at the side of a ravine. Cedar would outlast pine. Will had never come across a rotting cedar post. Cedar shed the elements and the bugs didn't bore in. You could split a long-felled cedar or an old greyed cedar post and find the wood inside healthy and strong. Will got off his horse. He took a hand ax from the saddle bag. He side-stepped his way down the uncertain ground. The tree was about two feet taller than Will, but, once he trimmed it down, it would be the size for the fence. Graylight sat on his pony. Will began to chop and cuss at the strength of the tree.

As the sun worked its way into their backs, Graylight said, "He is chased by the spring Grizzly."

The smell of cedar was as sharp as incense as Will chopped. Will thought he would line his closets and chests in his mansion with thick strips of cedar.

"It is our land, not his."

Will knew the old Indian, in his oblique way, spoke of Dixon.

Graylight swung down from his horse. He stood at the side of the tree, ready to steady it or prevent it from tumbling down the ravine.

"Can he not remember it is ours?"

Will straightened up. He picked up the cut end. The stack of chips at the base looked like the work of a beaver.

"Your Dixon we do not understand."

They carried either end of the dwarfed tree up the crusted soil, taking care not to slip. Once they reached level ground, Will took the ax and with quick strikes, shucked the tree of its bony branches.

"Not understand," Graylight repeated.

Will dragged the pole behind his horse. Graylight removed the shovel from his saddle and started to dig. He and Will took turns on the stubborn rocks. Will wished for a crowbar. He didn't want to break the shovel, was cautious with the pressure he exerted to pry out the pieces of shale and sandstone. They had a good three feet to dig out.

"He wants much."

Will wiggled the post into the deep hole. Graylight kicked rocks in and shoveled the dirt. With the handle of the shovel, Will tamped it down. They did this again and until the layers of earth and rocks again held the post. They fitted the old wire to the post. Will took three new staples from the handful in his shirt pocket and held them between his lips. He spit one staple out and placed it over the smooth part of the wire. He struck it with one stroke flush into the green wood. He did the same to the lower wires.

"From the weak ones—too much."

Graylight must have heard stories that he was leaving, Will thought, not that either mentioned any such possibilities.

"I will talk to my father," Will said, but, inside he wondered how far Dixon had already gone. There was no money for such expansion. It had not come up at breakfast. Not when he was there, at least. He seems to be railroading The Old Man—passing him over when he chooses. How much of it can The Old Man see? How much is he ignoring? He used to know what we were up to by the look on our faces. I can't believe he's lost that, Will thought as he rode home now along with Graylight, a man who allowed ample time for questions and answers.

Will tried to piece together what course Dixon must be taking. Of course, he said to himself. *The weak ones.* Dixon could be ponying around out there: smooth talking this one or that one, paving his way with bottles of liquor. Coaxing this one or that one into signing their allotments over to him for quick cash and booze.

"Why go through all the red tape with those boys at the Agency…you can deal direct with me," he could hear him say, "make your own deal."

It explained Two Legs at the cookhouse. And Evens sniffing around, some sort of hired lackey. Christ. Graylight knows. He knows how a white man can get the richest grazing land in the state without paying what it's worth. Will thought of Graylight, and he thought of his own interest in this land: we're in the same boat. How will I, when I'm off in some two-bit apartment, keep Dixon from converting all the leases and God knows what else to his own name? Will looked at Graylight ahead of him: he's letting me come to my own conclusions, and, at the same time, getting his fence mended.

## Chapter Fourteen
## Fishing Upstream

### May, 1930

Virginia spent the morning at loose ends, lonelier than if she had stayed in town without Will. She found his note written on the back of a check blank tucked in the toe of her shoe at the foot of her straw bower. It informed her that because of Graylight's unexpected call her grand tour to the sheepherder camps to meet Armitage had to be postponed and that Clara Matthews was expecting her to stop by the big house for tea. P.S., Dixon had left for town. She chided herself for the lazy sleeping in—scandalous for a rancher's wife, she was certain. She was disappointed, but grateful Will had thought to mention Dixon's whereabouts, so she was spared worrying about what she might say if she ran into him. She smoothed out the lumpy mattress, poked back the blunt bits of straw.

Rather than drive down to the big house and find something for breakfast, she sat cross-legged on her impromptu front porch and peeled one of the oranges she had brought from home. She picked off each strand of the white membrane from each segment before biting into the sweet juicy fruit. Will was right. The Crow had known the best place, she thought, as she took in the sweep of cottonwoods, the fields folding in on each other, the morning haze in the distance over the Yellowstone River. She ate one of Clara's perfect circle butter cookies and drank from the jug of lemonade. The sugar clashed with the tart citrus on her tongue. Once the sun cleared out the shadows, she unwound her hair and washed it in the clear, cold waters of Arrow Creek, and rubbed it dry in the hot sun.

Then, with her stationery box as desk, she worked on the last of her thank you notes and wove in references to apartment 301C one day, this deerskin tipi the next, as she gave thanks for pieces of china she'd already stored in the Yellowstone Avenue basement. Her only visitor was Argus, Clara's sheep dog. He'd startled her when she had seen only black ear tips and a tail weaving towards her through the golden meadows. He sniffed around the tipi and mattress and the note cards and the orange-rind pyramid and then, as if appointing himself her attaché, curled up at her elbow. When she decided to make what started as a somewhat formal call on Jeanette, she was glad Argus trotted at her side about a mile down the winding road to the little blue house.

Virginia knocked on the screen door. She had been to the house once with Will, but never on her own. The weathered door, not setting true in the jamb, rattled against the planks of warped pine. Paint on the siding blistered in the sun.

She could hear Jeanette at work in the kitchen, now trapped in the center of the tiny house since a mud porch had been attached to the west side, blocking the kitchen window. That made it a warmer spot in winter, Jeanette had told her, but, Virginia thought, it must be dim and claustrophobic. She had not wanted to peer uninvited into the living room, but the front door was open. There was no entry way, no polite buffer. Jeanette, it turned out, was bent on cleaning her immaculate forlorn house, scouring around the edges of sink and counter with an old toothbrush.

Virginia knocked again, called out, "Hello?" and Jeanette called back, "Virginia? Oh. Come in. I'll be right there."

Virginia stepped in. The room carried the onus of transients although Dixon and Jeanette had lived there nearly two years. The house was void of anything personal, except for the few amenities that signaled a baby, and even those seemed spare to Virginia. A wooden-legged card table and two folding chairs blocked access to the front window. A slumping couch against one wall had been covered with a green-fringed bedspread, two dark brown throw pillows were placed equidistant from either arm. A low three-cornered stool served as a footstool. There were no books. No photographs. The only decoration on the wall was a large Northern Pacific calendar. Virginia wondered if the one substantial piece of furniture, a maple rocking chair, might have been on loan from the big house. The worn maroon floral print square rug reminded Virginia of cheap hotels. If Dixon had his Masonic friends call, Virginia imagined he entertained them at the big house.

Jeanette came in with the baby on her hip, all apologetic. "Don't look too closely," she said to Virginia, who, while she did not think the room inviting, certainly thought it clean. "We've just finished eating," Jeanette said and she wet her thumb and wiped smears of jam from the little boy's ruddy cheeks. "Dixon doesn't always keep his muddy boots to the mudroom. Expects everything spit-polished."

"I should have given you some warning."

"No one ever does." Jeanette lowered the child to the floor and unpinned her own apron and, even in her loose house dress, it was evident she'd lost little of the weight she'd gained in her confinement. "How could you? There's no telephone."

"Do you feel stranded?" Virginia asked not meaning any disparaging word, but she noticed how the little blue house was separated from the big house by the commissary, blacksmith shop, bunkhouse, horse barn and corrals. A lovely walk on a warm day like today, but with a baby and for the nights there must be when Dixon would be off with the car, it felt isolated.

"Well, Dixon says not to worry about every little thing," Jeanette said, "Dixon says it's too expensive to have a telephone installed here when we can use the one at the big house anytime we want. You know what a penny pincher he is."

Is that it? Virginia asked herself. If Jeanette were making the point that while she might have a house to live in, there was little to envy, Virginia agreed to the unsaid.

"Let's have a cup of coffee—I need to stop for a moment anyway."

Virginia decided to ignore the "anyway" and Jeanette's inference that she was interrupting—what? her long day alone of working and cleaning and cooking in a house that looked, no matter how much Dutch Cleanser was applied, only one step above the bunkhouse. Perhaps I shouldn't have called, Virginia thought. But, on the other hand, it would be rude not to. Regardless of our husbands or where we sleep—Virginia felt she was lecturing herself out of her mother's antiquated *The Ideal Woman*—it's best Jeanette and I get to know each other.

"I hear you slept in that ratty old tipi last night." Jeanette said from the kitchen coffee pot as if reading Virginia's mind. "Like dudes from the east. I couldn't believe it! Even newlyweds and all. If I had the choice, like you do—" and here Virginia felt Jeanette's bookkeeperish tone, "I'd pick the big house. It's the grandest."

Has she no sense why we are not living on the ranch? Can't she feel the tension between these men? Virginia's short-lived dreams of a western odyssey were slow to evaporate and with Will about to be out a job, the whole scenario had seemed like something from a serial in *Collier's*, not her life.

"Will's a sheepherder at heart." Virginia hoped it sounded casual and jokey. Of course we would prefer soft linen sheets and feather beds. Who dreams of straw-filled mattresses and rats racing overhead? Or cramped noisy apartments? I would have been more honest, Virginia thought, to let Jeanette's comments float out into the hills unanswered.

"That's what Dixon says," Jeanette went on. "Says it cracks him up how different he and Will are in that respect. Says he's bound and determined to make this into the biggest

167

place in the valley," she said with a shrug. "To each his own, but sleeping in the tipi!" she gave another shrug. "When I've finished my work in the late afternoon, Little Andrew and I go up and sit with Mother Matthews and we see what we can get on the radio. Or listen to her gramophone. She likes the company, and Little Andrew likes to totter and take his falls on the soft rugs. And, I'm up there helping Alma put up things from the garden, stocking the commissary—we'd starve without all the garden things pickled and preserved. Don't even mind making blood sausage now.

"The big kitchen," Jeanette said as she filled two cups with coffee, "there's so much counter space. So, as I say, I'd stay up at the big house whenever I could. Dixon says there'll come the time—you know Dad Matthews (Virginia cringed) is seventy now and not getting any younger, and Mother Matthews…well, you can see she's not so well. Dixon says there'll come the time when there will be no choice: someone will have to live in the big house with them."

She will have the silver to herself in no time, Virginia thought, remembering Jeanette's compulsive polishing and counting after the engagement dinner. So, Will is right about Dixon's timetable. To Jeanette she said nothing, but looked at Little Andrew sitting on the rug stacking colored wooden rings on a peg, trying to master the symmetry of the larger red one on the bottom, followed by the blue, the green, the yellow.

"Dixon went to Billings," Jeanette offered, "for one of his Masonic meetings—he's moving up the chairs already, did Will tell you? and, they get over so late, and he's so much the life of the party always, you know, that he and Harry

Evens...you know Harry? from over by Pompey's Pillar? they'll stay in town."

It was evident she was proud to be married to the merriest of the brothers, the one quick on his feet when it came to dancing, the smooth one when it came time to procure another round of drinks, the one ready to initiate a madcap escapade. But if Virginia's memory of him at the Woolgrowers convention in Helena last winter was any indication, it seemed that Jeanette already was quite separate from the merry part of her husband's life. It appeared to revolve around organizations of men's weekly meetings at severe stone buildings where wives were admitted only for one obligatory evening a year.

"Everything must be spic and span when he gets home, that's why I'm rushing."

"Would you trust me with Little Andrew?" Virginia was eager for fresh air. "I have time on my hands this morning, I'll take him for a little walk, and you can have some time to yourself."

"You bet," she seemed pleased with Virginia's interruption. "When I was working in the bank, before we were married, I complained of no free time, but now, when I look back, it seems like luxury to me. Not that I'd change a thing."

Virginia believed her.

If the house wasn't much, Virginia thought as she walked to the small square window while Jeanette found the child's shoes, its view of the late spring grasses reaching beyond the tall shady box elder trees in the front yard to the low green hills was lovely.

"Where's Will?" Jeanette asked, as an after thought, as she tied the laces and tucked her son's little plaid shirt into his shorts.

"Off checking fences with Mr. Graylight."

"Oh, that old Indian. Gives me the creeps. These Indians coming and going as they do out here. That Graylight's so silent. Never know when he'll pop up."

"I haven't met him yet."

"Really?" Jeanette sounded surprised. "Dixon says that old Indian and Will are 'thicker than thieves'—said he'd have bet money Will would have had Graylight be his best man!"

Virginia didn't know what to say. But, she herself had not been surprised Will hadn't asked Dixon to stand up for him.

"Well, you know how Dixon likes to pull your leg."

Argus waited on the porch, stretched and then followed as Virginia, leaning over to hold both of the child's hands in hers, walked up toward the corral not minding the pace of one scuffed white shoe after the other finding their way gingerly between sagebrush as tall as Little Andrew himself. The fragrant purple alfalfa blossoms along the pathway brushed against his freckled nose. At the corral, Virginia picked up the little boy. The one old mare ambled over in hopes of a sugar lump. They scratched the long white diamond on her nose; both jumped when the mare tossed back her long narrow head and whinnied in gratitude and showed her big yellow teeth. "All the better to eat you with, my dear!" Virginia said and imitated the mare's big open mouth. Little Andrew giggled, mimicked her and clutched his fat little hand tight to Virginia's long braid. It had come free from its pinnings.

A landscape that could look barren, devoid of people, suddenly felt crowded, Virginia thought. At tea, Mrs. Treet came hurrying in and stayed even while she said she must go because "The Reverend" was waiting for her. It affronted Virginia's belief in brief farewells. Any chance for personal conversation was overshadowed with talk of the church circle that, as Mrs. Treet dissected in detail, was in the throes of making new linens for the communion table. Then Mrs. Treet turned to the matter of the newlyweds not living at the ranch. How had Clara listened to this rattling-on for, what, nearly thirty years?

"We wish you could talk Will into staying—but, we know how he itches for the more adventuresome place…" Mrs. Treet began.

"A more adventuresome place: the lavish apartment #301C above the ten-cent hamburger joint?" Virginia couldn't help blurt out with a laugh, but immediately checked herself, and Mrs. Treet continued, overriding Virginia's interruption.

"When I married Reverend Treet, I had no idea I would ever leave Philadelphia. But he couldn't resist the homestead bug. Isn't it something where we follow these men?" Clara made no response. She'd come to Montana from Scotland on her own to teach the children of a wealthy remittance man and his wife who had large holdings north of Billings. One sister and a brother came a year or two after Clara.

"You're more accustomed to the city," Mrs. Treet continued. "With your family in town and your travels to Europe."

Clara got to her feet, poured more tea, passed a tiny plate of cookies and hand-made butter mints. The talk made her uneasy, Virginia could see, but her mother-in-law kept her own council, so she followed her lead. Any attempt to set Mrs. Treet straight, when, Virginia realized, it was more-or-less still a mystery to her as well, seemed in vain.

"We had hopes you would join our circle," the minister's wife continued. "We can always use new blood."

I could ease out drops of communal grape juice accidentally splashed on the pure Protestant cloth, work out deep-set stains, erase creases with turns through the steamy mangle, lash my mercerized threads over fraying edges, Virginia thought. She pictured herself as the silent Puritan tending to the tasks of the congregation.

When Mrs. Treet finally left, Virginia thought Clara looked worn out. After clearing the tea things, Virginia excused herself as well.

The sun was shimmying low in the western sky. Will still wasn't back. She cautioned herself not to get in the habit of expecting him to appear like a bank clerk. I feel more a visitor than his wife, she thought. She walked down from the big house towards the junction. At the corral she stopped to visit the swaybacked mare. Emmet came around the corner from the cookhouse. "No sign of that husband of yours yet?" he asked.

"How difficult would it be to help me saddle the mare?" she asked. She was relieved when it didn't occur to the chore boy to take Clara's English saddle from its peg.

"You should be honored that Argus has taken you on," he said. "And, Poco here won't give you any trouble, either. Just don't let her get it into her head to come back to the corral, unless that's what's in your head."

Virginia kept the horse at a walking pace to the tipi. She stopped at the car, dismounted and rummaged in the trunk for her fishing pole.

Poco took her far up Arrow Creek. If they stayed by the creek, she wouldn't get lost or turned around. Why didn't I think of riding earlier? she asked herself. Exploring on her own made her feel less of a visitor. Although her seat started to feel sore after thirty minutes or so, she rode until she found what she thought must be a good fishing hole. She untied her bamboo pole from her saddle and stepped from the horse to the moss that grew like big soft eaves beyond its roots at the bank. She wrapped the reins to the trunk of a twisted willow. Then, she waded far out. The water was never deep, not rushing like the new mountain water she was used to in summer. She felt her way on stones slipperier than those in fast water; strands of moss rippled invisibly downstream. She hoped she wouldn't lose her balance, feel her feet slip out from underneath her and land quite unladylike on her bottom. She limbered up the line, wet it in the water, then, in sweeping zigs and zags, dried it in the air, not allowing it to snag a bit of willow. She let out more as she cast up stream and into the current, letting her line snake over and along the opposite overhung bank where she imagined a big trout might camouflage himself, speckled spot upon spot blended with the pebbles. Light through the rippling water made even the rocks seem fluid and moving downstream. She saw the fish. It barely moved, held itself with a flick of its cold steely tail, its gills searched the water for oxygen churned up by the water itself, its eyes looked out the sides of its still stone head not giving itself away. But, in the end, the fish was not able to resist the delicate bits of feather furled in disguise about the tiny hook, and took it swiftly, swallowed it whole and there could be no changing of its mind. So, on her first cast she had a bite and played it, not knowing how firmly it was lodged, then, walking gradually backwards, feeling her way with the soles of her feet feeling through the soles of her boots, then walking sideways to the bank. She reeled it in.

It was then she saw Will on the sandbar. He waded across.

"I found your note."

Virginia had printed "gone fishing" on one of her engraved informals with a stick-figure picture of herself dangling off the round descender of the "g." She left the note on her side of the bedroll.

In the end she had four nice-sized ones.

"Think your parents would like a trout dinner?" Virginia asked.

Will watched as she slit each fish open, and, running her thumb flush up the cold backbone, cleaned each on the spot, and rinsed them in the cold water.

"At the lake, no one's allowed home with their fish not cleaned."

The cook hurried Emmet off to town to find lemons. Alma filleted and served the fish with fresh wedges of lemon to Will and Virginia, R.T. and Clara in the dining room. Virginia was seated in the spot she knew was Dixon's. She felt he might suddenly bound in and demand his place. Not his absence, but the avoidance of much mention of him seemed unnatural. She was curious as to what the atmosphere was like when it was Dixon and Jeanette and Little Andrew at the table.

The conversation that night was the weather: the unseasonably hot days and sun bent on burning the new hay crop and the lack of moisture and the perils of another year of drought and the fear of early hailstorms and then an incantation of peculiarities of seasons past. "The summer of 1903 was so wet ferns sprouted in the fields." "You could almost walk across the Yellowstone, stone by stone, and keep your feet dry in 1912!" This was the tragic poetry recited by weather-bent ranchers, Virginia thought. The evening was punctuated with long silent stretches. No toasts. No lines of Shakespeare. Virginia felt the most for Clara Matthews. It was clearly not for the first time she was caught between these stubborn, silent men. Virginia wondered if it would not be this situation, rather than the Sunday silver, that she would be bequeathed by Will's mother.

Both Virginia and Will were weary when they returned to the tipi after dinner. They slept hard far after midnight.

Until they heard the car. It roared up the long gravel road that followed not the natural contour of the land, but the rigid legal perimeters. It screeched suddenly at right angles at the section corners, skidded in the gravel. This night interruption, ricocheted like rounds of artillery. Will bolted from bed. Then, the instant he knew where he was, he lay back down. Both brothers were familiar with taking that home stretch late and fast.

"He's drunk—and making sure we know he's back."

"No tiptoeing in with shoes in hand?" Virginia murmured.

The night was silent again. Will slept within reach of Virginia. He touched as he turned, her elbow, her soft shoulder, her thigh, but he had few fitful nightmares of enemy shells lighting up the skies above his sagebrush hills.

Virginia, on the other hand, after Dixon's interruption, was awake. She imagined Jeanette awake now in her cleaned house and sympathized with her. Then, as she remembered the night's trout dinner, she couldn't help but compare it to the merry engagement dinner.

## Chapter Fifteen
## Camp Tenders

### May, 1930

"Well, look who's not sleeping in this morning," Dixon said as Virginia came in to the dining room. The three men rose and stood until she took her place alongside Will, and with the early May morning light behind him, Dixon became a silhouette. She couldn't see his expression, or the look in his quick eyes, but he sounded uneasy in his merriment. No one made mention of the late night screech of loose gravel.

After an abbreviated breakfast at the polished mahogany table, Virginia excused herself and walked into the big kitchen to ask Alma about a lunch. When she saw Alma was baking bread and filling the boxes for the herders and cooking eggs to specifications for the breakfast table, she announced she had come to make her own sandwiches. There was cold roast beef and hard-boiled eggs, crisp cucumber pickles, tart dried apples, biscuits from breakfast; she had no trouble assembling a picnic.

A far cry from the peanut butter sandwich and orange and Hershey bar she would have stuck in her back pockets for a day's hike from the cabin in the Beartooths. Emmet was there to help load the truck with the cartons Clara had labeled for each sheepherder, with the week's eggs, bacon and milk and sugar and canned goods.

The sky arched like a pure robin's egg blue before them. At last she and Will were headed off to make Virginia's acquaintance with the sheepherders. They were scattered like skipping stones across twenty-five square miles of grassy uplands. After the first mile of the jarring ruts on what Will called roads she was grateful she hadn't accepted his dare to take horses and a wagon the first time.

They bumped through yellow fields of the arrowleaf balsam root. "It's certainly spring," Virginia said as she pointed to a string of what she thought must be deer on a distant ridge.

"Elk," Will said as he handed her binoculars from the jockey box. "Heading to the high summer range in the Bighorns. We're not the only nomads out here."

"Gypsies, all." Virginia said. "Do they return in autumn?"

"Yes. The snows force them down to this lower country—for food, and companionship. They're in the rut come fall, stay with their harem for the winter."

The herders were the most courteous, the most reticent men she'd ever met.

Armitage stood large and white, stock-still and quite

Biblical. Straight from the Old Testament to Arrow Creek,
Virginia thought when she first saw him high on a sandstone
outcrop looking out over his flock. She could picture stone
tablets, thunderheads. Will took her hand and they climbed the
narrow way, stepping through the prickly pear and wind-wrung
sage. Up close, Armitage was all heavy white mustache and
whiskery eyebrows and weather-worn ice gray beaver hat that
sheltered his eyes in all seasons from sun and the blinding glare
of snow, and it was that wide felt brim he tipped quite grandly,
in lieu of any verbal greeting, when Will made the
introductions.

Virginia felt little need to speak. It seemed appropriate
to just be there with Armitage on his god-made cairn, to
admire his fed and watered fat ewes and their licked-clean
lambs, all corralled by his black border collie. The dog had a
white clerical ruff about his neck, he panted with his pink
tongue out, and his face had an honest-to-goodness smile. The
dog ran off down to the sheep and then back up through the
rocks to Armitage. She took in the tranquillity and tried to
imagine Will's years out here. The dog came up to her and she
reached down and scratched behind its black ears, and said,
"Look at his smile," as they walked back down to the wagon.
Armitage didn't change expression, but said, "Old Quick
Jaws?" Virginia turned to him. These were the first words he
had spoken. He looked down at the dog at her heels and then
toward the coyote pelts stretched out like scalps, tacked to the
side of the wagon.

Will had taken some quixotic reassurance in seeing
Armitage and Virginia and the dog together in the light ruffled

wind, seeing how she fit in.

Armitage helped Will unload his provisions from the truck.

"Ah ha," he proclaimed. Virginia turned to see him handle a tube of six tins of Copenhagen, then a fat quart jar of Clara Matthews's thick orange marmalade. He held it high to let the sun stream through the sweet rinds. "A man of his word," he said, and then to answer her quizzical look—"You picked the smart one. He pays up."

"What's this all about?" Virginia asked. Will hadn't told her of the encounter with Armitage yesterday.

"Come. See for yourself," Will said. She walked closer to the men and the wagon. "Take a peek in the wagon," Will said, grinning, "with your permission, Armitage?"

The herder, a man of about fifty-five, Virginia guessed, stepped aside. Will gave her a little boost as she stepped up warily. She'd been in all sorts of dwellings—from the lava-stilled homes in ancient Pompeii to the just-deserted summer nests of black bears where park rangers took the curious. Although it took her a second to adjust to the windowless place, her first sensation was of the heavy odor that hung like an old blanket in the stifling space. She couldn't equate it with any other smell. Stronger than the closed smell from a hibernating winter that hit when they opened the lake cabin one spring, and found, after prying free the kitchen floor boards, the remains of one cyclopean, rotting woodchuck. The odor did not lessen, but Virginia's concern for it was diminished when she saw the two pairs of eyes open. The large leafy ears lay flat on the speckled smooth heads, the long aristocratic sharp noses pointed out from the tattered tartan flannels on Armitage's narrow bunk which was practically hidden by the stack of unrinsed saucepan, black crusty fry pan and tin plates and spoons on the cold coal stove. It was so cramped she couldn't imagine a man the size of Armitage in it. She thought if he stood straight up, his big salt-and-pepper head and shoulders would rip through the bowed canvas crown of the wagon. She could not imagine him spending the hours, the days, the whole seasons he must in the tight space. Virginia took one step in and found herself kneeling, putting herself at eye-level, not knowing if she should pet these wild things. With the tip of her finger, she touched one on its forehead and petted it. She felt the soft head ease back into the flannel. When she touched the other fawn with her other hand, she saw their eyelids go as limp as the alley kittens she had found as a child.

"Did ya' know this man o' yours such a soft touch?" Armitage sang into the dingy cavern.

When Virginia backed out into the sun, she took several extra steps to take in full breaths of fresh air. She listened to Will and Armitage embellish the finding and feeding of the fawns. The two storytellers had almost transformed the sagebrush into bulrushes. She was right to think they were teasing her about Armitage's knack of getting the fawns to mother-up to a ewe. Armitage admitted he milked "that old biddy you almost tripped over on your way in" and fed the fawns by letting each suck his finger dipped in the tin of warm milk.

"Some wet nurse," Will said.

"Tell me more about Armitage," Virginia said as they drove off and down the coulee and out of earshot.

"I don't know much," Will said, "but that he's a rattlin' good friend of mine." He let it go at that for a mile or so, then he added, as if there had been no pause in the conversation: "He's pretty heavy on the booze at times. One time I ran into a man on the Hi-line near Malta or Hinsdale right in that country up there who had a sheep outfit of his own. He said Armitage could have stayed there on that ranch as a partner."

"Why didn't he?"

"I didn't think it my place to ask."


Will spotted McLeod. Gave the horn three short staccato taps. McLeod gestured by waving his herder's crook wildly, but he stayed out in the midst of his sheep with his dogs, one a black border collie like Armitage's, and the other, pure white.

"Looks like this is about as close as we'll get to McLeod."

McLeod, a herder at the furthest reach of the grazing circle, nearly ten miles across the flat prairie from Armitage, didn't want much to do with men *or* women. He had run sheep over by Miles City for years, Will said. "When he came over here, just before I left for the war, he said to The Old Man, 'I herd sheep. That's all. I'm tired of being boss.' He refused to give anybody any orders, he would not run a lambing crew and he would not tend camp, he would only herd sheep."

Will and Virginia unloaded the provisions themselves. They checked his painfully neat cupboards, the antithesis to Armitage's, to see what the man was running short on. Others would have lists ready—with snoose underlined and usually at the top—but McLeod left all matters of civilization to others.

Virginia felt perhaps he and the other herders spoke more when Will was there alone with them. He said it wasn't so, except for Armitage. "It was different," Will said, "when I was younger and not, in so many words, his boss."

They drove on. The hills rose and fell like a grassy roller coaster. "Now, this one," Will said, "is Rattlesnake. He's the toughest little New York Irishman you'll ever see." When Virginia reached his tidy camp, he reminded her of a compact, stubby street cop in the movies. He regarded her as he might a new teacher, or a registering nurse at the infirmary. He shook her hand as if nudged by a distant voice from his growing up days instructing him how one greets a lady.

Will accepted Rattlesnake's offer of coffee.

"I'll get Alma's cookies," Virginia volunteered and went back to the truck for the tin of round butter cookies.

They sat out front of the camp wagon. Rattlesnake poured coffee from the dented and dinged gunmetal pot that hung over the coals of the campfire.
As he handed her the hot tin cup, he said, "You'll want to let it settle."

Virginia realized there was nothing filtering the coffee out here. When she took the first sip, it was the richest she had ever tasted.

Rattlesnake regarded Will formally, Virginia thought. Will was often the only human being Rattlesnake saw for months on end. They talked about work. The sheep were heavy with wool. The lambs were full of independence and ignorant of the pair of coyotes that worked the place as attentively as the herder. Both men feared drought.

"We could use a rinsing," Rattlesnake said. "The creeks slowed-up early."

"He quits in summer—goes off prospecting for silver and gold," Will said after they left. He felt like an itinerant preacher, filling her in on the stories. "Takes himself off up the Stillwater. Then, up the switchbacks of State 32 to Cooke. But, as a rule, he's back down in this country by late September."

"No one minds that he comes and goes as he pleases?"

"Well, these men have their own patterns, so to speak," Will said. "There's no guarantee of a job when he returns. Fact is, he leaves assuming he'll strike the rich vein and never be back. When he comes back, no one rubs it in. Of course, at the same time, there's an unwritten law, that a herder, once he signs up for the winter season, say October through April, he doesn't leave his band of sheep."

Virginia wondered about Rattlesnake's formality. Although he himself left, did he fear that she might cause Will to take his own leave? What had Rattlesnake heard out here where there was no one to hear anything from? She felt she was not imagining the look in his eye, a look the other herders had too. It was one of quiet respect, a being at ease with this young man who ate with them from their tin cups of hash, traded stories and pitched hay to the gravid ewes huddled noonday when the temperature remained well below zero. *A chill no coat, however stout, of homespun stuff could quite shut out*, she recited to herself from Whittier's *Snowbound*. The sheepherders could relish as well the hot summer days. Will had said he had come across Armitage a time or two on a July day, the man basking bare, his pale pink skin open to the sun.

They were men who preferred, at least nine to ten months of the year, to have little or nothing to do with women.

"Have any of them ever married?"

"Most—at one time or another," Will said. "Rattlesnake told me once—'I go prospecting every spring.' But he's back—single, broke, and in time to take on a couple thousand sheep for the winter."

Let's hope, Virginia thought to herself, you don't follow suit.

Chapter Sixteen
The Last of June

1930

On the last day of June Virginia took the train to Ballantine for the final days of shearing. She had stayed behind at the apartment in town to fill in for Orpha at the law firm transcribing dictation, typing deeds and filing carbon copies to earn what extra she could.

A life divided between ranch and town was unpredictable. When Virginia expected Will in town, there could be many reasons why he could not be. A pileup was rare, but the most tragic. If one lamb got rattled, others might blindly follow. A ravine could fill with animals trampling and smothering one another. If Virginia drove out to surprise Will, it might be the morning he had to bring in a herder (now a little drunk with medicinal doses who wouldn't admit to a nasty fracture) to the hospital. So, when things worked out as planned, such times were received as a gift. Such was the case with shearing.

Will was waiting at the station. "I don't know when I've been so glad to see anyone," he said. She held on to him, paid little attention to onlookers whose presence might have curbed a public display of affection by Virginia. She wished the drive to the ranch could be as slow as the engagement drive cross country last fall.

Shearing was long hard hot days. Will had strung electric lights above the pens and alleyways in the shearing shed. The shearers worked well into the sweltering nights, thick fleeces falling as of one piece to the floor. The place looked like a county fair—the shearers like Gypsies. Will had been working twenty-four hours a day, against the threat of afternoon rains. No one wanted to wait for a band of soggy sheep to dry out.

Virginia had a Thermos of ice water, a book, Will's tarp from the trunk of the car.

"Stay outside and in the shade," Will advised before he went back into the shed.

She settled near the red shed in the shade of the spring-fed willows. The balsamroot, wilted and drying, crackled as she spread her tarp. Yellow buttercup-like dots on green shrubby cinquefoil were the only bright flowers. Green gooseberries were starting to turn. Flocks of baby tree swallows bobbed on the branches. There was no breeze. The big meadow had been trampled by the eight thousand unshorn sheep. One band at a time was ushered in. The air was stagnant and dense with pollen and dust. Hatches of deer flies hovered about her arms and ankles. Virginia couldn't concentrate on her book for long. She got to her feet and walked toward the low drone of the shed.

The hum of blade sliding against blade slicing through the thick, sticky wool vibrated from the weathered wooden building: inside, the hollering of the shearers, the shutting of gates and chutes, the bleating and blatting of the sheep. She walked in. It was a maze of pens and aisles, sheep and men. Everyone had a job. She wished she knew enough to help. She perched on a railing, her feet pulled up and out of the way of the nervous hooves. From the opposite side of the shed, Will gave a wave while he talked with the red-headed captain of the shearing crew. If Dixon saw Virginia, he didn't acknowledge her. He was preoccupied with the tallier, who went from pen to pen marking cards, keeping track of the number of sheep sheared by each shearer. There was no sign of his cohort, Harry Evens. The shearers were stripped to their waists, sweat ran from their bodies. The ones near her grinned big shy gaping grins. She tried to ignore the stench. But she could not ignore the calling back and forth, the separation of ewe from lamb. It could last for hours while the lamb was held motherless in an outside corral. Virginia watched the assembly line—the ewe shorn, its wounds dipped, its back painted with the hieroglyphics of identification. Close up, it could be brutal. While the shearer would cradle the ewe in the crook of his elbow and clip the wool within a quarter-of-an-inch of the skin, there could be blood from the chance nick of flesh, the severing of ear or teat caught in the elongated sharpened triangular hand-held blades. The shearer did not stop. He was paid according to the number of fleeces that slumped to the floor of his pen, and the faster he finished, the quicker the wound could be treated. Virginia couldn't help wince when the bleating changed to a sharp cry.

Only Emmet, the chore boy, who kept coming through, stopping at each man, giving each sweaty shearer a long drink from the canvas water bag, had spoken to her. "Anyone offer you a turn at one of these cranky sisters?"

Minutes after Virginia had heard the sound of the truck, Alma, the cook from the big house, and Jeanette stuck their heads in where the wide sliding door had been shoved open to catch any breeze. Virginia waved, kept one hand on the railing. She bet her sister-in-law was surprised to find her here. Virginia reluctantly went outside. The women were covering tables with cloths, setting out pails of roast beef and ham sandwiches, deviled eggs, coleslaw, potato salad, sliced tomatoes and cucumber, fork-tined peanut butter cookies, congregation-sized urns of lemonade. She realized she should have offered to help with the food, although she preferred watching the men work. She thought of Emmet's comment, wondered if she ever would have the chance to calm a resistant ewe.

"Dixon says you've forsaken us for the city lights," Jeanette started right in, and started her sentence in her requisite *Dixon says*. She was, it turned out, the only one that day to mention their residence in town,

"Well," Virginia paused. "Now when you come to town Saturdays, you'll have a place to bring Baby Andrew—I'll watch him at the apartment while you do your errands."

A generous offer was not what Jeanette had expected. "I'll take you up on that," she said. "Since your walk to the corrals," Jeanette continued, more enthusiastically now, "he opens his mouth like a big yawn and snorts through his nose."

"Oh, I didn't think Andrew would tell on me," Virginia said. "I tried out some silly whinnies."

Will and Virginia spent the night between shearing and loading in the tipi wound about each other. Will fell asleep before the moon rose. Virginia lay awake looking at the mere promise of a new moon. The air was weighted with the acrid smells of cured grasses, the odors from the shearing shed. The insects didn't quiet down. Crickets called to her from every direction. Two seemed right under the board floor. She made herself listen beyond their vibrations, beyond the sheep. Once there was the piercing neigh of a horse. Towards dawn she heard coyotes. She knew Will detested them, but she awaited their answerings—a den of hungry pups yipping, then the further off howls. She wondered not so much what Will would do for a living, but how the last day at the ranch would sort itself out.

While Will was about to be out of a job, he was a man given to finishing one job before taking on another, and to Virginia's unspoken concerns, he had only begun to figure how he might make a living away from the ranch. He had his stock, his share of the place, but to expect dividends was folly. Cash out, he knew wasn't until The Old Man died. If then.

What Will had wanted most that last day—the day of loading and hauling and weighing and shipping the wool—was for the day to pass like any other. He wanted no farewells. From Dixon, from The Old Man. Nothing to mark the day with any finality. Perhaps no one—least of all himself, perceived it as such. So, it had been, on the surface, another day of work. A day of settling up with the wool buyer. Meldrum, both guest and buyer of the year's work, would be watched, not in distrust, but to prevent any misunderstanding that might jeopardize the mortgaged once-a-year check.

"Take your time, my dear, another biscuit? if you will, and, then perhaps you will ride in to the loading station with me," R.T. said to his new daughter-in-law. Virginia, Will, R.T. and Dixon were eating breakfast at the big dining room table. "You can help me," he said, keen on his mission of the day, "see that Meldrum doesn't short us."

"Will says you have been besting him for years." Virginia was not surprised at how bright and brisk everyone was this morning.

Meldrum had been out at Arrow Creek for a day or two of the shearing seeing what he was buying "on the hoof." He would separate the thick wool on the woolly back of a compliant ewe, note what attention the Matthewses paid to the sorting and separating of tag ends, black wool, broken wool. R.T. and Will had toured him around, so the buyer was expecting few surprises in the quality of the wool.

"Out here a man's word outweighs his signature," R.T. continued. He was grateful to have a new listener to his old maxims.

Dixon sat unwontedly silent, making columns of figures alongside the commodity prices in the paper, dissolving sugar cubes in his tea.

"All the same," R.T. continued, "he knows we read every word of our contract. We live up to it, know he will follow suit. Meldrum may be the epitome of decorum. He has traded with us for years, and even though we trust him, we never forget," R.T. said, looking her in the eye, "that he would return home the greater hero if he returns with one more penny in his pocket." His eyes were bright. "So," he turned to Virginia, "you and I, we'll keep our eye on him as he records the weights and measures the length of our wool."

"You boys be off. We'll be along." He dispatched his sons like scouts.

For as long as Will could remember, Meldrum had been buying or bidding on the Matthewses' wool. Will remembered back to 1919. He was just home from France. Even now, eleven years later, Will could feel Meldrum's tug at his lapel, feel his thick scratchy uniform judged by Meldrum's expert fingers. He could hear the Boston accent embellish accolades (for "giving your old man something to brag about besides his goddamn wool clip") and congratulate himself and all the woolgrowers of America on the high grade of the worsted wool, on doing their part for the war. More than once Meldrum and The Old Man had set to calculating how much wool had been sold to the Army. They'd toast the high price— it had more than doubled since the war began to around 58 cents.

That last day, Will took fresh note of the wool buyer: how the man from Boston dressed in fine, custom-tailored summer weight woolens—as if his skin would tolerate no other fiber; how Meldrum spoke not only with R.T., but with the hired men loading the wool bags, and with Dixon and Will— the second-generation sons he would expect to deal with in the future. *I know wool and weights and strength of staple as well as he,* Will thought. *Hell, maybe that's what I'll do—strike a fair deal with a Summer Street wool house, then ride from ranch to ranch, a man respected for his knowledge and his word. Sign up contracts with the big ranches, nail the wool pools.* It sounded good.

Even if the family was not good at goodbyes, the loading went well. It turned out to be one of the largest wool clips in the history of the ranch. Will could take pride in that, however, with the market down to 22 cents, the check was the lowest it had been in eight years.

Early the morning after the last day Virginia and Will herded thirty-one lambs about two miles up the road to a fresh pasture. They walked back hand in hand. They packed. Virginia returned the quilt to the big house. If the men were stoic, Clara and Virginia allowed themselves a minute to weep on each others' shoulders in the upstairs hall. R.T. called up, "We're ready." He and Clara drove Will and Virginia to Ballantine. There were only minutes to wait for the 2:15 Northern Pacific to town. The senior Matthewses waved goodbye almost as if they expected the younger couple back on the next day's train. Late that afternoon Will and Virginia would drive from Billings with Virginia's parents in the big

Packard for the Fourth of July. The Hartwells always celebrated Independence Day at the cabin in the Beartooths.

Book III

Book III
Chapter Seventeen
Cadillac Showers

January 24, 1940

Will walked out the front door of the little stucco house, his blue-striped towel rolled up under his arm. Virginia and the baby were still asleep. It was four below zero. Will's breath, like cirrus clouds, pierced the dry dark air. The peg-legged man next door who had lost both legs between uncoupled boxcars, was the only one on the block who had shoveled his walks. Although daybreak had not yet touched the rimrocks that enclosed the valley like a Roman wall, the nearly full moon was just setting on the western horizon, and the whole sky was brightening. Looking ahead beyond the first faint line of the wild Pryor Mountains to a cluster of stars in the east, Will could pick out the Summer Triangle. He thought of Armitage and the old sheepherder's readings of the night skies. Will recited, like a line of poetry—*Vega, Deneb and Altair*, and, in his mind translated the fragments of constellations into flying vulture, swan, and wing of eagle. But as his footsteps squeaked in the dry grit of snow against the pavement of Broadwater Avenue, Will switched back from the home place on Arrow Creek, barely sensing his dexterity.

On a morning when you wanted everything to go right, Will thought, nothing beat a shower at MacNeil's Cadillac-Pontiac dealership. Today, January 24, 1940 was such a day. It was a day deserving of water not interrupted in volume or temperature. And pressure enough to wake a man to the task at hand. Today—the 1940 White Sulphur Springs bid. Today Will would spell out his calculations to Meldrum for the big wool pool, nail down his deal to represent the man's fancy Boston wool house for another year. That was the plan.

He stepped into the showroom, gave Mac a short salute, and headed to the back bay.

When Will was in town—when he was not working the rutted ranch roads between Roundup and Harlo and up into Two Dot and Martinsdale where it began to seem like the old river Meander rather than the Musselshell he was following, trying to make a living buying and selling yearling ewes and lambs and wool—he had taken up the habit of stopping by Mac's dealership. On the nights when the new models were unloaded after dark at the Northern Pacific depot and driven on a circuitous route from Montana Avenue down alleys and side streets to the glassy showrooms, windows all blotted out with butcher paper until the official unveiling, he'd cross to the way point in the intersection, sense the commotion behind the cloaked showroom windows and find his way into MacNeil's

Cadillac and Pontiac. To Will one of the few pleasures of living in town was being able to be the first to examine the pristine V8 engines, the first to run a hand over the new chrome curves, the first at The Northern the next morning to say to Red—"you won't believe what they've done to the two-barrel carburetion on the new '40 Torpedo." And, although none of it could match the effect on a man's soul, say, of a stab of lightning sending a herd of antelope streaking in sharp zigs and zags across the sage plateau above Arrow Creek, it kept his mind off the ranch.

Will would settle himself in the soft leather seat behind the steering wheel in a new deluxe sedan, adjust the height and angle. Adjust the rear-view mirror. Gauge the headroom with and without his city Stetson, let his legs reach out. He'd roll down the window, and Mac would lean down and peer in. Will would monkey with the gadgets on the dash. He'd open the glove box. He liked a roomy glove box. He'd punch the cigarette lighter. Find where they'd put the ashtray. Push buttons, fiddle with the radio dial. See if he could pick up KGHL. When he'd finished his inspection, he'd get out, shut the door, and with a degree of reverence, lean back against the car and fold his arms alongside Mac.

"I like a heavy car. A man needs one on these roads," he'd say. "Day before last, I was on the Musselshell, heading home from Ingomar and that country up there and the wind was changing its mind on me," he'd pause and Mac would shake his head, "...and you know that black ice in the shadow of those mud cliffs where the road damn-near falls into the river—there's only that rump-sprung two-bit guard rail, those lily-white crosses. Now, that's where you need a heavy car."

Mac's head kept time with Will's words and he agreed as if he were the buyer, not the seller. Mac was rarely on the road. The older man took Will's close calls, his witness to highway drama and threaded them into his sales pitch.

Will took notice of Mac's shower. It was back alongside the service bays, a roomy shower and locker setup that Mac had installed for the grease monkeys. Will told Mac about his shower at home: the shower head hung adjacent to Virginia's wringer washing machine in the basement so that all washings and rinsings in the household could share the same drain on the alkali-buckled floor. Its feeble drip reminded Will of snow melt seeping through pinholes in the camp-tending wagons at the ranch. The flimsy J.C. Penney shower curtain, draped from the low-slung exposed pipes between the floor joists barely above Will's head, clung to his skin.

"Use ours anytime," Mac had said. "Anytime."

That Will could not yet afford a Cadillac or a Pontiac was no impediment to his being offered such neighborly munificence. In return, towards Christmas, he would bring in a gift-boxed bottle of Johnnie Walker Red Label, a pocketful of shot glasses on loan from Red the Bartender and help Mac and the showroom boys toast what they all bet would be the end of the Great Depression.

Will stepped into the shower.

As the hot water pounded and the Palmolive lather shot off his back, Will stacked up the figures in his head. He tallied pounds, freight, percentages, shrinkage and commissions and profits. Surges in the water pressure accelerated his calculations. Say, twenty-eight cents. Would they expect an extra quarter of a cent? Everyone's betting now that the Brits are in—make it twenty-eight and-a-quarter cents per pound—could shoot the moon when Roosevelt jumps in. OK, at a hundred-pound weight—at roughly three-hundred pounds per bag, OK, allow one percent shrinkage, stay on the safe side, round off the whole clip at 700 bags, up a fraction from last year. Will shivered. The bank draft. I'll worry about the draft later. OK. Take the full commission. A quarter of a cent per pound. Watch Meldrum. Don't let the bastard talk me down. Jesus. Last year's bid—a fraction under Meldrum's recommendation. The finesse worked. Knew in my bones it was right. Kept Meldrum singing my praises to those fancypants in Boston. Bet my last silver dollar on any wool pool in this part of the country. Especially the White Sulphur clip.

Before shearing, Will would cover the limestone gulches of that Smith River country as he had the year before. He'd stop at each ranch whether to check a hundred head or a couple thousand ewes. He'd walk into the band, finger his way into the woolly backs. He'd lean on the fences and adjust his hat and figure prices in his head and talk to the sheepmen and their sons. He accepted invitations for lunch at the ranch houses, charmed the wives when he tipped his hat and removed it and his galoshes, and stepped into their kitchens in spotless oxfords for the big noon meal. Will poured it on when he told the wives their mulligan stews and biscuits split open hot in thin, light layers and plum jams came so close to what his mother had made. He knew the livestock, the people.

He knew who tagged their sheep, who put their wool up in the best condition: no black wool, no ends tossed in. He knew what he was bidding on. He knew how clean the countryside was, how to figure shrinkage from dirt and lanolin. And, when it came time to take delivery, he'd find few surprises when he slit that long black knife deep into the wool bag. Will would plunge his hand into the oily stuff and pull out hunks of strong Montana wool. It'd stink from the heavy, rich lanolin left sweltering in the summer warehouse, but it'd bring a good price in Boston. But inside he worried. Would he get the order? Could he put the deal together again this year? Lose it once, lose the confidence of the hard-ass boys in Boston.

He rubbed the bar of soap into his hair, his knuckles kneaded into his scalp.

At one year past forty, born the last year of the last century, Will had enough age on him to hold the respect of the old-time ranchers who knew his father from the days when R.T. Matthews ran up to 35,000 head of sheep on the outfit at Arrow Creek. He knew his way around a band of sheep as well as any commission man: he could cull the ewes, pick the best ram in the pen, bet money on the age of any animal in the lot, judge the grade of wool. Of himself as a salesman, Will was less sure. It was here he felt at odds with Dixon; while he was not immune to conjuring up the rewards of a good deal—the signed contract, the commission, the pride in having it known—he thought his kid brother had come to live only for the deal.

He turned the hot water up to see how hot he could stand it.

Dixon seemed to be on a rampage to acquire any land adjacent to the ranch. Before Christmas he had wanted Will to go along with him to have The Matthews Sheep Company acquire a section of reservation land.

It always came down to the land.

They met at The Northern. When Will walked in, Dixon was already well-attended at the bar; he must have come in early from the ranch. Two pals of his were standing on either side, leaning down, listening. Dixon was not a tall man even in his boots: "… So it turned out his sister, someone of importance back east—she was always trying to get him to come home. Made attempts, sent money. Even came out to get him once, but Armitage just rode off. But, then, there came a time, second thoughts, I suppose, that he did think of going back. He quit, went as far as to buy a ticket, and then, to celebrate, went on a drunk. He blew all his money, wanted to cash the ticket in. Agent told him he couldn't, that he'd have to send it in to St. Paul or Chicago or some damn place. He got mad. And he can be ornery. He came back to the ranch all sobered up and wanted his job back. The Old Man knew nothing about any ticket, but was happy to have him back." Dixon took a drink of his coffee. "Then, in a week or two…if the inspector for the Burlington doesn't show up at the ranch. Asks The Old Man if we have a herder camped near the railroad line. There was a hill there east of Ballantine, and Armitage, it turned out, had got himself a gallon or two of oil and he oiled the track up for a hundred yards—Christ, when the big drive wheels hit a slick spot, the motor would spin out.

They were having a devil of a time getting up the hill and they were out to find out who was sabotaging them. The Old Man declared himself arbitrator. Well, he got Armitage to put away his oil can, and the Burlington man to give him his ticket money back that same day, right out of his pocket. Everybody loved everybody after that."

It was one of Dixon's favorites. Will had to admit, Dixon could tell a good story. The men hurried up their laughter, nevertheless, when they saw Will, exchanged pleasantries with him and moved to the far end of the bar.

Both Will and Dixon ordered a triple club. Red poured each a shot of Scotch, a tall water on the side. Dixon unsheathed his fountain pen and drew the perimeter of the land in question on the linen napkin, held the nib long enough to bleed in little dots where the reservation land joined the ranch, to underscore the temptation. He presented the deal as a *fait accompli*. An advance would be made to a relatively new foreman Dixon had on the place; the foreman would in turn buy the land from the Indian owner, and in turn, after a period of time—and, here Dixon slowed his pace to emphasize the degree of caution at work—sell the land to the Company. All standard methods.

"I don't like the smell of it," Will said. He took a Lucky from his breast pocket, left the pack on the bar. "I'd rather wrestle the bastards for it, than steal it from them."

"Where's the stealing? They want to sell; they want the cash. What Indian doesn't want cash, Will? Be honest. There's not a rancher in the valley who wouldn't give his right arm for this deal. Not one who wouldn't sign up if he were in your shiny shoes. How do you think a man like Simms keeps gaining on us?"

Will was used to Dixon having both the questions and the answers, but didn't relish his brotherly use of the pronoun *us*. While he couldn't prevent Dixon making such a transaction in his own name, he didn't want land owned by the Company acquired in that manner. Still, he wasn't so naive to think that title to various parcels on the ranch was clean, as it was. He guessed he'd never know until it came time to sell or settle the estate.

"You know how it works," Dixon baited him as he shook a cigarette out of Will's pack. Will flicked his hand in assent. Dixon continued, his voice tighter. He toyed with Will's matches, "What makes you suddenly some goddamn virgin?"

Will had become one to avoid a fight, especially with his brother, but on this he wouldn't give. Although it had been a good ten years since he'd worked or lived on the ranch, he was still a stockholder with Dixon and The Old Man, but his signature was rarely needed, and only sought now since The Old Man was of late no longer so predictably in Dixon's corner, Will thought. He let his brother do the talking.

"I'll never know what happened on those holy fields of France," he said, sticking his finger in to see if he could find his old feistier brother—the brother who had pummeled him with the boxing gloves after R.T. had drawn a circle with his walking stick in the thick corral dust, punched the knob on his gold pocket watch and watched the two boys go at it for a two-minute round. Each had envisioned himself Jack Dempsey taking the title from Jess Willard. Each swung as hard as he could. When R.T. called it quits, the boys knew to hang up their gloves, wipe their bloody noses and shake hands. Often they didn't exchange civilities for days.

"Was it those German SOBs or those *re-fined* French whores that drained it out?"

Silently, Will cursed his brother for his MovieTone version of the earlier war, but he didn't bite. The bodies still piled up like wind-riled sheep into a gully. Sent him on his night walks. But equal to the bitter taste in his mouth was his knowledge that Dixon, not one to be bested, had never recovered from what he considered his bad timing—born a couple of years too late: missing the war—and overestimated the heroic acts he might have attained if it had been he, rather than Will, who'd managed to get himself in uniform and shipped out to France.

The two brothers each shelled out a silver dollar to pay the tab.

"My regards to Virginia," Dixon said.

"And mine to Jeanette."

Neither asked about Christmas. It would be up to Will to call The Old Man, make their own plans directly. In the mail, Will would likely receive notice of a renewed subscription to *Reader's Digest*; Virginia, in return, would send a tinfoiled coffee can of her peanut brittle.

Will finished his shower with a blast of cold water—it recalled the ice cold square shower room at St. John's Military Academy where his father had sent him at fifteen to memorize irregular Latin verbs and the gentlemanly ways of battle. He shivered, shut off the water and scoured himself with the rough terry cloth.

Regardless of his disdain for Dixon's way, Will thought as he rubbed his thick head of hair with the towel, he envied his confidence. He was so certain.

Will's self-assurance could wane in this business from the lengthy gestation period a deal could require—the span between one summer shearing and the next, between one spring lamb crop and when the band of yearling ewes would be ready for market. The dark idle winter months were tough. Snow could pile up, hem him in. Ranchers wouldn't get to town. He spent time on the telephone, checked his trap line: he talked to his wool pool managers, the ranchers, other buyers, and, most of all, he talked to Meldrum. Since Meldrum had driven his Buick out from Boston last summer, and Will chauffeured him around that rich triangle from Ashland to Big Timber and back by way of White Sulphur, and Meldrum plied Will's woolgrowers with prime rib dinners, Will spent his time trying to get a purchase on the man. He was smart. He bought wool—tons of wool—from Australia to Montana. And, he wanted only two things: the best wool at the lowest price and no shenanigans when it came to delivery.

So did Will. He worried about the bid. The timing. The international market. The war. Australian imports. Subsidies. And, the delivery. In his sleep, Will rode the rails with the carloads of yolky wool as they inched across the plains: he saw bridges wash out, trellises collapse, ice-loosened sandstone slide onto the tracks, trains derail, cars sidetracked and jackknifed, sodden, rotted bags of wool, unfathomable costs.

In the bare locker room outside the shower, he stepped into his pressed tan wool gabardine trousers. He buttoned his shirt of the same cloth, tucked it in, fastened his belt buckle easy. As he pulled on thin wool stockings over his not-quite-dry feet, he went over the peculiarities of bank drafts, the liability of signing his name to a draft in the tens of thousands. Deals could go bad. Commission men like himself had been ruined overnight from the odd financing system. Ranchers had been known to renege on a price. A wool company could go bankrupt as well as anyone. Will wouldn't relax until the deal was done, the sheep or wool delivered, checks cashed, everyone paid. Then, the circle started again.

He slipped into his Florsheims, gave Mac a salute on his way out.

Still ahead of the sun, Will thought as he stepped out of MacNeil's. As he waited for a truck to pass at the corner, he looked straight up—there, a star so orangey bright, "It must be Arcturus," he said out loud. He snapped his towel in the ice-white air. Now, Meldrum. Snap, snap. He'd get the go-ahead, get Meldrum's word, get to work—drive out into Meagher County, take a room at the hotel and start in with this year's manager of the pool. The man would expect some coddling, say prime rib at the White Sulphur Springs Hotel. While it was a sealed-bid sale, there was more to it than price. He felt he had an edge. He had a good name up and down the valley— he'd once been on their side of the deal, and, earlier in the

month at the Woolgrowers annual meeting in Helena he'd
bought his share of drinks and not taken too many at poker.

The house smelled of buttered French toast and soap
bubbles. Virginia was giving Jack his bath. Will took a cold
triangle of toast, dabbed it in the sweet syrup left on his son's
Humpty-Dumpty dish, and stood at the doorway to the
bathroom. Virginia, her dark hair springing from its braided
coil at the nape of her neck, knelt on the green and black tiled
floor with a firm hold under the youngster's curly head as he
splashed and slid in the tub. Her slender ankles were covered
by long folds of Will's flannel robe.

"Hey, Bud, soon you'll be old enough for the big
Cadillac showers."

"Lac-a-lac-a-lac," the little boy sang. Will and Virginia
were late starting a family: first by not marrying until she was
twenty-seven and Will thirty-one, then through the
miscarriages. They'd had almost as many miscarriages as
different apartments since their marriage in 1930. By the time
this healthy baby boy who had Virginia's brown eyes and Will's
curly hair was born, Will again believed in miracles. He bent
down and kissed Virginia on the top of her head.

"I'll hold a high thought for you today," she said. And
pray it goes through, she thought. There were bills: expenses
piled up in winter against little income, few sales, and although
both expected it, the long days in January and February when
the phone didn't ring. It could pull Will's nerves to the edge,
and even if he kept his worries to himself, Virginia could sense
it. Before the baby was born, to help out she'd fill-in at her

208

father's old law firm. Eventually, Will would take out a short-term loan like the other livestock buyers did. He always paid it back, but he nursed it like a thorn in his foot. Watching Will's silence could be worse than the debts themselves.

"Page me if Meldrum calls."

Chapter Eighteen
The Pinioned Birds

January 24, 1940

R.T. Matthews bathed before sun struck the iced windowpanes. He stropped his straight-edge on the leather that hung from a brass ring above the basin, shaved, and with a sharp pair of Clara's darning scissors that looked too delicate for his large knuckled fingers, trimmed his short pepper-and-salt mustache. He dressed in a clean set of long underwear, fresh starched white shirt, tie, thin wool hose and tweed vest. He held the gold ridges firm between thumb and forefinger as he wound his pocket watch. He looped the chain into his left vest pocket. The big house was silent. He walked down the stairs on the cushioned maroon Oriental runner, careful not to wake Jeanette and the little boys. Dixon was apt to be already out, or not yet in. The latter, he recalled: his son had gone in for Harry Even's stag. Well, damn him for not taking me, for not giving this old albatross a ride to town. I'll call Will if need be.

At the foot of the banister, he paused as he pressed the gold knob of his pocket watch: the engraved cover sprang open like a sea shell, the Roman numerals stood thin and straight as The Old Man himself. It was six o'clock. He was an hour and forty-five minutes ahead of the sun, and ready to pursue what had become his prime responsibility—the feeding of his pet birds.

R.T. believed the prudent man saw that his livestock was fed first.

In hat, scarf and tweed wool overcoat, but ungloved hands, he walked out into the sharp morning air. Light from the one exterior electrical pole burnt through the freezing air. Little wind blew in this protected coulee. He and Clara had chosen this land in the Yellowstone Valley when it was released for homestead to whites in the early years of their marriage, and the early years of the twentieth century. R. T. crossed the frozen front yard, past lilacs leafless as broom bristles. At a low weathered shed, he leaned down and unsnapped the tempered clasp. The birds didn't stop to scratch for food beneath the crusted snow, but followed him, cac-cac-cac-ing back towards the front steps.

"Why, look at you little beggars, lining up for a handout, not putting in a lick of work. What will you do the day I don't come out?" One pair of the sharp-tailed grouse came closer to coax extra bits of dry feed from his hand. "Hey, you greedy bastard," he singled out the bolder of the brown birds, "where are your manners?" Beaks clicked and pecked and gulped. R.T.

spoke with a brand of English like the vernacular he used in his conversation with horses: intimate and interrogative and confessional. Often it was his longest conversation of the day. "Next you'll expect a drop of cabernet." He lifted a laced oxford as barrier to the greediest. "And, you, this may be your last supper." He played at begrudging them their bits of grain, but he himself had held the hot wire and clipped their wings when each was only days old and met his responsibility when snow covered the ground. "Be grateful I don't make you sharpen those beaks on Armitage's biscuits."

R.T. still paid a bounty for any coyote carcass a herder or Indian brought in, and tacked up the hide on the barn like a trophy scalp. Wild bird hunting, however, was forbidden at Arrow Creek. Even the pheasant or duck, the immigrant Canada goose, were off limits. R.T. was not opposed to editing his private flock of grouse himself for worthy occasions, and was proud to offer the platters of stuffed and roasted delicacies to Sunday guests. Clara had bet she could have a bird's neck twisted, its feathers plucked, and the plump carcass roasting in the oven from the time she first saw dust or twirling snow on the long road tunneling to the ranch buildings to when the guests stepped onto the porch. Those were good times. A shot of good Scotch in the den with Mr. Lochwood.

The Old Man lifted his willow walking stick, struck the thin ice in the stream that ran past the house, opened circles of spring water to slake the thirst of his flock. He turned the pinioned birds over to Argus, Clara's border collie. The old dog took daytime supervision of the birds, keeping them safe from the cats or others on the dole.

Until Clara died six years ago, the heart of the ranch had been her dining room and its attendant kitchen, pantry and gardens, but now R.T. felt the pulse of the place more in this den with his books, his desk and the oak telephone box mounted on the wall. Cubbyholes held the rolled maps and plats defining each section of land added through lease or purchase. He bent down at the black steel fire-proof safe. At the center of the gold-leaf eagle talons and wide-spread wings was the brass face of the dial. He worked the combination—1-24-81. The numbers were not contrived of dates of wedding or birth, but that winter day in Kalispell in 1881 after a shift at a logging mill when he didn't have a dime to buy dinner until he saw a fifty-cent piece in the snow in front of the boarding house. It was like gold. He was never broke or so hungry again. The lock clicked. The door swung open. He cursed as he had the day before. Dixon had still not returned R.T.'s stock certificates, his shares of the Matthews Sheep Company.

The fool thinks he's outsmarted me. Tells me to leave them in the bank in Billings if I won't sign them over. Doesn't set right, he told himself as he fingered the long slender safe deposit box key he wore as his watch fob. He'd use it today in town. R.T. might have slammed the heavy door shut, but he preferred to prolong the quiet and the sleep of his co-inhabitants. So, he closed it as if handling an explosive, like a charge of dynamite, say, as he often had in the days of blasting a new road on the place, or excavating the reservoir.

The ranch safe was not empty: it held the deeds, the leases, the silver dollars, the gold pieces. R.T. believed in precious metals. If war ever came he wanted something of real value to barter with. And, if the banks closed their doors as they had in the Thirties, he could put his hands on gold. As he twirled the dial, he re-worked the combination. Christ. 1-24-81. Fifty-nine years ago to the day. The temperature hasn't improved a hell of a lot, he thought. It was four below.

The office walls were papered with Northern Pacific calendars, never discarded at year end, but saved for the photographs of the land the railroad crossed—herder and a band of sheep in Paradise Valley, a head of cattle fording the Yellowstone, a sleek passenger train snaking its way through the Continental Divide. R.T. had a fondness for the railroad. It had saved his hide more than once: delivered tons of coal and feed to his door in the worst winters; shipped his lambs and wool to market; stopped for Clara and him even where there was no station.

He might have to flag the North Coast Limited today, he thought.

R.T. took no notice of the set of Huffman enlargements behind his desk. Years back he'd commissioned the photographer to spend time at the ranch. These were not family portraits taken each Christmas, but places on the ranch: plump sheep quilting the banks of Arrow Creek, thunderheads on the horizon from the plateau, the home place itself. One of those heavy black Speedgraphix had condensed the big white house, the orchards, the willows, the ponderosa pine, the lilac hedge, the fence line, the high-reaching elms to an 8-by-10 negative, and, from the perspective of looking down on it, the home ranch became one-dimensional as if it had been pressed flat between leaves in the family Bible. It looked cold with its pinch of snow, stern in its Quakerish black and whiteness, and lifeless. Not one sheep or one person or sleeping dog was in the picture. In those later years, R.T. had prided himself on keeping the sheep out of sight from the main house.

There was the first smell of coffee. R.T. turned down the narrow hall to the dining room. Armitage had come over from the cookhouse as he did every morning to make his breakfast.

"Any sign of Dixon?" R.T. asked.

The answer was a slow shake of his big white head from the old herder whose baking powder biscuits were as hard as parched clay from the creek bank. The biscuits made him miss Clara more than anything—Clara, who would shoo the hired girls out of her way and stir up biscuits so light they separated like flutters of fine marked papers—but R.T. didn't complain. He welcomed a breakfast without Jeanette starting out the day. He cut the cold unsalted butter so thin it curled. He covered the biscuit with the butter, and the butter with orange marmalade. At least someone kept up with one of Clara's recipes, he told himself. He poured his own cup, didn't muddy the black coffee, but took a spoonful of thick yellow cow's cream directly into his mouth, just to hear Clara admonish him for doing so.

R.T. folded his napkin. He placed it in the silver ring alongside *The Gazette* with its stern garamond bold headlines of warnings from Roosevelt and Churchill.

Morning, when his mind was most clear, was the time for memorizing, R.T. felt, and evening the time for reading. In the still-quiet house, he switched on the light beside his oak office chair. Armitage stoked the stove. A soft leather pouch filled with buckshot held his place open in the thick volume of poems. He glanced at the worn pages as if to prompt himself. The solace of the songs his mother chanted to her children in Nova Scotia winters came over him. She would move from *O, My luve's like a red, red rose,* to *Green grow the rushes O,* her voice wrestling Bobbie Burns into his memory.

And Burns had been welcome company when, as a kid, R.T. worked from outfit to outfit crisscrossing the country, and lastly, the long, filthy cattle drive the width of the Dakotas, through the Badlands, the Powder River, then trailing the Yellowstone into Miles City that October of 1880. It wasn't much of a town, a dusty place, always a string of horses, or a herd of cattle trailing through main street. Yet the lights that first night looked as bright as Times Square. He was worn out. It had been his job to wash up for the cook, sleep without shutting his eyes, take a two hour watch on the horses, then, before daybreak, find wood for the fire and ready the cook tent. The cranky cook spoke to R.T. only in sharp cries and a wave of his knife. R.T. was a kid too poor to buy liquor and the Chinese cook threatened him to be the one to stay sober. But, with a swig of cheap bourbon that first night in town, R.T. started in with *"...While we sit bousing at the nappy, An' getting fou and unco happy..."* and, with little encouragement, went on to *A man's a man for a' that* and took it all the way to the bitter end. He woke up in the warm ante-room in a Miles City flophouse, and, although it bore little resemblance to Nova Scotia, he felt as if he'd come home.

A clang from Jeanette banging breakfast things brought him back to this century. He pushed the book to the front of his desk. After poetry, he wrote formal letters to grandchildren on their birthdays or senators needing direction in Helena or Washington. This morning he wrote to his newest grandson, a note that the child would not be able to read for years, but the boy's father, his eldest son Will, would, The Old Man hoped, read it to him:

> *My Dear Grandson: I am very glad that you are my grandson and that you are getting along so well. I had a notice on my calendar that you were going to be having a birthday January 12 but I didn't think that the date was going to be so soon; after you get grown up you know that birthdays and every other kind of days keep coming along so fast that you just cannot keep track of them all; it's like riding on a fast railroad train and trying to count the telegraph poles, some of them get by no matter how sharp you keep your eyes on them.... I will come to town when the roads clear.*
> *With my best love to you. Grand Dad.*

And, at times he composed notes of affection to lady friends of years past. While he realized Dixon considered correspondence to the ladies foolish, he didn't mind making Dixon dance. R.T. felt the fuss was leveled at the future of his estate, rather than any romance in the here and now. R.T. pulled out a sheet of ecru paper and with pen began, *"My dear Mrs. Lochwood ..."* He remembered the evening before last.

There was Jeanette, sitting in her floral print catalog dress too tight now across her thighs, opening and sorting bills, interrupting, as she often did, the pleasures that might occur during a night by a fire crackling with split logs of cured cottonwood.

"What's this?" Jeanette had said as she slit open the florist's bill. R.T.'s monogram glanced from the letter opener. "Nosegays? Nosegays in the dead of winter?"

R.T. sat still as the sphinx. More than once had he overheard Jeanette, worrying outloud to Dixon, "What if Fanny Lochwood corners The Old Man?" R.T. was unruffled by any remark over how he spent his own money. Instead he thought of the pleasures of cornering and turned the worn pages to a favored stanza of Hardy's....*A dream of mine flew over the mead...to the halls where my old Love reigns.* He refrained from reading out loud, for although Jeanette was a worthy helpmate to his son, she was not the sort of woman who would bend to a line of poetry.

R.T. cleared his throat and went outside to think. He liked a girl with spunk, but Jeanette's way seemed disingenuous. That's what he gets, The Old Man thought, for marrying one of those German girls from the greasewood flats of the Project. R.T. much preferred Clara's way. He recalled the time he came out from a wager at the Yellowstone County Fair the owner of a dozen blue ribbon pigs. He sent them ahead to the ranch by train. The stationmaster must have called Clara and she must have sent the boys down to Ballantine with wagons to bring them back. However, by the time R.T. saw his prize pigs again, they hung scalded and skinned from hooks in the meat locker. Clara had not come all the way from Scotland to live on a pig farm. Neither R.T. nor Clara ever found a need to mention it again.

As he walked, he heard the men in the horse barn. Old snow blew across the rippled ice. Sticks of yellow stubble poked through drifts. Snow not worn off since Christmas. In an earlier year, R.T. would have hitched a team of horses, set off down the coulee, taken a turn at bringing provisions to the herders. He would have traded the hemmed-in feeling of the winter ranch for the open glistening prairie, the quiet welcome of Armitage. But now he and Armitage were both tethered at the ranch, one practically to the other, and the possibility of surprising him with an extra jar of marmalade tucked in by Clara, had been just one of the things to have vanished from his day.

It's time to get to town, he thought.

Two things preyed on his mind: his stock and his will. He muttered as he marched: "I want my stock. Won't sign it over. What fool would? I want a new will." Once R.T. took up the notion he was captive, he began in earnest the steps to freedom.

Chapter Nineteen
That Waterhole

January 24, 1940

He returned to his den. Dixon was back. Damn, he would have to wait him out. Dixon was writing figures down the side of the adding machine tape. He struck each thick black number, cranked the handle. A brutal assault on the silence of the room, R.T. thought. Why can't the fellow do his calculations in his head like Will?

"Morning, Dixon," R.T. called out in exaggerated loudness over the crash of the machine, "do you find yourself coming close to balancing this outfit once and for all?"

"Morning, Sir," his younger son replied, not lifting his eyes. "Perhaps it would balance," he said, but his tone belied his poker face, "if I tally in your herd of fat grouse?"

The Old Man's eyes were bright.

Dixon tore the tape, tucked it in his breast pocket. "Last night, at the stag—Evens led me to believe he's closing in on that quarter section beyond Ten Mile Creek."

It would be major reserve of water. Dixon knew that owning it could one day increase the resale value of the ranch. "Some dude could grab it," Evens had cautioned. "Weaken your position in the valley."

"Still chasing that one?"

"The spring. It's a gold mine."

"Yes…I coveted it for years," R.T. paused, "but these days it could be costly."

"Evens says not."

"Legally, I mean."

"I know, I know," said Dixon, as if it were not the first time The Old Man had cautioned him. "Evens knows how to work it. He's clean. He holds no title to land on the reservation. He buys this piece. No obligation to anyone. Right? Then," he said, leaning back on the heels of the chair, "it's just a matter of time until Evens will decide—all of his own accord, of course," and he allowed himself a smile,"—to sell it to us."

Evens had grown up over by Pompey's Pillar, knew who owned what, who wanted what, and what they'd pay. He let it be known around town he would make loans to Indians. He made it easy. No questions. He lived unobtrusively in Hardin, but knew the benefit of throwing a stag in Billings.

"I'd advise against anything that down the road might put our title in jeopardy."

"That old law would never hold up in court. Even the cranky bank lawyer says so. Everyone ignores it. Even the

BIA. You've ignored it yourself." Dixon was referring to Section 2 of the Crow Act passed by Congress in June 4, 1920.

Dixon knew that the initial sale of land to Evens must be free from any trace to himself or the ranch corporation. He knew if anyone could show a white man had instigated such a two-step deal, it would be declared a sham; the land would be without good title, and, there were criminal implications. No intent on Dixon's part to be the second white owner of the land must be discernible. Even so, such a sale was common practice. And, if it went against the intent of the old 1920 law that limited the number of acres any white could own on reservation land, that law seemed unrealistic to Dixon in 1940.

"Don't worry—it wasn't the legitimate rancher who was the object of that old 1920 statute," Evens had assured Dixon at the stag. "They were after the land speculator—the outsider who came in and bought it dirt cheap."

"Well, it's not 1930 or '35 anymore. I doubt Charlie Graylight ignores it," R.T. continued. "He hasn't forgotten the intent of land laws."

"You've always had it on your list," Dixon said. "Don't start talking like Will on me. And, as for Graylight—leave that to me."

The Old Man looked wooden.

"He's my pal," Dixon said, reverting to his jokier tone. "Every year he gets a check from me on his leases, a pint, even a Thanksgiving turkey—he's not going to squawk."

With his chin anchored between thumbs and poised index fingers, The Old Man sat with his elbows planted, palms against each other, doubled fingers spread and pointed like a cathedral.

Leasing was one thing, Dixon knew, and Graylight's opinion on the sale of Indian land to any white man was another. Even he had heard Graylight talk of Plenty Coups saying "But when the buffalo went away the hearts of my people fell to the ground…" and equate it to the fate of reservation land sold to whites.

"Okay," Dixon said, as if he and his father had reached an agreement. "You and Argus keep out of harm's way. I'll be back for dinner."

Neither mentioned the empty space in the safe.


"Keep an eye on The Old Man," Dixon told Jeanette after he left R.T. in the den.

"Easier said than done, lately." She rested one hand on her hip.

"I may be back late from Hardin." He didn't tell her the nature of his business, and he didn't leave Evens's phone number. If she needed him, he knew Jeanette would call the Four Aces Bar, and word would reach him soon enough.

Today, January 24, 1940, was the day Dixon would make the cash advance to Evens in anticipation of getting the deed on the spring above Ten Mile Creek. At the same time, he would have Evens sign a deed to him. Dixon wasn't new to such dealings: he would make sure Evens didn't run off and sell it to someone else. Then, once Evens turned the deed over to him, Dixon would let it grow "old and cold" in his desk drawer before he recorded it at the courthouse.

Dixon settled himself in his car, a new 1940 Buick, its title held by the Matthews Sheep Company, and, heading south east to Hardin, left the ranch less than an hour after returning home that morning.

The Thursday before, Evens had run into Dixon in town: "That waterhole up above Ten Mile Creek there—still on your most wanted list?"

They agreed to meet for a drink after Dixon's Masonic meeting.

The bar was nearly empty. Evens was seated on a bar stool at the end of the smooth mahogany. Dixon stood, forearms overlapping on the bar, looking ahead, not at his companion. Red mixed their drinks, turned the radio up and went back to washing glasses.

"I remember your mentioning that waterhole," Evens said and tilted his head backwards toward the Pryors.

Dixon nodded. He was accustomed to Evens' careful wording, spoken so it could never be said Evens was acting as agent for the white or for the Indian.

Evens was in no hurry. "I have no interest in it personally, of course, but one of my clients...," Evens paused, took a drink from his tall bourbon and ditch. "One of my clients," he repeated, "may be in need of some cash."

Dixon was listening.

Neither man changed expression.

"If I happen to come into that property," Evens went on, "I may give you a call."

"Don't scalp me on this one." Dixon studied the nude above the bar.

Nellie Pretty Feathers's father had been killed—thrown through the iced-up windshield into the sluggish Little Bighorn outside of Wyola—in a one-car accident on the reservation the month before Christmas. The quarter section property naturally fell to her. The mother had died in a similar accident years back. Evens wasn't surprised when, sometime after the accident, Nellie came in to his office. The father had known of his interest in the land. She was strapped for money. Could she get a loan? "Have a chair, Miss Pretty Feathers," he had said. He proceeded with his condolences. Evens was a reader of weddings and obituaries, and, from the list of family in the write-up on her father, he knew she had not only her own children to care for, but now would take on a set of younger half-brothers and sisters. He did not insult her by asking if she were interested in selling the land. Instead he said, "Yes, we could arrange a loan, but you'll need collateral." He didn't explain the terminology. "You'll need a patent to that land of yours."

In the 1887 allotment act, each Crow Indian had received 320 acres of land from the U. S. government. Indians born after that date could inherit the land from their family. There were two steps involved in a Crow selling land to a white. First, the Crow must apply for a patent in fee-simple to the land; if the government declared that the Indian was competent to settle his or her own affairs, the government would issue a patent. Then, the white would make payment to the Indian and receive a deed from the Indian. This was the "cleansing process" of the title. If the white was not in violation of the 1920 act—if the white did not own in excess of the 1280 (farming) and 1920 (grazing) acres—he received a clean title. Then, he was free to turn around and sell it to anyone he chose. It was only if the first white buyer could be shown to be acting as agent for the second white buyer that the title was tainted.

Nellie Pretty Feathers nodded.

"Then, you can be assured I'll loan you the money, but, you understand, I can't loan on the land while it's in trust patent. That is a standard procedure, as I'm sure you are aware. I can't loan anyone anything without a patent."

Nellie Pretty Feathers did not blink or take her eyes from him.

"You can apply for the patent yourself at the land office at Crow Agency."

Nellie Pretty Feathers sat motionless in the straight-backed chair.

"Then, you may come back when you're ready." Evens stood.

Nellie Pretty Feathers stood, and Evens shook her hand.

"Again, my sympathies for your loss."


Evens knew Nellie Pretty Feathers would get questioned at Crow Agency. But, it was better for the Indian to initiate the process than a white man. The government clerks would be apt to try to talk her out of getting the patent. They could predict the outcome. In such cases, the Indian would take the loan from Evens, or whoever the lender was. The money would be spent. When it would come time for the loan payment of interest and principle, she would, in time, as Evens had anticipated, not be able to come up with the money. At that time, Evens would tell Nellie Pretty Feathers he had no recourse but to foreclose on the land. What he would not tell her is that if he did foreclose—but if she did not agree to sell— she would have a year of redemption, during which she could at any time come up with the money and claim her land. There is no year of redemption for Nellie Pretty Feathers. He is sorry. But, when the time comes, the good news, he would say is—he doesn't have to go through the foreclosure action: he'll tear up the note if she will sell. Then, Evens would release the mortgage. He would get the deed.

Once he heard Dixon's car shoot out on the ice, R.T. set about the steps for his twenty-five mile trip into Billings. I won't be here when you get back, he muttered to himself. You're not the only one going to town. I have urgent matters. I'll not stay for Jeanette's fussing. I'll get a ride. Go to the Northern. See who's in the lobby. Page Will. We'll have lunch: my usual triple-decker club. I'll sign. Then, the bank. Will knows a smart man keeps his stock within reach. Then, a lawyer. And, if the Widow Lochwood were free on such short notice...

With swift strokes of his pen and his hand firm against the blotter, he readied a note, enclosed it in one of his fine envelopes. And for the third time that morning, he put on his overcoat, tucked his paisley scarf in about his neck. He put on tinted glasses to guard his snowburned eyes. He walked towards the corrals where the Lamont boy was changing hay. The boy will like a break, R.T. thought. A nice drive to Ballantine. Once there, R.T. imagined, he would flag the Burlington on its way west from the Twin Cities and remove himself to a more sociable place.

Refusing The Old Man was awkward. "I would, Sir, if I had a car…" A second hand begged off. Armitage shook his head, left The Old Man standing. They would not report to Dixon his father's requests. It would bring out not only the idea that The Old Man was getting senile, but that he was angling around his younger son.

"Afraid of their shadows," R.T. grunted. The cold bit at his cheekbones.

He walked back to the office. He had no recourse but to pick up the telephone and call Will.

Chapter Twenty
Switching Horses

January 24, 1940

When the call came to Will at the Northern bar, it was not Meldrum, the Boston wool buyer. It was Virginia, relaying R.T.'s message. Now, as Will drove the icy road to the ranch, he repeated his father's words like a mantra to himself: *Tell Will to come and get me out of here.*

At the fistful of low morning lights of Ballantine, he turned south, his back to the river, and left the highway. The snow-rutted rat-a-tat-tat washboard road followed the linear dictates of the homestead tracts. As he straddled the ruts, Will retraced, as was his habit on any drive back to the home ranch, the end of that long, premonitory January in 1930—the winter of his engagement, his quitting. It seemed like day before last. How had ten years passed? Paled sky and bits of snow erased the gentle inclination of the land. It felt bleak and white and flat. Only the gray perpendicular cottonwoods along the creekbed offered any relief. He felt the numb winter knife into his own blood. My God, he thought, The Old Man could freeze to death—he hoped his father had enough wits about him to wait in the big house.

Where the road took a sharp right turn, Will saw the tall rangy figure: The Old Man had walked down to the first section line, was brandishing his walking stick as if flagging a train. He must have started out when he put the receiver down, Will thought. His father stood like a lone willow against the hills. He wore his overshoes, had his stick, but even so, the ruts were solid ice from the thaw yesterday and last night's freeze and the temperature had not since wavered. Will was surprised The Old Man hadn't fallen. The sky was as bleak as the hills. There was no horizon. Jesus Christ, he thought, how did they let him get this far from home? He shifted into low, brought the car to a gradual stop and took a deep breath before he got out.

"What in hell are you doing way down here, Boss?"

"What took you so long?"

R.T. took Will's arm and walked to the car and got in and sat down. If his cheeks weren't frostbit, they were close to it. Will was grateful the Chevrolet had a first-rate heater; he turned it up until it poured hot air to The Old Man's ankles. He took his flask from the glove compartment and gave his father a drink.

"Thanks, Bud." The Old Man looked at his son. "Lunch is on me."

Will pulled the red plaid lap robe from the back seat, wrapped it around his father's legs and tucked it tight in around his arms and waist.

"You'll have me looking like a goddamn papoose."

It took some doing to turn the car around without getting stuck or high-centered.

The Old Man dozed on the way back to Billings. He must be exhausted, Will thought, but even as he slept, he didn't look peaceful. He'd go rigid, then give a big shudder. Will could see he must be drained from such exposure, not to mention his state of mind. How would he handle his father's demands? Dixon would read it capture or defection or both. Will remembered his last corn beef hash dinner at Armitage's camp, then the flukey run-in with Dixon and Two Legs. He revisited that night again and again. How had he been ambushed, caught so unawares?

Will drove straight to 42 Broadwater. At the narrow icy driveway, he cut an abrupt turn, jumped the curb, sliced a clod of frozen grass from the boulevard, then righted himself.

"Close call, Bud," The Old Man said. "You could have put us in the river."

Backtracking ten years on the twenty-mile ride home had set Will on edge—"three goddamn dummies" he muttered— he was angry with Dixon, had little mercy for his father and was fed up with himself. All at odds and here was The Old Man, dazed and bundled up in a blanket, looking out at Will and Virginia's boxy stucco house with its pointy roof and truncated Tudor leanings, its frozen geranium stalks left dead in the window box as if it were some sort of mirage.

Virginia came out of the house to help Will help R.T. navigate the slippery step. The heat from the roof had melted the icicles onto the front step. "We need new gutters," she told R.T. They held his elbows as if he were a china teapot. Neither could let go of him, but three abreast they were unable to get through the doorway. They looked ridiculous. Finally she and Will had to laugh at their trio.

"You made it a hell of a way down the road on your own," Will said to his father, "but we think we have to worry you up these stairs."

Virginia poured R.T. a cup of hot Ovaltine and cut a rich flaking brownie with gone-to-sugar mint icing. He saved the icing for last and laughed with Jack. She put on a pan of Quaker Oats.

Will placed a call to the ranch. He got Jeanette.

"You could have taken a minute to drive down and let me know you'd picked him up, for Gods sake." She was screaming. "I have the men out looking for him."

"Where's Dixon?" Will asked as evenly as he could, but his voice hardened as Jeanette kept on. She seemed incapable of answering his one question; he said, "Well then, if you would, please, ask Dixon to give me a call when you hear from him." He hung up.


When Dixon had arrived at Evens's office in Hardin, Evens's first words were, "Jeanette called. Can't find your father. He wandered off." Dixon took the phone. Both men looked irritated by the distraction. After three words from Jeanette, he called Will.

232

"What the hell is going on?" Dixon said.

"You tell me," Will said.

"Jeanette is livid."

"He was almost frozen. Jesus. A coyote could have taken him down."

Dixon let go a string of blasphemies.

"Okay. He's okay. Settle down. He's in the kitchen eating hot oatmeal with Virginia and Jack. But, look. The Old Man's all riled up. Wants to see a lawyer. Wants his stock. Says you want him to *sign* his stock." Will didn't believe Dixon would have had the gall—on that he thought The Old Man must be exaggerating.

"Christ."

"If the man wants to see a lawyer, he sees a lawyer. Right?" But Will thought to himself—he can't go alone, and I don't want to be the only one with him: Dixon would misconstrue any outcome. "It will calm him down. Come in to town. We three will go together." He paused, let that sink in. "He says he wants to change his will. Wants more than one executor."

After Clara died and Dixon and Jeanette and their little boys had moved into the big house, R.T. had named Dixon sole executor. Will had been living off the ranch for six years by then and figured no matter who was executor, Dixon would rig it.

"I know. I know," Dixon said on the telephone. "Christ, you're not the one who sees to him day in, day out. He has a hundred little worries. He gets hipped on one thing.

233

Today it's his will.  Tomorrow, it will be something else.  You spend an hour with him, now you're the authority."

Neither said anything.

Dixon broke the silence.  "I'll be there by three."

"Look, on second thought, he's had quite a day.  We all have.  Come tomorrow."

"You set it up with the lawyer.  Doc Richards might be better.  Either way, afterwards, I'll bring him back down here where he belongs."

Will let it go.  Goddamn right, he thought: It *is* where he belongs.  But not held captive for his goddamn stock, for Chrissake.

If R.T.'s mind was failing, there was nothing wrong with his hearing.  From the kitchen he called to Will.  "Tell him to feed the goddamned birds."

Not until he put the telephone down did Will remember: "Christ, Meldrum."


It was spitting snow.  The morning weather was turning into a blizzard.  This time Virginia was watching for Graylight.  She didn't want him waiting outside like he had earlier that morning.  She had the door open when he came through the back gate, snow collecting on the brim of his hat, the ridges of his blunt shoulders.

R.T. was taking a nap in the back bedroom.  Will and Graylight settled in the kitchen.  Will stood with one elbow on the top of the refrigerator.  Graylight stood, arms folded.  The blanket hung like wet wings from his shoulders.  Virginia had set a stack of sandwiches out.  She was down to a couple of tins of deviled ham, and she put that and what chunks of cheese she had between the heels of bread. They ate standing up. Will added a spoonful of chokecherry jelly to the top of his sandwich. Each drank a tall glass of milk.

"Nellie Pretty Feathers. The mother was killed. The father. Before Christmas. Our family now." Will was familiar with relations in the tribe, how families adopted one another. "No money after the father. Only land. Evens got her." The Indian spaced each word as a show horse would its step. "She sign. He make it easy. Gave her ten dollars. Says she can't go back now. Says she lose the land—owe Evens—go to jail."

The two men stared out at the whitening trees. They knew where it would lead. Will didn't know what Graylight thought he might do. He knows I don't have that kind of money, Will said to himself. He lit a cigarette. He put an ashtray on the top of the refrigerator. It was silver and had two cranes with long beaks to grasp the cigarette. Will fiddled with it while Graylight talked.

"After Evens. No money for food. None for children. I am old. Nellie go to the shacks. If she could keep the land...no listen. Believe Evens." Graylight shrugged. Will thought Graylight ageless, but in the last light of afternoon, he looked tired. Will knew he was close to his father's age.

"This Pretty Feathers land you're talking about is that quarter section beyond Ten Mile Creek? Who leases it now?" As Will asked the question, he knew the answer.

Graylight gave a nod.

"Since?"

"Before you left."

235

"Christ." He felt like an idiot. So we know who's lined up as eventual buyer, Will said to himself. The greedy bastard. "Your Nellie Pretty Feathers is caught in the barbed wire."

Twenty One
A Man in Town

January 24, 1940

It was after dinner.  His father was camped out in the
nursery, exhausted from what he now referred to as his
"Byzantine escape" from the ranch with Will that morning.
Virginia was reading to Jack, and when Will walked into the
living room it sounded like she was at a stopping point, but as
she came to

> "...Yet gentle will the griffin be,
> Most decorous and fat,
> And walk up to the Milky Way
> And lap it like a cat..."

she began again:

> "The moon? It is a griffin's egg...

237

*Hatching tomorrow night.*
*And how the little boys will watch*
*With shouting and delight.*
*To see him break the shell and stretch*
*And creep across the sky.*
*The boys will laugh The little girls,*
*I fear, may hide and cry..."*

singsonging Jack to sleep.

The child's eyelids were closed, his dark lashes still, but Virginia felt from his breathing that he was not asleep. She wanted Jack fast asleep when she put him down in his unfamiliar cubbyhole in their bedroom. She was beat. She relished the hour when the telephone and doorbell would not ring, when no meals needed to be prepared, no dishes done. The college girl had retired to her room off the laundry. That was a blessing as there was little privacy in the stucco house where archways rather than doors led from kitchen to dining room to the front room. Virginia envied the girl her basement retreat, and had mixed feelings when she went home weekends to her family's sugar beet farm south of town, but didn't know how she'd manage without her. She would not be able to go to Congo Club. No Tuesday afternoons with her childhood Gillygouch Girls who now ate molded crab salads, darned their husbands' socks and banked on each other for gossip and solace in a world of war and good works. No moment to herself without help. The girl had morning classes at Normal School, but was home afternoons to watch Jack. If Virginia wheeled Jack in the cavernous navy blue baby buggy, as she often did, regardless of flooded gutters, to visit her mother, then the girl started on dinner—fixed the potatoes, cleaned and cut up the chicken, ironed dry the damp shirts hanging like scarecrows from the exposed pipes in the basement, and picked up the house, so that when Will came home, the house didn't look like a wreck, and Virginia wasn't exhausted.

Pregnancy at thirty-seven hadn't been easy on Virginia; she did not have the energy of the younger mothers she saw playing with their children in Pioneer Park. She looked forward to the hour when she and Will could talk over the day by themselves. Will would listen to the radio and she could rest her feet on her father's old cracked leather footstool, finish her story in *Woman's Home Companion* and sort through the contests in the advertisements.

When she glanced up, she knew Will was going out. He looked tired, but restless. She wouldn't mind, she told herself, if only he didn't stay out late. But she blamed herself for a husband who consoled himself at the Northern Bar. From Will's comments about which men were out playing poker or at the all night stags at the Hilands, she knew she wasn't alone. But it was not a topic at her sewing club. To discuss it would be a breach of privacy. So she let the slight shame of it hover as she read her library books, worked her crossword puzzles, contrived her contest jingles, mended pillow slips and lay in her bed alone. On such nights she wondered if this would be the case if they had stayed on the ranch? On such nights, if she'd fall asleep reading in bed, then wake from her light sleep and he was not home, she'd reach for the knob on the light clamped to the headboard and turn it off and not resume her reading because she didn't want Will to see the late light. That way, in the morning, they could avoid mentioning the hour.

A man in town is not the same as he is on the prairie. His shoes shine. He puts on a clean shirt, knots a silk tie beneath his chin, even if he has nowhere to go. Will, however, had a destination. The Northern Hotel, his own redoubt in the city. There was an art in knowing who was in town, whose lambs were for sale, which rancher was prone to selling in the ring, what offers were being made, whose accepted, whose not, how to read the market and how to keep one's own counsel. That was the reconnaissance side of Will's business.

Will eventually would take up his worries with Virginia, but tonight he sought the companionship of Red and the solitude of The Northern. There'd be room there to winnow through the events of the day, the mellow accompaniment of Gracie Caldwell at the organ in the lobby, and if he felt so inclined, a shot of Scotch. It could do little harm.

The snow had subsided. Will wanted to walk. His shoes squeaked in the dry grit of the snow. The air was clear, the night sky bright. Perseus was in flight above the rimrocks. Ah, the power to rescue, behead, cast to stone. Will gave an exaggerated sigh, lit a Lucky Strike. He passed the Cadillac dealership; that morning's shower seemed light-years away. The janitor was on his hands and knees waxing the floor.

Will was thinking of Dixon. Back seven, eight years ago in the early Thirties when Will had left the ranch, he was taking

any work he could find.  He herded a trainload of Talbott's
yearling ewes and lambs to South Dakota to fatten one winter.
He did the legwork in the upper Yellowstone checking
livestock for the farm credit corporation's loans for two years.
All the while, he was bidding on this band of sheep, that wool
clip, bit by bit putting together a reputation in the commission
business.  But, if anyone asked Dixon, "How's Will getting on
in town?" according to second hand reports, Dixon would
answer, "I can't honestly say…don't know what deals—if
any—he's coming up with.  Virginia is back at her father's law
office some, I hear.  That may be it." In a town of easy
information, Will would hear of Dixon, how he'd welch on a
deal—balk at the price of feed long after it was delivered, claim
one bag was rotten, for example, and get the man to whittle
cents off his bill.  Or, how he'd work a way to buy wholesale
before anyone else had thought of it.  It left a bad taste in
Will's mouth.

The worst for Will was the time there was talk of a big
pile-up on the ranch.  More than a hundred spring lambs, it
was said.  It signaled neglect.

But, while men might roll their eyes at Dixon's business
practices, he was magnetic in getting others—including Will, he
himself had to admit—to do his bidding.  When times had
been hard in the early Thirties both on the ranch and for Will
in town, Will had gone back and filled in during shearing or
lambing.

"You have a stake in it, don't forget," Dixon would say,
admonishing him into coming back to help at low pay.  In
return, Dixon might give him the contract to sell that year's

spring lambs in the fall. Will was a rep for two companies—
one out of Council Bluffs, the other from the Chicago yards.
If there were no local buyer, he'd sell the lambs to a trader who
would ship them out to the river markets and then to a feed
lot. Virginia was irritated that often Dixon would short Will on
the commission, or hand him a check, but say, "That should
cover your share of the ranch dividends, as well, this year."

As Will walked, he sorted through the day: his father was
anxious about his stock and had fled the ranch; his brother was
peeved at the both of them, and could turn on Graylight, too,
if he knew his neighbor meant to meddle with his land
acquisition deal. But Meldrum. At least that had gone right.
How in hell he'd managed to get that call through to Boston
between his drive to the ranch and the sob stories at home, he
didn't know. Pure adrenaline? He should be in White Sulphur
Springs, start the real work on the wool pool bid.

Will thought of his brother. Dixon was out to extend
The Old Man's dreams of a vast spreading ranch even if it
meant prying the man's stock from his hands. Until recently
Dixon controlled the stock: he could count on R.T. going his
way, thus had little need for Will's consent on company
dealings, but now R.T. felt threatened, his position tenuous,
and Dixon questioned The Old Man's sanity as well as his
loyalty.

Dixon was practically stealing the land, Will thought,
from the Pretty Feathers daughter. It went against Will's grain,
but, he asked himself as he took his time walking towards the
center of town, why? It's how it works, he answered himself as

if taking his brother's side. It is not the first time a white man has taken land from an Indian down on his luck. And white from white in similar circumstances. American as apple pie. Darwinian—survival of the fittest. Commonplace during the depression. Someone was standing by to pay the lowest price to the heartbroken homesteader. But the case of Nellie Pretty Feathers had one important twist, Will reminded himself. She doesn't need to sell her land. She needs a loan from a reputable banker. Not some charlatan.

When Will left the ranch, back in the summer of 1930, he had little money. It surprised him how easy it was to get a modest short-term loan. He had avoided Lochwood's bank where the family did its banking because he felt Lochwood had cast his lot with Dixon. He went to Billings State Bank. The banker knew the ranch, knew R.T., had knowledge of the sons. The only collateral Will had was his share in the ranch, but he didn't have to put that up. He got the loan on his name. The banker's thoughts would have run along the lines of "well, Will's coming into the money some day." He opened an account. Every year, although he and Virginia struggled, they paid the interest and paid down on the principal, and the banker renewed the note, and they started over again. Nellie Pretty Feathers's name, however, was not the right name for such a collateral-free bank loan. It was the exactly right name for a quick Evens-and-Dixon-backed loan against the grassy spring-fed 160 acres adjacent the Matthews sheep ranch.

He's so good at what he does, Will thought. No price too low. No land out of bounds. I should know that there's no limit. Will remembered the time in 1932 when the

Reverend Treet was about to default on his loan on his modest homestead. The minister's salary was minimal, and the drought relentless. Low prices on wool (down to 9 cents a pound) and lambs rung his cash flow dry. Dixon—gallant at age 30—offered to rescue him, buy him out, and allow that the Treets could live on their place, in their bungalow, for as long as they wanted. He asked only a nominal rent, which, he explained apologetically, he needed for taxes on the place. The minister and his wife were grateful. If R.T. objected, Will was ignorant of it. He supposed his father thought a minister should be a minister, had no business trying to run a ranch, in the first place. Dixon was methodical. One section at a time. He laid low during the worst of the depression. Cut back on the help, worked himself hard. But when the wool prices turned in 1933 and 1934, he could pick and choose.

Well, I don't know how, Will told himself as he crossed North Broadway, but I'm going to do my damnedest to see that he doesn't get this land under these circumstances. Huge snowflakes sifted through the yellow circles of light at the corner and peaked like white frosting on the light globes at the hotel entrance. The bellhop was sweeping a path on the worn red carpet. He flicked his cigarette into a snow bank when he saw Will approach and opened the door.

The lobby was quiet. Couples were finishing late dinners in the dining room. A mid-week handful of salesmen deposited by yesterday's Northern Pacific from the Twin Cities were in the bar. A notions salesman had samples of new fasteners, and pinned-in underarm perspiration pads to leave behind with the black-dressed drygoods clerk at Coles Department Store. Another salesman was supervising inventory at the International Harvester implement dealership. No ranchers. The snow had them drifted in. The only live spot at the bar was Hap Zimmerman. He wore his three-piece dark wool suit and white starched shirt and dark red bow tie. He was finishing a cup of tea. The slight, bespectacled academic-looking man had Red smiling.

"Getting Red to write your headlines again?" Will asked.

"Now he's after a byline."

"You may work your night shift cold sober, but I need a drink for mine."

Red turned to the phalanx of bottles lined up against the mirror.

"No Scotch that strong—those Germans keep any man sober," Hap said.

"What's new on the Nazi's?"

"It's the Finns and Russians now—that's what's coming over the wire tonight," Hap said as he buttoned his overcoat. "Nearly press time. My best to Virginia." The reporter took the side door. It was a shortcut to the fire escape across the alley that zippered up the back of the stuccoed building at the opposite corner of the block which he used to reach the second-floor newsroom. Hap and his wife knew Virginia from college, and Hap and Will had become friends; the couples played bridge together, bowled an occasional line in the basement of the Babcock theater.

"Still coming down out there?" Red asked as he removed Hap's teapot, saucer and cup and spoon and sugar bowl and milk pitcher and floated the dishes into the soapy water.

"The sky's pink and full of snow. I'd say there'd be a foot by the time your byline hits my front door." Will didn't toy with the jigger of Scotch Red sat before him. He pushed the empty glass back. "Now I'd take a big glass of your free water."

Neither man said anything. There wasn't much of a crowd in the bar. You could hear the piano from the lobby. *Gonna take a sentimental journey, gonna set my heart at ease, gonna take a sentimental journey… sentimental jour-ur-neee home.* Will was whistling along under his breath. Red replenished the drinks of the salesmen.

"All the wars are over water," Will said. "People think it's land everyone wants. It's water. The goddamn land isn't worth a dime without water. They baptize you in holy water, not grains of sand. Some boys, however, have the mistaken notion that there's water for the taking in parts of this desert."

"Old Man ornery as ever?" Red asked

"In some ways. Fighting for his life, this time. Sees salvation in safety deposit keys and stock certificates. His boy Dixon is after 'em, but The Old Man's not one to hand them over without a fight. He's siding with me, now, on that account…crime to see it come this way. Right now he's sound asleep—booted little Jack out of his room. Yes, sound asleep. Or we'll get a call from Virginia."

Red was listening. He leaned forward, his big arms against his side of the bar.

"And," Will said, fiddling with his keys, "it's not only the white folks who can't get along out there. Turns out I've got some work to do with the Indians."

Red cocked his head to one side and nodded. "I saw your Graylight taking his time walking Minnesota Avenue towards the depot late this afternoon."

"Hell, I've turned into the BIA today," Will said. "Refill my water glass, if you will, please. We have work to do."

Will outlined the situation for Red. The bartender folded his arms across his chest and shifted his weight back against the counter. "You've had more on the docket for one day, I'd say, than the ordinary stiff."

"And not a helluva lot of time," Will said. "I haven't a history of outrunning that brother of mine, and—Evens," he coughed and continued, "he's out of the gates before the gun goes off."

"So," Red said. "Looks like you might just find yourself in the lease business."

"That *would* queer the deal." Will took a drink of the water while he considered Red's suggestion. "How, in hell? I'm not made of money," he paused, "just yet, you know. And I'm no squealer."

"Well, couldn't you lease it as well as the next man? Tell me how that works."

"It *is* leased. Pretty Feathers—the father there—leased it to Dixon for years before he died."

"Lay it out for me," Red said.

Will did.

"So, what's to prevent you from getting a lease in your own name from the Indian woman," Red added.

"Get him at his own game?" Will said. Red was a mind reader.

Red gave his go-ahead nod.

"Well, she'd have to agree to it. Nellie Pretty Feathers would have to have a reason to untangle herself from Evens. I have little use for that lease in my own name—if I could get the lease, I'd want it back in the company name—in The Matthews Sheep Company name." Will was figuring as he talked. "I could do that, you bet. I could get a short-term loan. Dixon's got the lease, but if I upped the bid—paid an advance against the lease—then, I could wangle the next lease. But," he paused and began whistling through his plan. Red had plenty of glasses to wash while Will worked on the deal in his head. "How do I make her see the dangers of putting up the land as collateral with Evens? Talk her into sticking with leasing? She needs money now." Will ran his hands through his hair. "I know that feeling."

"If you loaned her the money up front, she'd still keep the land?"

"Yes. She could put it against the loan. But how can I convince her? I doubt if she knows me from Adam. She'd have little reason to trust me over Evens. Those damn Indians go to Evens even when they see what happens to their friends."

"What about Graylight? He got you into this deal. If he wants it to work, make him work for it."

"You're right, sonofabitch, you are right." Will stood, hooked his keys on his thumb. "Now, I'd better get home before I get kicked out of my own bed."

He walked through the lobby. It was dead. He signaled a cabby from across the street. He stretched his long arms out in front of himself, cracked his knuckles, took in a breath of the clear cold air and realized he wasn't ready to go home. He had all this figuring. He canceled the taxi with a wave. He'd walk. Instead of turning west and following snowy Perseus and the obliterated Milky Way, he turned east. No one was out. At the corner of North Twenty-Seventh Street he stepped down the rock-salted cement stairs to Benny's. He'd see who was in, how his luck was running, maybe pick up a little walking around money.

The boys were in the midst of five-card stud. Half of them were over from the Legion Hall. "Anti-Nazi, Anti Fifth Column and Ante-a-penny" was their game. Benny ran a clean game, but called for a quarter to ante-up. Will pulled a chair around. He watched. He bought five dollars worth of chips. Benny dealt him in. Not a bad hand, not a hand he'd win a fortune on, but a hand that kept him in the game.

When he'd get in a poker game, which of late had been more often than was prudent, while in his head he was playing for sport, allowing himself a respite from the naggings of the commission business, in his heart he would let loose on what might come of the winnings. If he should hit the jackpot, well, he'd buy Dixon out, take the whole place back. Dixon, he knew, had a price. Or, if his winnings were one rung down, he'd stake out a share of the place, buy a band of sheep, a truckload of beet tops for winter feed, hire a good herder—someone like Armitage had been twenty, thirty years ago. He'd build a house. He and Virginia and Jack might spend winters in town, but the better part of the year, they'd be on the ranch. Jack wouldn't grow up knowing only concrete beneath his feet.

Will's weren't errant musings. When it came time and the estate was settled, he would come into his half ownership, and that could be cash or land, livestock, equipment. Will doubted the cash would amount to much. Dixon would have seen to that. Will would go for the land. At the thought of *the land*, Will relinquished himself to the delights of pipe dreams, riding the glens and gullies, fording spring streams. He was back sitting on the razor-hot sandstone with Virginia, again hand-picking the best place on the ranch. It was like isolating the flawless emerald on the jeweler's velvet tray of precious stones. There was Ten Mile. There was Spring Creek. There was Pryor Creek. He held each to the light. Will could not, however, allow himself to tempt fate and float too near the hills and sage plateau encircling the home place on Arrow Creek.

Will's chances of winning big were slim. He was clever at poker. He'd practiced his straight face against the Ballantine boys, at boarding school, from the narrow bunks of the slow troop-hauling ships, twice crossing the Atlantic, but his impulsiveness could override common sense. At times, if he won, he didn't think it sport to clean someone out. He'd be apt to play, as he rationalized the late nights to Virginia, until things evened out.

Will's philosophy, however, allowed for following one's luck. One never knew when luck might come—but a smart man realized when he had it.

Will sat down and went about winning. The first hand with two pair—queens and nines. A big pot at Benny's might be $20 to $25 dollars.

On the first hand he pulled in close to five dollars. The next hand he played he got four to a straight: he thought he could bluff—wondered if he could bluff, decided it was too early to bluff, and he folded.

In the next hand, he came up with a pair of tens showing. Around the table he saw a pair of deuces and a pair of fives—but the man with the deuces, had an ace and a king showing—ace/king, deuce/deuce; the man with the nines had queen/jack, nine/nine. Will had a hidden ten. He had trips for sure. He was winning on the board. He had clearly won. Three of a kind beat two pair. When Will got his ten down, and saw he was the clear winner, then he knew two things: he knew he had to bet enough to make it worthwhile, but not so much that he'd scare the other two out of the game. He had to make it seem like he was bluffing, that he only had two pairs, say tens and eights. He had the eight/seven, ten/ten showing; the third ten was face down. He couldn't horse it so much that he let them know he had trips. It was Will's bet, he had the high hand showing. He mustered his courage and bet. He had a neat stack of $1 chips and fifty cent and quarter chips. One $5 chip. He tossed the $5 chip in. The other two men hemmed and hawed and lifted the corners of their down cards two or three times to make certain they'd remembered right. Shorty, to Will's left, put in five $1 chips. The other, the man across the table from Will, put in three $1 chips and two fifty-cent chips and four quarter chips. The pot was right. It was time to declare. Will turned over the third ten. He knew he couldn't be beat.

"Damn I thought he had two pair."

"Looked like a bluff to me."

"I knew he had it all the time."

No one talked to the winner. The losers talked amongst themselves. There were six around the table. Three players, three onlookers. Will stacked his chips trying not show his excitement. The disgusted one with the nines dug in his pocket, slid five silver dollars across the table. Benny traded him the chips. The fellow with the deuces who couldn't afford to play in the first place signed another marker for $10 and passed it to Benny.

It was a big win. After three hands, Will had $33 dollars sitting in front of him with an investment of five dollars. He was tickled. He'd made a good two-weeks worth of walking around money, but more urgently, he felt this string of luck, and he knew he had to bet it hard enough to win, but not so hard that the others cashed out. But, in the next hand, he was dealt a five and then a seven; he tossed in his cards. No use testing lady luck with those.

It was late. They pitched in their quarters. Will drew a ten first, then an ace; a pair of queens showed up for Shorty; and, quickly, across the table, the fellow who couldn't afford it, had a pair of kings up. Two other aces showed around the table. Benny folded. The fellow who couldn't afford it with the two kings, on the second go around, started betting hard. He was trying to force the others out, Will thought. Shorty with two queens wouldn't budge: he might have been able to beat the kings. Will's third card was a king. He met the 75-cent bet. Two of the legionnaires dropped out. Smart, Will thought. Will watched his straight filling, felt his run of luck could take him all the way—to beat three kings or two pairs. Will knew he could face three kings or two pair across the table, or three queens or two pair from Shorty. The betting had come around and on the fourth card, the fellow who couldn't afford it bet $1 on his kings. Will followed. His fourth card was dealt and, bingo, he got a queen. Will was raised by Shorty. Three queens could be part of a full house; so the fourth card could double up and make a pair; the kings man, the man who couldn't afford it, the best he could have had would be three kings, but he could also have had a lesser hand of two pair; so, the best bluffing hand was Will's. But he was feeling his luck. He was itching to test it. The fifth card was dealt. With the fifth card, no one spoke. The card came to Will—it was a beautiful one-eyed knave. It filled his straight. The kings man bet $1. Now it was up to Will. Will followed. He would see the bet, put out his $1. Shorty said, "I'll see your dollar and raise you three," so Will knew he had three queens or two pair. The kings man said, "I'll see your $3, and raise you two more." A $5 bet to Will. Would he just call or would he want to teach them a lesson with a raise? He stopped and thought about that for a minute, and knowing how much he'd won already, how much was in the pot, and how he'd feel when he won, he didn't raise, he just called. He flipped in his $5. Tension was big. The place was silent. Shorty was confident. He showed he had trip queens; the kings man's face fell, he just turned his cards over. Will kept his eyes down and turned over his jack and showed his straight.

"Jesus Christ."

"Good hand, Will." They had to acknowledge this luck. They'd played with him enough to respect him for his not horsing the bet. They knew he could have made it worse on them. Slowly, wordlessly Will gathered in the chips.

Will stayed in the game. It was late. He should have been home. But he waited, lost a couple of hands. "Goodnight, gentlemen," he said and finally called it a night.

It was cold and late and the snow was still piling up. Will took the cab. He tipped the cabby a buck. He felt better than he had all day.

Virginia didn't. She kept her breathing steady and was grateful that at last one of the cars gained traction on the slick street had stopped and pulled into their narrow driveway of two strips of concrete that straddled the fresh snow covering the old ice tracks there since before Christmas. The three generations of Matthews's men in her life were for one night asleep, alive and safe in this one little house.

Chapter Twenty Two
Devise and Bequeath

January 25, 1940

Will paid attention to his first thought of the day. It signaled the rank of his uncertainties. That next morning it was not the granite face of his nearly eighty-year-old father, or the resolute face of his brother, or the darkly circled brown eyes of his wife, but the jowled face of Evens. Will felt the shyster shadow-boxing his dreams all night. Will's usual nightmare had the crack of artillery glance off the rimrocks. He had incorporated the sound of his father clearing his raspy throat in the front bedroom into the dream-like gunfire, but even in that rotted landscape the phantom Evens seemed the trespasser. Will felt Evens hover like a pesky jay over his shoulder as he relived his lucky streak at poker the night before, and Evens again as he anticipated today's meeting with Dixon to escort their father to the lawyer's office, and Evens again as he became absorbed in the particulars of this extraordinary job of land adjudicator he had accepted.

Will was neither meddler, nor matchmaker, but he could not ignore Graylight's request of last night. His old neighbor wasn't one to ask a favor.

Evens, in contrast to Graylight, was the sort Will would cross the street to avoid—the sort whose word meant nothing, the sort who preyed on the weak and the greedy.

However, all was not sacrifice on Will's part. One of the pleasures would be pulling the reins on Dixon. Detouring Evens would be pure retribution. He thought of the pair of them: on the one hand they paraded around on the Indian relations panel of the Hardin chamber of commerce, and on the other, sniffed out the vulnerable land. The high bright beam of luck shone in his heart as he reviewed the logistics.

*It seemed a fair deal.* Graylight's Nellie would have a second chance to keep her land. Not that she feared it endangered. Not that there wouldn't be the next exploitive landman. *Dixon and Evens would be thwarted at their sport.* Not that it would be their last attempt. *Will would return the lease to The Matthews Sheep Company.* Not that it would make things equal between the brothers. Dixon's converting leases from the ranch to his name had lessened the value of The Matthews Sheep Company. On paper, Dixon had laid claim to a large number of acres the ranch had once leased directly. By bringing the Pretty Feathers lease back to the company, however, Will wouldn't come empty handed when it came time to settle the estate. It had been nearly ten years now. He had a good name in the commission business and was making more as prices increased with the new war in Europe, but he had to admit his dream was the ranch. Even Virginia would say, "all you talk about since you left is how to get back into the sheep business." *The Old Man would find satisfaction in the deal.* It would not elude R.T. that, even at this late date, his vagabond son was returning the ranch company name to one of its traditional grazing leases. If R.T. had once seen Dixon's acquisitions as a boy following in his footsteps, he had become more territorial when he felt Dixon moving in on his stock. Will smiled. He felt his father the peppiest when his sons vied for his approval: the ranch, the bait and the beneficiary. If his luck held, Will thought, Nellie Pretty Feathers wouldn't have her land in fee patent yet. There were advantages to the unhurriedness of the government agency which, paradoxically, rivaled the vagaries of "Indian time."

"Do me a favor?" Will asked across the predawn shadows from his side of the bed towards the soft shape of Virginia covered in the rumpled quilt of roses before either knew if the other were awake.

She suspected sometimes when Will would come home from downtown not only late but in an amorous mood, he'd be hesitant to disturb her, but if he awoke with the same sentiment, he'd persevere. He'd send his toes underneath the folds of the sheet as emissaries. Often she felt it was a peace offering, and she was rarely one to refuse, even if she could have kicked him for going out and staying so late. But this morning, when there were no probing toes, when a romantic awakening seemed an unlikely way for this day to unfold, she turned to read the look on his face. It was quite business-like.

"A lease to type." The moment he spoke he realized what had crossed her mind. Had *favor* become synonymous with *love-making* in the vernacular of their marriage? He could only imagine his father mistakenly stalking in through the bathroom between the two bedrooms with its confusing doors in either direction. Not to mention Jack asleep in the corner.

"Keep your good thought," he said, "we'll celebrate tonight—in the meantime I'll take care of breakfast for this bunch," he added, and gave her a pat on her bottom.

Her slight flush of embarrassment disappeared as she stepped barefoot onto the ice cold hardwood floor and walked to the bathroom. "A lease?" she called over her shoulder. "What's all this about?" She washed quickly, twisted her hair into a chignon at her neck. "I wish I had gone out for a shampoo yesterday," she said to her hastily-assembled self in the mirror while she buttoned her warm wool paisley dress with quick fingers. She dabbed her face with a powder puff, put on dark red lipstick, thought it too severe for morning, and blotted it on a piece of toilet paper that she let flutter to the toilet bowl.

While Will shaved she brought her half piece of toast and orange juice in and sat on the edge of the tub in the steamy bathroom. He lathered his face with his bristle brush and as he made long clean swathes down his jawbone, he gave the gist of the plan. She took it down in shorthand on the back of an envelope. He reeled off the legal description of the quarter section like it was his own address.

"You know the files with the lease agreements, water rights and all?"

"Yes," she answered as in her head she composed copy—*Bathroom steno. On call twenty-four hours a day. No request refused*—for a hypothetical advertisement in the bleak position-wanted notices of *The Gazette*.

Will dried his face. "I'll go out and get the car warmed up."

At the front door Virginia bent down and pulled on her overshoes. She sorted through her handbag for keys and gloves and coin purse. She flicked on the porch light, rubbed a spot clear on the frosted window and peered at the thermometer nailed outside.

"Eleven below," she said as Will came back in. He had shoveled the narrow parallel strips of the driveway and was brushing the snow from the newspaper.

"*Another English Destroyer is Sunk. Exmouth said lost; fear 200 men perished; War Vessel is Britain's twenty-second naval loss in warfare with Nazis.*" Will read the stacked headlines out loud, shaking his head.

"Destroyer destroyed," Virginia said under her breath. "This shouldn't take me long," she said. "Maybe Jack will sleep in."

"You've got a world of time; we're not due to meet Dixon until ten." He helped her on with her coat, pulled up her collar around her neck and kissed her on the cheek.

"You can see how women fall for their bosses," she said. "Ones who warm up their cars, fix breakfast, and baby-sit."

"What more could you ask?" His blue eyes brightened, then he cautioned, "Take it slow on Broadwater, it's glass under that new snow." It hadn't been that long since he had come home in the cab. But, regardless of his warning, she took the length of the driveway at full speed. Her back wheels spun when she hit the slick gutter. She let up only to ease the car into the jagged winter-long ruts. Will often gauged her mood by the velocity and character of her exit. Today's made him think the idea of ambushing Dixon appealed to her.

The streetlights were still on. The snowplow worked its way back down North Broadway. On its first pass, it had scraped clear in front of the hotel; Virginia parked there to avoid getting stuck. She stood on the swept curb beneath the hotel marquee while the plow made its second run, the concave blade sending snow like a cresting winter wave down the middle of the wide empty street. Then, like the first one out to play in the new-fallen snow, she climbed the high, white ridge. When her boot sank deep in the snow, she extracted it without the snow caving in on her leg. She stomped her boots clean at the threshold of The Todd Insurance agency. Will sublet a small space in the back. She hung her coat behind the partition on a hook by his gunmetal gray desk, but set her notes and handbag by Mrs. Todd's big shiny black Underwood typewriter in the front of the office. She opened the slats of the clattery wooden Venetian blinds and allowed in the awakening North Broadway—the night lights inside Chapple Drug, the drifted-in alley, the fogged, brass studded hotel doors. The eastern sky was turning a breathless pink. This wasn't the first time Virginia had beat the sunrise downtown. When she had work to type for Will, she often came down before business hours.

At home, for her own letters, recipes, minutes for her Congo Club, she used her college portable and spread out on the dining table, but for professional work she preferred the office. She liked its quiet orderliness, the weight of its fireproof safe securing alphabetically and in fine print the premiums the better part of Billings held against disaster, acts of God not excluded. There was nothing, Mr. Todd liked to say, that he could not insure, nothing he could not insure against. Virginia sensed Will trusted the provisions in Mr. Todd's policies over the heavenly hopes in Mr. Treet's sermons. Will had progressed from taking out short-term insurance policies on a carload of sheep or wool in transit to putting a rider on his policy whenever he did something unusual, like take a winter road trip through Wyoming and Nebraska to Iowa to buy lambs. It would cover any business debts, he explained, as well as add to his own life insurance. "So, if you were to expire in your sleep or drown in the shower at Mac's dealership," Virginia teased, "it would not be so beneficial to the beneficiary." This morning, Virginia caught herself thinking that Will might up his coverage while he rolled dice with his brother and the pros on reservation land swaps.

The rich aroma from Mr. Todd's tobacco pipe reminded her of her father. She helped herself to the Beechnut gum she borrowed by the half-stick from the pencil tray in Mrs. Todd's top drawer. (Virginia brought her Christmas peanut brittle in exchange.) She felt at home in a place that never ran out of good water-marked paper and yellow copy paper. She coveted the industrial-sized three-hole punch, the weighted Scotch tape dispenser. Above all, Virginia liked solitude with an assignment.

She set to work. Will had given few preliminaries, but she sensed the importance from the urgency and hour of the request, and presumed Graylight's visit behind the new lease. She was not unhappy to see Will sticking his neck out in this regard, although she loathed the necessity of it. Disregarding her frugal nature, she bypassed the limp, used carbons embedded with their own histories, and counted out three glossy new sheets of carbon paper from the thumb-holed box in Will's drawer. She layered the thickened black sheets between thin white onionskin paper, careful to face each inked side down (or suffer the mirrored backing of her original), careful not to press her fingerprints into her work. She typed with the determination of a child making certain her mother hears her finger exercises, insuring that each stroke carried each serif and semicolon through the pages. She typed without lowering her eyes. She bent to the hypnotic cadence: the retort of the determined backspacer, her little finger's reach to depress the shift at each proper name or new sentence, the little bell warning as she neared the right margin and her right hand's swift command of the return carriage. She rolled the layers of legal-sized paper backwards—one line at a time—to check spelling and punctuation, careful not to let one piece of paper slide ahead of another. It was like feeding fresh bedsheets through the mangle. And today, more satisfying.

When she finished, she tidied up Mrs. Todd's desk. She returned the used carbon paper, itself now a blackened record of the terms of the lease, and closed the blinds. As she let herself out, Hap Zimmerman called to her from across the street and touched the brim of his hat in greeting. "You taking the morning shift, too?" She smiled and waved. The sun felt good on her face.

For Will, the greater part of the morning of January 25, 1940, was devoted to getting R.T. to the lawyer. Dixon came to town as he had said he would, and Will and his father met him in the dim hotel lobby. The three looked like pallbearers. Backs straight, chins jutting. Dark winter wool topcoats, neck scarves and abbreviated city Stetsons. Will's coat was from Filene's in Boston where he had spent a winter after the war. He'd worked in the woolen mills and acquired a taste for oysters on the half-shell, tiny pink scallops and exquisite diamonds but not the multitudes of the city. Dixon's coat was a newer cut, bought the previous winter at a men's store near the Brown Palace when he went to the Denver stock show. They walked three abreast—R.T. flanked by his two sons—a half a block north to the Stapleton Building. They waited for the elevator. Balls of ice clung to the buckles of their galoshes, then sloughed off, leaving puddles on the pink and gray marble floor. Will bought a pack of Lucky Strikes at the newsstand wedged in the corner back under the stairs in the foyer. "Remember the day Bud Farnswoth shot old Tilson waiting for this elevator?" he asked. They all knew the story. The Old Man had on his stone face. Dixon kept any thoughts to himself.

The meeting was uneventful. Will had relayed R.T.'s preferences to the lawyer, and the document had been readied for the meeting. Virginia could have written it, Will thought. It was two pages triple-spaced on legal-sized paper. Standard stuff. The lawyer directed his queries and comments to R.T. and set the document on the table before him with little fanfare. Dixon and Will knew how to sit silent in straight-backed chairs. R.T. took his time. He sat back at the end of the last page.

The lawyer asked, "Any questions? any changes? additions? subtractions?"

"No, sir." R.T. wasn't one to wave his dirty laundry in public, let alone in front of a lawyer. He got what he wanted. A new will with three executors rather than, as in the will Dixon had drawn up for him after Clara died, only Dixon.

"It's my practice to read the document aloud," the lawyer continued. He cleared his throat and proceeded, his tone resembling the capital letters of the first imperative:

*KNOW ALL MEN BY THESE PRESENTS: That I, R. T. MATTHEWS, of lawful age, of Ballantine, Montana, being of sound and disposing mind and memory, not acting by reason of fraud, duress, menace or undue influence of any person whatsoever, having in mind the uncertainty of life and the natural rights of others and my obligation to them, and it being my intention and purpose to dispose of all the property, real, personal and mixed, which I may own at the time of my death or which I may have the power to dispose of by Will, do hereby make, publish and declare this to be my last Will and Testament in manner following, to-wit:*

The delivery, Will thought, a cross between judicial caveat and a come-to-Jesus meeting. To liken it to a caution to warring nations or naughty boys, one would have to read deep

264

between the lines, give weight to both the written and the omitted. *Duress? Menace?* Well, you could make a case. But, *fraud?* Too strong. At this point. But, yes, *the uncertainty of life.* Will extracted *the natural rights of others and my obligations to them* as bolster for the work he had undertaken on behalf of Graylight. The oration insisted both he and Dixon think on the final words in their father's presence. Will felt R.T. must find satisfaction in hearing his intentions presented uninterrupted to his two sons. During the reading, R.T. himself seemed drawn toward the horizon limned by the below zero air—beyond the white marble facade of the Electric Building and beyond the brick and sandstone stacked stories of The Northern to the old-friend foothills. Up they rose beyond the banks of the Yellowstone like leavened bread, and R.T.'s gaze carried him to his backyard Pryors and their great canyons of wild horses, and still further south to his neighboring Bighorns cast purple against the steely blue sky. The clouds were traveling fast for a winter morning. R.T. might have seemed mesmerized more by the old territory than the document. Will felt each word spoken was embedded like a cut gemstone in The Old Man's *sound and disposing,* if unpredictable, brain.

Will saw the three of them sitting with the land of their discontent laid out before them as the lawyer repeated *in equal parts, share and share alike* three separate times. And with the alliterative poetry—*all the rest, residue and remainder*—time sifted through his fingers. Will could visualize the residue of his own life—the poker table, the late-night bars empty of wool buyers and sellers, the driven roads, the barbed wire, and now Evens. What residue, he wondered, came to Dixon's mind? Will stumbled over *die seized*. He'd ask Virginia to translate this legal oath. In its elaborate wording, it seemed the law favored the triplicate—*I give, devise and bequeath*. It lulled him, like the drone of hot summer morning scripture in the Ballantine Congregational Church when the air was suffused with cut hay and the lavendered perspiring women one pew removed. His ears pricked up, and he sensed Dixon's did with the *I hereby nominate and appoint Dixon Matthews, The Reverend Everest Treet, Virginia Hartwell Matthews, the Executors and Executrix, respectively… to serve without bonds*. His father's chosen triumvirate. Will was grateful that The Old Man had known not to let Jeanette worm her way into the legal paragraphs of the family. Although she would, in her way, be omnipresent. And himself? Not named executor to his own father's will. *Serves me right. No balls. Not weathering the storm. No fighting back. Can't blame The Old Man. Or could he?* He was having trouble convincing himself all these years later. But, no matter today's wording, regardless the thrice repeated trilogy of *in equal parts, share and share alike* sounding like the fixed response of the congregation—it would be a battle. He'd put money on it: a match, he feared, without cushion of the old gloves.

The lawyer finished. The stenographer and clerk stood like stanchions at either side as witness to R.T.'s signature. The stenographer clenched her fist, squeezed her notary seal, and raised the date and the seal of the great state of Montana up from the white paper.

R.T. stood. He shook hands with Will and Dixon and

said, "They say you never know a man until you have settled an estate with him."

It had taken less than an hour. They walked to the corner, both sons closing in on their father lest he catch an icy heel and slip on the glazed pavement. They crossed Second Avenue and then North Broadway, and walked into the foyer of the bank. They removed their hats. R.T. rang for the elevator. The outer door opened. "Mr. Matthews, gentlemen" a pale, properly-suited attendant who looked to be R.T.'s senior addressed them as he pulled back the expansion grill with his white-gloved hand. The three stepped into the square cage and were lowered to the basement vault. Here there was a small carpeted anteroom, and beyond that a low-walled section behind which Emma Warwick sat at an abbreviated mahogany desk behind her large oak card catalog. Will and Dixon stood back. R.T. proceeded to the latched gate, as the henna-haired Emma Warwick pressed a button on her desk to unlatch the low mahogany gate.

"Good morning, Mr. Matthews, we haven't seen you in quite awhile," she said, and asked, "snowed in, I bet?"

"Hobbled," he replied as he shook his head.

She peered behind him and acknowledged the sons. "Please have a seat," she said to R.T. who did. He asked after her health and the health of her mother as she retrieved his card from her file and set it out for his signature; she compared his signature to that on her signature card as she had for the past twenty years. She initialed the card by his signature and noted the date and time. "May I have your key?" she asked, and when he produced it from his silk-lined vest pocket, she said, "Please follow me," and R.T. proceeded to follow the well-girdled Emma Warwick into the vault.

"Now I understand The Old Man's attachment to his safety deposit box," Dixon said.

R.T. surveyed the aisles flush with metal boxes and as she fit his key and her duplicate into the two locks, retrieved and withdrew the large thin metal drawer, he said, "All the trappings of a mausoleum." She made no comment, but showed him into the first of the private rooms and placed the box on the desk. "Thank you, my dear," he said and after she left, he closed the door.

He took his time. He unbuttoned his coat. The top of the box opened like a child's school desk. He lifted the lid and he took the items out one by one. There were old canceled deeds he kept for nostalgic reasons. There were stock certificates from defunct enterprises, rueful reminders of early heady investments. Gold claims. One old miner's map from his years in Philipsburg that a prospector had sold him late one night. A reminder against cash deals between drunks.

The deeds from The Matthews Sheep Company. Clara's homestead claim. Deeds to homesteads he had arranged and then bought. Up and down the creek. A ranch never settled into one fixed place, he thought. The buying, the leasing, the bartering of land was as much his job as the livestock on it. *Getting and spending we lay waste our powers,* he agreed with Shakespeare on that. He cleared his throat, soon it would be the dividing. Weighing the worth of one piece of land versus another. Does one spring-fed half section equal one full section of rich dryland prairie grasses? Or vice versa. The boys will have one whale of time, he thought. *Share and share alike*, the legal verbiage floated in. I can hear them. Both, in their own ways, as stubborn as their mother.

R.T. believed in cash. Silver dollars were kept in the ranch safe at the ready. He fingered the velvet pouch. His souvenir coins were here. Coins from Nova Scotia and England. I wish I had kept that lucky cold half-dollar from the Kalispell boardwalk, he mused, but then I would have starved. The fifty cent piece that saved my life. He picked up the twice-folded paper. His birth certificate. Nova Scotia. 1860. No one need know yet that he'd never become a United States citizen. As a child, he had moved across the Canadian border into the United States with an aunt and uncle, not his parents. Two brothers had married two sisters; after his father's first wife died in child birth, he married her third sister; R.T. had half-brothers who were cousins. It confused him still. If he had moved as a minor with his parents, he would automatically have become a citizen. This secret kept him from filing for a homestead in his own name. The original homestead of the ranch was over Clara's signature. The other initial homesteads that made up the ranch he bought from relatives. It didn't keep him from voting and no one ever questioned his citizenship, but he knew better than to risk running for office. He had been asked. "Anyone who can make a dime running a ranch with the Democrats running things, could run the country," was his pet reply. Knowing that he was something of a guest kept him on better behavior than he might have been inclined, especially in his early days as a horse wrangler and coal miner. He'd never spent a night in jail, which was more than he could say for his friends. Once or twice it had cost him. He tucked his birth certificate in with Clara's from Scotland, and her U. S. citizenship papers. He wondered if anyone would notice the void. Clara hadn't made much about his citizenship. Well, it was his own business.

He'd never had to prove his citizenship to enlist in the army: he had missed the wars of his century—too late for the Civil War (he was five when Lincoln was shot), and a teenager at the time of the Custer Battle, and a man with family by time of the Spanish Civil War. He had shaken hands with Teddy Roosevelt when the wild man hunted in Big Horn county, but R.T. had little use for blood sport. Killing animals was work. Outsmarting a particularly clever coyote or wolf was work. Here was a packet of red, white and blue pins of candidates he'd voted for—Teddy Roosevelt, Hoover, Landon. He'd vote for Dewey this year. Damn FDR had overstayed his welcome. Here, the marriage certificate. Three perfect arrowheads. He rubbed his hands over the thin, sharp rock. "Christ, looks like a school boy's pocket emptyings," he muttered. In a folded yellowed envelope was the 1876 silver dollar his father had given him the year he left home at 16. That, it turned out, had been his inheritance from his father. Well, he thought, no one did much fighting over that.

At the bottom of the box were the stock certificates. He rubbed his rough fingers around the embossed circle of words. Dixon thinks I am nuts, he said to himself. Thinks he could sweet talk me into signing my shares over to him. Tried it once. Threatened power of attorney. Only a feeble-minded fool would stand for that. He can wait until I die. R.T. folded the stock certificates in thirds, fitted them in the inside pocket of his suit coat, and straightened his tie, and pulled down the sleeves of his suit jacket. Then, just as carefully, R.T. put his newly signed will into the safe deposit box. It deserves some distance, he muttered. Makes sense to keep the stock and the will separate, he reasoned. I don't want to get my hands—or anyone's hands—on the will in haste. But, the stock certificates, they belong with me at the ranch.

As the three walked back to the hotel, Dixon said to his father, "You can take a rest at Will's. I have two appointments; after that, we can drive home in time for dinner." He turned to see if that was agreeable to Will. "Jeanette's making your mulligan stew…"

"Will will drive me home," R.T. interrupted in his morning "stand to" voice.

Will was not overjoyed at first. He had Meldrum, the wool growers in White Sulphur Springs, the Pretty Feathers deal to work on. But, then he realized that not only was his father making a statement, but that the drive down would give him the chance to run into Graylight. Will could no longer come and go from the ranch without raising questions. Nor could he afford to track Graylight down by telephone. He doubted Graylight had one of the telephones the ranchers used. In any case, there were no secrets on the party lines of Ballantine. Or the switchboards of the Billings phone company.

"You call it," Dixon said to his father.

"What are they asking for a new Pontiac?" R.T. asked Will as they drove past the bright windows of MacNeil's.

"Close to $800, if you take delivery in Michigan—you thinking of a new car?"

The Old Man beamed.

They went into the house. Will changed from his coat to his quilted snow jacket with fur-trimmed collar. Virginia handed Will the envelope with the typed lease. Will tucked it in the inside chest pocket of his coat. R.T. began his courtly goodbyes to Virginia and Jack, then straightened up and said, "Is your college girl on duty?" When Virginia said yes, R.T. said, "Honor us with your presence for lunch. I must start off on good terms with my new executrix."

"And I with my testator," Virginia said in the same spirit, relieved not to have to think of something for lunch for herself or the three of them.

When the three were settled in a booth at the Northern, they placed their orders for club sandwiches. "Don't short me on the bacon," R.T. said to Darla.

Chapter Twenty Three
The Tallest Cottonwood

January 25, 1940

One's father is always one's father. Regardless how frail, how daft. The mix of feelings Will felt for this straight thin man, his gloved fingers interlaced in his tweed lap, his blue eyes fixed straight ahead, were as impossible as ever to sort out. They drove in silence. The Yellowstone was widened with ice. Only when they were on the bridge could they see the thawed channel of exposed current cutting its narrow way down the riverbed between the stripped cottonwoods. Frozen silt clung to the river rock. As the two men crossed the bridge a pair of blue-black birds flew against the wind and landed on the metal struts.

"Early for buzzards," The Old Man said.

"Ravens," Will said.

"Early for them, too."

Will pushed in the lighter, cracked the window, and was

shaking a cigarette from the new pack of Lucky's. What satisfaction must The Old Man take in the brothers at odds? What satisfaction at proving a degree of independence from Dixon, if only in the matter of the stock? In naming the additional executors? But wasn't it sadness Will felt for the father? In his own exile, he held his sons with the arid acres, the bands of bleating sheep, the water rights, the mineral rights, the grazing rights, the shares of stock.

"It's popped out." R.T. said. Will took the glowing coils, lit his cigarette.

Will felt he was as much a pawn as ever—that his father favored him now to shame Dixon for threatening his shares of stock, for taking his right to the land for granted. How the three of us play one against the other. Would he himself be, Will asked himself, so intent on the Nellie Pretty Feathers land if it were Evens and some other dumb bastard, not Dixon? Maybe. But, he had to admit, the reward would not be so sweet. Will felt his father would take some pride in his undertaking. In the end, Will expected Dixon would not say one word to him about the Pretty Feathers land. To acknowledge it would be to acknowledge a victory.

"You're figuring hard in that head, boy," R.T. said.

"The road brings it on."

"This road? Ye gods, you know it by heart."

"It's every road I've ever been on."

The Old Man raised his tufts of eyebrows.

"When I was in France, I'd be crammed in the middle of a truck with a bunch of carsick soldiers pissing and puking and crying. I'd close my eyes and lean back against the rattling sides of the truck: I'd be on this road, on Highway 10. I'd look up one gully after another for a stray, stand in the wind at every outcrop, dig my heel in the sandstone, smell the scrub cedar. Hear you cuss at the broken fence, at deer pawing down the haystacks. I'd see the railroad signal lights, the turn off to Huntley, and Riley's sway-back gas station at the Ballantine corner, and then the willows up Arrow Creek. All green-tasseled. I wouldn't stop at the home ranch to get chewed on by you; I'd head to Crow Meadow and bang on Armitage's beat-up wagon until he'd come out with a hatful of biscuits. "

"Homesick for those goddamn biscuits?"

"Saved my life."

"When it comes time, I want a simple pine box," R.T. said. "Don't waste money on anything from Smith's front parlor. The Congregational Church in town, in Billings. I know, not your choice—you've earned a military funeral, one day, but the Masonic is the best I can do. Dixon can take care of that." R.T.'s voice was strengthened. He spoke as if the audience were not only his son, but the snowed hills, the ice-struck highway, the frozen ponds harpooned with cattails dead since fall.

"You used to say 'wrap me up in my old tarp and stick me in the fork of the tallest cottonwood down by the Creek…' " Will was pulling The Old Man's leg a little to cut the dour topic. " 'Let the elements…' " But R.T. would not take the detour.

"Bury me next to Clara in the plot at Mountainview," he said. "Good thing I didn't marry Fanny Lochwood. Not that she didn't hint. Yes? But as it stands, there's room for all of us in the plot—you and Virginia, Dixon and Jeanette. Clara's already in her place. Room for six. No room for the next generation. They'll have to fend for themselves."

R.T. backtracked to the details of who would speak and who would not and how he only wanted *The Crossing of the Bar*, "Tennyson, no deadly passages from the Bible." Will quoted "*When that which drew from out the boundless deep/ Turns again home*," and R.T. picked up, "You did learn something in your brief stays at those expensive schools," and, yes, not to think that he'd gone soft on them, but "find the most beautiful soprano to sing *The Old Rugged Cross*," and he began a growly hum that went staccato when the tire chains hit the blacktop. Will was suffused with the memory of his mother's funeral. Clara's funeral was six years ago, now. He heard not what was said or sung in the church, nor saw the casket. The circle of Crow women was what he saw. They stood that hot July day in wool blankets in the shade of a great green cathedral-branched elm on the freshly-mown yard of the Congregational Church on the corner in the heart of downtown Billings. They gave a long low melodious wail—some taking it to a high wild wind. That circle, that mournful voice sent goose bumps down Will's arms. The women sat as if blind to the black crepe women of Billings and their blue serge husbands walking on the sidewalk and up the painted wood stairs and into the sanctuary.

Jeanette was standing out on the porch. Argus was sunning herself, her tail thumped on the swept-clean boards when the car door opened. The sharp-tailed grouse didn't look up from their pecking at the crusted snow. Jeanette came down the step, fluttered about R.T., helped him with his parcels. He held his briefcase close. She ignored it. Didn't offer to carry it. The Old Man was polite. He told her about the slick roads from Huntley on, the river ice, the threat of flooding. Buzzards from California. Jeanette listened. Will tipped his hat. She said nothing to him. She did not invite Will in. He was grateful. He had no interest in the house. He began to tell his father goodbye at the front door. The Old Man said, "No, come in." Will followed him down the hall to the office. His father took off his coat, faced the dial of the big safe. He worked the combination. As the heavy door swung open, R.T. stepped closer. He put the portfolio he had carried from his safety deposit box into the safe. He shut the safe, twirled the dial. "There. Thank you, Will." He turned then and walked Will to the front door and onto the porch. The Old Man affected a cheery wave, almost a salute. Will returned the salute. Jeanette was at the door again, trying to get her frail father-in-law in out of the cold. The two of them reminded Will of the wooden figures in a cuckoo clock.

There was no room to turn around. Will opened the car door a crack, held it open, kept his eye on the tracks as he backed down the rutted road to the cookhouse.

"Any sign of Graylight today?"

Armitage dried his hands and cocked his head and poured him a cup of coffee. "Must be up at his place. Came back on the seven o'clock last night."

Will couldn't ride up to Graylight's himself, he couldn't have Jeanette see any goings on between the two from her perch in Clara's big old kitchen.

"Let him know I was asking after him," he said. Then he saw the Indian riding in from the tipi meadow. A pack of blankets surrounded the big black hat. Graylight shook off the snow on the wooden steps of the cookhouse. Armitage left the two men to their business. It was brief.

"Meet me in Hardin—still this afternoon? With your Nellie Pretty Feathers?"

The old Indian gave a slight nod. "You bet."


Will dug the chains out of his trunk. There could be bad spots on the county roads to Hardin. He didn't want to end up in the ditch. Armitage came out, stood like a white totem pole against the fading light. Will jacked up one rear tire, then lay on his back on the ice ruts outside the cookhouse and tugged and cussed at the chains to fit them around the rigid tire. "Not much give to those damn contraptions," Armitage said, but did little else to help. "Easier to shoe one of them pedigree colts out of Pryor," he concluded. While Will wished for the days when Armitage would have stooped down and given him a hand, he appreciated that there was someone on the place who'd at least come out and commiserate with him in the steel gray January day.

"Keep The Old Man on a short rope," Will said when he finished.

It was crazy he couldn't give Graylight a ride, Will thought once he was underway. He drank from the Thermos Armitage had filled with hot gritty black coffee. He had no idea how Graylight would get to Hardin, but he'd bet his old friend would beat him there.

The chains set up competing rhythms on the glazed snow. Will talked out loud over that syncopation and the radio: "Don't go and make this another one of those three-point drop kicks for the other team." He was back some twenty-five years on the football field at St. John's. It could still make him wince. "Let the ball fall short on its own." He often thought of that play—his heroic lunge. He realized how much he wanted to see Nellie Pretty Feathers sign on the dotted line and see that lease back in the name of The Matthews Sheep Company. It's all in order, he told himself, as he lighted a cigarette from the stub still in the corner of his mouth.

The weather held. He cut across to Ten Mile. Drove to the old Corinth station. Then, the road to Fly Creek, and along the Burlington Northern line past the cemetery and on into Hardin. Nothing but wind-blown snow.

"Graylight could beat the North Coast Limited." Will smiled to himself. He saw the bundled-up Graylight crossing the big wide main street of Hardin. It was a street built for a city, for returning heroes, wider by three times than the Appian Way. But droves of sheep and dung-splat cattle were its travelers, not Roman soldiers. He couldn't meet Graylight and

Nellie Pretty Feathers in a cafe. That would be a red flag. But he was hungry and knew chances were they would be, too. He pulled up in front of the Hotel Becker across from the train station. He walked into the bar to see who was about, had a shot of Scotch.

"Can you pack me some sandwiches?" he asked the barmaid.

"Roast beef? Meat loaf? Cheese and salami?" she asked.

"A couple of each, and give me a bottle of milk, fill this Thermos, if you will, and throw in a handful of cookies or Hershey bars."

He left her to getting the food together, and went off on foot. The street was nearly deserted. He came face to face with Graylight. "Can you meet me at the Congregational Church over two blocks?" Will wanted a place he wouldn't run into Evens. He figured Dixon would still be in Billings. Will wasn't much of a churchgoer, didn't know if this paralleled the money-changers. He thought it might seem safe to Nellie Pretty Feathers. It was usually hard to read Graylight's face, but with the mention of the church as meeting place, Will saw he had caught the man unawares. He could hardly wait to describe the wry look on Graylight's face to Virginia. "And Nellie Pretty Feathers? In ten, twenty minutes?"

"Yes, Sir," said Graylight.

Will's was the only car at the church, but he saw a light in the office. Will knew the minister from funerals. "I've shouldered a few sheepherders in and out of here," Will said by way of introduction. The minister asked after Rev. Treet and Will's father. Then, Will got around to his question: "Mind if I borrow one of your pews? I have a meeting with some of my neighbors."

"I don't keep the furnace going in the sanctuary unless it's Sunday," the minister apologized. He didn't seem fazed by the request.

"We'll keep our coats on," Will said. "And keep the crumbs to a minimum," he said indicating the brown lunch sack and Thermos.

"The cat will be glad to clean up after you," he said. "Let me get you some cups."

"We won't be long," Will assured him, and went out on the front steps to have a cigarette while he waited for Graylight and Nellie Pretty Feathers. The day was sliding into darkness, winter cutting short the crepuscular hour.

At first Nellie Pretty Feathers kept her eyes on her knees. Will asked if she wanted a sandwich? No. "Coffee?" he asked. She declined both, but she broke off four squares from the Hershey bar Graylight passed to her. Graylight started to eat a sandwich. He stopped and poured Nellie Pretty Feathers a cup of coffee. She accepted. Will didn't feel hungry anymore, but he knew that if he didn't eat a sandwich, Graylight would stop and Nellie Pretty Feathers wouldn't eat. He wanted them well-fed. He bit into a meat loaf sandwich.

"I'm new at this," he started out. He explained part of the arrangement. "But, Graylight has explained your situation to me. What you need, in my opinion, is time. Some time on your side. I've had some money troubles myself in recent years. Believe me." He felt she was listening. "This arrangement will give you time. It will make it possible for you to keep your land." She looked him in the eye when he said, "You may want to sell your land at some point, or keep your land for your own children. But the arrangement you have now is not in your best interest. It is not safe." Will did not want to insult her, but he wanted to make his point. He keep repeating the phrase "your land." Graylight said nothing, let it be Nellie Pretty Feathers's meeting. Will knew Graylight would have talked to her on the walk over. "Graylight here has known me almost as long as my father has."

Nellie Pretty Feathers looked at Graylight. She and Will signed the lease agreement. Will gave her an envelope with the advance money. She opened it and counted the cash. She didn't say thank you, but when Will reached out to shake her hand, she took his hand. "Graylight will go with you to see Mr. Evens, if you like," Will said. She said nothing. Will took that as agreement. They finished their sandwiches.

Chapter Twenty Four
Divinest Sense

February - 1940

This time it was Dixon who called.

He started right in. "The Old Man's out of his head."

It was after midnight. It had been eleven days since the three had met with the lawyer. Will's first thought was that Dixon had learned of his agreement with Nellie Pretty Feathers.

"He won't listen to reason. He's throwing things. Breaking windows. Yelling about his stock certificates. He's hipped on it. He's turned on me. Won't have a thing to do with me. He wants you to come down and get him." Dixon sounded tired. "He's got it in his head that Jeanette's in some sort of dope ring—because she makes him take his medicine, I guess. He's nuts. He could kill himself, or all of us."

"Jesus Christ."

"He needs to be in a sanitarium."

"I see." Will stood in the dark living room in his BVDs, the cold black receiver pressed hard to his ear. He had trouble hearing his brother, although it felt like he was practically shouting. "You couldn't wait to move up into the big house to take care of him," Will said evenly, feeling his voice echo in the quiet house, "and now you want to ship him off to the loony bin."

"You aren't with him every day." For once Dixon sounded worn. "Look, I'm asking you to come home and help with The Old Man."

Will let a moment pass, his brother's words suspended in the air.

"I'm on my way."


R.T., Dixon and Jeanette sat as if holding their breath in the cold living room. R.T. had his wool overcoat on over pajamas and bathrobe, his beaver hat with the fur earflaps pulled down to meet the paisley wool scarf coiled around his neck, his pants stuffed in the tops of his buckled overshoes and his sheepskin gloves pulled over his long thin hands. But, despite all that padding, he was a paltry figure in his overstuffed leather chair. Dixon was red-eyed and punchy like he'd had too much to drink and not enough time to sleep it off. But Will knew Dixon had never been more sober. Jeanette and Dixon sat on the hickory-rimmed davenport opposite R.T. Jeanette, wrestled up in an ivory chenille robe, looked like a resolute old ewe facing off a predator. It was like a sad spoof on a beleaguered waiting room. You expected the Marx brothers to start opening and shutting the doors, hopping harum-scarum in and out the window.

"I'm damn glad to see you," R.T. said when Will
came in.

"I'm damn glad to see *you*, Boss."

The plate-glass window was shattered.  Big triangular
pieces of broken glass had been pushed to one side toward the
wall.  R.T. had come down in the night, after complaining all
day that he wanted to go to town.  Dixon had double-locked
the doors when he went to bed so R.T. could not wander away.
Dixon and Jeanette and the little boys woke when one of the
dining room chairs crashed against the window.

His father looked a little weepy, Will thought.  He must
be exhausted from all these heroics.  The letdown after his
Pyrrhic victory.

Dixon got to his feet and Will followed him into the
hall.

"They're going to decide what to do with me," R.T.
called to Jeanette as if she were deaf.  "Don't blame them.  I
hate old things—old men, old stiffs.  They smell.  Toss me in
with the heap of offal."

"Now, Father Matthews."

"He was in a rage," Dixon said to Will.  "When I came
downstairs he had his damn stick and was stabbing the glass as
if it were ice in the pond.  He was ready to step through the
window."

The two brothers were in The Old Man's den.  They
stood side by side, not looking directly at one another, like they
were watching from a distance one of the hired men break a
horse.  They stared out into the empty black night. They both

had lighted cigarettes, Dixon with a lighter, Will with a wooden match. There were great spaces between the words. "I had one hell of a time pulling him back without killing us both; he can be strong as a horse." Great silences between the sentences. "We can't keep him here this way. Jeanette is afraid for the boys. I can't blame her. He belongs in a sanitarium."

"Sanitarium? Do you know what you're saying?" Will said. "I can't do that."

"Don't go sentimental on me—it's the only outfit that could handle him."

"We might as well take him out to the corral and put a pistol to his forehead."

"Pack him up—take him to live with you and Virginia— let's see how long that lasts."

"He should be here, on the ranch. It's still his house, isn't it? for Chrissake. He can afford a practical nurse, if he needs one."

Dixon made no answer.

"Well," Will said and ran his fingers through his hair, "we don't have to decide tonight. Loan me Armitage. I'll take the pair of them to town. Get Dad in to see Doc Roth. See what he says. Maybe run The Old Man out to the Mayo Clinic."


R.T. was, as Will told Virginia, "as a docile as a lamb" on the ride back in. She was awake when she heard the car in the driveway, but surprised to hear the third door slam shut. She was expecting Will's father, but not Armitage. He dwarfed the living room. Armitage said nothing, but removed his old beaver hat when he saw Virginia. It must have been nearly three in the morning. Virginia didn't want to think how fast Will had driven on winter roads. She made hot chocolate and wondered where everyone would sleep. She told herself not to let the pan boil over because there wasn't much milk. She put out what oatmeal cookies there were from the bottom of the Dutch girl cookie jar. She transferred Jack to the middle of their bed while she and Will collapsed Jack's crib. Virginia pulled cotton sheet blankets from the stack in the linen closet and made up a bed for R.T. on the spare cot in the baby's room where she slept if he had the croup. Will had brought his bedroll in from the trunk of the car and fixed it for Armitage on the davenport in the living room.

While everyone took turns in the tiny bathroom, Will stood at the kitchen sink. He felt the vibrations through the linoleum under his feet and could hear the coupling of boxcars from the tracks a few blocks south. The graveyard shift. He worked the fifth of Scotch out from the top shelf of the spice cupboard. His jigger was in with the juice glasses. He ran the water. He poured himself a shot and drank it back. He filled a tall glass with the ice cold water and drank it. After all these years, the water, compared to spring water, still tasted bitter. He cupped his big hands under the faucet and splashed his face a half-dozen times. He dried his face and hands on Virginia's tea towel, the cross-stitched Tuesday's Child brushing across his face.

Virginia relaxed when she could count the snores of three men, one grinding his teeth, and Jack purring and sucking his thumb. But she did not fall asleep. She went over what she had in the house to fix Mr. Matthews and Armitage for breakfast. Then she thought of the ramifications of Will's words—"sanitarium or hospital." *Much Madness is divinest Sense,* she said to herself as she imagined the scene at the ranch, the broken window, the three men. She wondered how long The Old Man would last away from Arrow Creek, confined in one way or the other. She thought back through the years she had known R.T. Matthews: why had this man's life come down to these two choices?

Will went to sleep with his own diagnosis. He thought his father's recklessness and troubles stemmed from malnutrition, loneliness and brooding about his stock certificates. Any animal goes crazy if he's not fed properly. Any animal thrashes about to free itself. He supposed Dixon was rarely home to eat with him, and that his father preferred to eat alone rather than listen to Jeanette. Or, perhaps Jeanette fed him before or after she and the boys had supper.

Will was down to Spear's before the sun was up. The butcher shop was dark but he hammered on the back door: he knew Mr. Spear would be in there. "I've got a couple of hungry bums to feed," he said. "Give me a string of little pig sausages and a dozen eggs." The speckled brown eggs looked fresh from Clara's hen house. "What do you have in the way of T-bones?" Spear swung down the side of beef he was working on. "Cut me four, if you would, please—The Old Man likes them thin, about the width of your little finger there."

When he got home, he mixed flour and baking powder and salt and cut in the cube of butter with a fork. He added

288

the milk and turned the oven up. He dropped spoonfuls of the lumpy batter on Virginia's heavy cookie sheet and put the cast iron skillet on to heat.

R.T. came into the dining alcove fully-dressed. "Beautiful day," he said, winding his pocket watch. "Beautiful day." The sky was clear. The sun was aiming for the icicles. He helped Virginia put in the extra leaves and sat and watched as she set the table. She scooted Jack's highchair up next to his grandfather's chair. R.T. helped himself to three of Virginia's thin, emerald green, bone china bouillon cups. He started a little shell game on the wooden tray of the high chair. The little boy kept his eyes on the long, veiny fingers with knuckles like walnuts as they pranced around his tray. He watched his grandfather put his key chain on the tray. The boy was about to reach for it, but R.T. covered it with one cup. Then he moved it and lifted what seemed like a different cup, then moved that one and shifted them in circles. The art of the shuffle mesmerized the child. The Old Man teased Jack. "Is it here? Or…is it here?" The little boy didn't know what the game was about at first, but when he caught on, he would jab his finger at the cup he thought was covering the keys, and clap his hands if ever he was on the money. "Keep track of your safety deposit key, my boy." R.T. repeated it like a mantra. Jack mimicked, "Key! Key! Key!" and banged on the tray while Virginia squeezed the orange juice and Armitage supervised as Will browned the sausage and fried the steaks and eggs.

The morning sun on the outside snow threw Baby Jack into silhouette. Will saw his child in profile. In this stilled bit of time, Will felt the compression of future and past. Here in the unfettered joy with safety deposit box key as clanging symbol, Will could recognize a trace of jutting chin, hint of dimple. In that way the child could be said to take after this old distrustful grandfather, and the boy's hands, like The Old Man's, were long and slender. But there was his high great plains forehead—a likeness to his lawyer grandfather. The boy, like his maternal grandfather, Will thought, could take a watchful eye to the world even as he studied a piece of biscuit or as he banged any gavel. But, if he turns out like me, Will thought, I'll skin him alive. If he closes down the bars, if too many barmaids know him by name. What chance has he got? Three greedy Matthews men whittling away any inheritance. You'll only amount to anything if you take after your mother there. If you have to be like your grandfathers, make it be the men they were when they came West—beholden to no one. Find your own land. All you've got is one skinny city lot—no horse or a dog—not much more than bare branches scratching against your storm window. All you know is cement. Some tenderfoot. Well, your mother will see to it that you know her mountains, but if you're at all like me, you'll want your space more uninterrupted. Will looked away. Who says you need a piece of land? What good did it do me? Well, he countered to himself, the boy deserves a choice—let him live where he damn well pleases.

Doc Roth said: "Arteriosclerosis." Both Will's and Virginia's families had entrusted their hearts, livers and appendices to Dr. Roth over the years. There didn't seem to be any use of a big trip to the Mayo Clinic.

"Hardening of the arteries?" Will asked.

"Yes. It's a chronic condition. The arterial walls thicken. There is a loss of elasticity. The result is impaired blood circulation. It affects the brain. Common in old age."

That confirmed Dixon's verdict.

"He needs bed rest, a calm place. His system reacts violently to worry, any agitation," the doctor continued.

"That we know," Will said.

"We can give him medication to insure rest."

The choices were as Dixon had said: hospital or sanitarium. Will couldn't go with the idea of the sanitarium. He wanted to try the hospital first and see if that might work. He called Dixon: they agreed that The Old Man should go back to the ranch for at least a night and be told there that he needed to have a complete checkup and a rest in the hospital. "It will be easier to get him to accept the idea from the comfort of his home," Will said. They would have a family dinner, they agreed, to soften the night of broken glass.


Will asked Virginia to go along when he drove R.T. and Armitage home the next day. Even under the circumstances, Virginia welcomed a long drive. Will was a steady driver. Once she told him she felt he fit behind the wheel of a good car. He had not disagreed. The college girl had classes, but on short notice, Virginia's mother offered to take care of Jack. Sugar cookies, piano keys, a generous lap and sliding on the smooth staircase on Yellowstone Avenue would do Jack good, Virginia thought. The morning was overcast, right at freezing. She could see her breath. Virginia didn't mind a winter day, but hoped for sunshine for R.T.'s sake. The road was patchy. Virginia settled into the back seat with R.T., and spread the Black Watch plaid lap robe across their knees. She was happy not to be up front where she would anticipate each square of black ice. There was an awkward moment when Armitage assumed R.T. would sit up front with Will, but hesitated when it seemed awkward for Virginia to be in back with a sheepherder. R.T. sensed Armitage's unease first and insisted he sit with Virginia: "We'll let these boys chauffeur us, won't we, my dear?"

Once they were underway, Virginia realized she hadn't been to the ranch since Clara died. That had been nearly six years now. Even before Clara's death, the number of visits had diminished. Clara had been ill. There had been a woman to dress and help feed her. Jeanette oversaw this care, but while she hinted at the burden, she had developed, Virginia felt, a proprietary hold on Clara. In those early years, when Will had business with Dixon, Virginia would accompany him—partly to see Clara, and partly because going back alone put him in such poor spirits.

She wished Jeanette could see such visits as free time. Virginia coveted the time alone with Clara when they could sit in the sun-flooded round upper room. She'd read aloud clever excepts from the current serial they were following in *Colliers*.

"What a breath of fresh air," Clara would say, laughing and wiping the tears from her eyes at something funny in the story. "No one here has much time for a good story."

But it seemed to Virginia that Jeanette had time to stick her head in frequently for little reason. Once, Virginia remembered, she and Clara were drinking hot black tea and Clara had begun to reminisce about leaving Scotland. "We lived simply there. Father taught at University. But once he signed a bank note for one of his students, or a family member, I can't remember now. At any rate, the man couldn't pay. It was up to Father. After that there was no money for a large family. America sounded so promising. One by one my brothers left, then my sister and I."

Clara hadn't needed any prompting, but Virginia said, "It must have been hard on your mother."

Clara replied, "I miss her voice. We wrote letters, she sent cards and small books to Will and Dixon, but I longed to hear her call, 'Clara. Clara,' like she did. She always said it twice. If you think I roll my r's," she laughed, "you should have heard her. I have dreams of her voice." The frail woman looked at the flames in the small fireplace and said, "I've been away more than fifty years."

Virginia was hoping for more, but Jeanette had appeared at the doorway, saying, "Are you getting tired out Mother Matthews?"

There had no longer been family dinners, no phone calls to come for Sunday fried chicken picnics, only this feeling they were intruding when they came to visit. When Virginia thought about it, it had seemed to her like Dixon's house years before he and Jeanette formally moved in.

Before Clara's final illness it had become easier for Will and Virginia to see R.T. and Clara in town. They came to dinner at 42 Broadwater or they had prime rib at The Northern. After Clara's death when Dixon and Jeanette and the little boys moved into the big house, Will went to the ranch only on business. When Dixon came to town, R.T. might drive along and have lunch or dinner with them. Or with just Virginia and Jack. Will could be out of town a good two to three days a week. R.T. might catch the milk train at Worden and come in for the afternoon, and return on the CB&Q in the evening to Ballantine. However, Jeanette took Virginia up on the baby-sitting offer when she came to town on errands. Virginia was glad for Jack to know his little cousins.

The men relaxed on the ride, even though Will had the radio on. The news was filled with "the Finns" and "the Reds" and "Scandinavia may get guns from the U. S." Virginia listened half-heartedly. She was engrossed in the land.

"A temperamental winter," she said as she looked at the snow crusted over the mounds of sagebrush in one ravine, and then the land blown barren the next.

"All fits and starts," R.T. replied.

The barrow pits were filled with winter trash tossed from cars, the old cattails wind snapped. They reached the gravel road to Arrow Creek and clattered across the ice-clogged cattle guards. As they passed each ranch building and shed, the corrals and horse barn, to Virginia the ranch seemed altered. But, she couldn't pin it down. Nothing new, no shacks hauled off. The fences, weathered gates, the forked fields looked as they had these ten years. Clara would say the big house deserved a coat of paint, but otherwise it was unchanged. What was it? Well, maybe it was only February that cast a pall—the dirt-laced snow, the threat of blizzard.

But, Virginia felt the change like a draft across her shoulders as Dixon opened the front door. She had once thought nothing of using the back door, walking through the wooden lean-to affixed each winter outside the kitchen door to keep the brute cold out, wedging her coat into the huddle of slicker and sheepskin. Now, Dixon took her coat at the front door. She realized when she saw him beckon from the front porch that she had become a visitor. He asked after her mother. "And how's Jack?" None of this was unusual. The Matthews men had good manners, but his voice was formal. She felt perhaps her status as executrix had shifted the balance.

The living room felt like a lobby. The furniture was heavy and imposing. The lined velvet draperies, pulled as insulation against the cold new glass, snuffed out the daylight.

"He can't take the glare," Jeanette explained as she came into the dim room. It was as if she could feel Virginia's wanting to pull the weighted gold tassels and let in the sun.

I can't blame her, Virginia thought, for not wanting R.T. tempted, like an acrophobic drawn to the parapet, to dive into the glass again.

"I tell him he has cataracts," she continued, "he insists it's snow blindness."

Virginia was irked at Jeanette's talking about R.T. as if he were not within hearing distance.

Virginia noticed Clara's collection of china plates that rimmed the buffet was missing. All the "good things" must have been packed away. But, Virginia thought, it was more than that. She wondered if the ambiance had simply floated off with Clara.

Fanny Lochwood was there. Jeanette had asked her down to spend the day. They were doing everything they could think of to make it easy on The Old Man. Virginia sat down with Fanny and Mr. Matthews on the couch and the three held hands. Will thought R.T. pathetically jovial. Jeanette had cooked a turkey dinner. It seemed to Virginia that it took forever to get it on the table and to eat it and to clear the table. There was little conversation. No wine. No toasts. There was the silly moment when R.T. barked out, "This same meal would run you 79 cents at the Northern Grill." Jeanette didn't blanch. Afterwards Fanny fussed over Jeanette about her clear gravy, and Jeanette shrugged off the compliment and asked forgiveness that the candied yams were out of a can. Will whispered to Virginia, "The condemned man ate a hearty meal."

On the everyday silver, Virginia noticed.

Virginia took R.T.'s arm and walked upstairs with him to get him settled for his afternoon rest. He stood with his arm around her shoulder as they looked at family pictures framed in the hallway. There was Clara in her last summer. She sat on a straight-back dining room chair set for her in the orchard wearing a freshly-pressed white handkerchief linen dress, the wire-framed glasses, her thin hair brushed up and knotted. Dixon's little boys sat at her feet on the grass. Virginia wished Jack had been born in time for a picture with Clara. There was R.T.—he would have been about fifty-five, just before Will went into the army—standing proud in front of a long wagon train slung high with fat wool sacks. There was Will buttoned-up in his military school uniform, leaning at the wrought iron gate. Lilacs in bloom behind him. There were Will and Dixon, somber faced in starched shirts, short pants and wool jackets, posed by a photographer in town. Virginia could not help her tears. When one escaped down her cheek she thought that if she didn't reach up to dab it with her handkerchief, maybe her father-in-law wouldn't notice. R.T. reached over with his ironed linen handkerchief and took care of the tears himself and she had a good, quiet cry.

When Virginia came down the stairs she went to join the women on the couch. As she approached she heard Fanny say confidentially to Jeanette, "I'm so glad I didn't marry him. Just think!"

It was R.T.'s first time in a Catholic hospital. It was the only room Doc Roth could find on short notice. Will worried he might balk. It went against his Masonic leanings, but at least it diverted him somewhat from his situation. With all the attention, R.T. was cheerful and polite about everything but the wait for breakfast. He buzzed. No tray appeared. When the first pink light of morning spread beyond the sandstone bluffs along the Yellowstone River, but no food, he turned to flattery and flirtation.

"Which of you fine and all-knowing women," he addressed the nuns, "will bring an old man breakfast in a timely fashion, as God intended?"

They giggled, but did not answer. When that did not work he cursed and buzzed his buzzer relentlessly. He expected his breakfast first thing. What kind of place would starve a man until midmorning, he asked each doctor or nurse or aid or janitorial worker who came past the room.

When Will came on the fourth day he asked his father if there was anything he could do. R.T. said, "Bring me a couple of your coyote firecrackers and I'll see if that hurries up these black habits." But, by the time the cereal, steamed to a light paste, came by dumb waiter from the basement kitchen to the tin tray at his bedside, The Old Man turned away and pretended to doze.

"Get me a room at The Northern," he ordered Will on the fifth day.

Will explained his father's routine to the Sisters of Charity, but there could be no exceptions. Eventually, they had no choice, the nuns explained, but to unplug his buzzer.

"They're starving him," he told Virginia.

Will worried about the food. He worried about the medication. He'd go on his late night walks and, although it wasn't visiting hours, he'd take the back stairs and look in. His father was "out." Even in the day time The Old Man was "out." They used hypos on him to keep him calm, to keep him in bed. R.T. looked unconscious for the better part of the day. Will realized that he couldn't handle his father at home, but it didn't seem as if the hospital's way was any solution.

That night, Will told Virginia what it felt like when the nurses repeated his father's words: "Send for Will. He'll get me out of this damned trap."

It was early. The hospital was quiet. Will took the back stairway two steps at a time. As he walked down the marble

298

floored corridor, he saw his father had a visitor. At first he thought the straight, dark shape was a priest. Had The Old Man died? God forbid, last rites! But, as he walked into the room he saw his father seemed peaceful, not drugged, not dead. The Old Man looked out toward the ranch. The sun cast a warm rosy pink to the eastern sky along the sandstone Rimrocks and the Pryors. The visitor was Charlie Graylight. The old Crow sat like a petrified stump in the metal frame chair next to his father's bedside table. Graylight was dressed as always. Thin braids tapered to fine points like moistened paint brushes, his same domed black felt hat was planted square on his head. His dark red Pendleton blanket was wrapped about him.

The two old men were silent. R.T. looked like a blue heron, pencil thin, great wings folded under overlapping sheets. He was surrounded by a bunker of pillows, pillows under his knees, pillows rolled thin behind his straight neck. He looked like he might disappear into the whiteness the nuns unfurled at every eight-hour shift. He seemed as peaceful as Will had seen him in months.

"Good morning, Boss."

His father's blue eyes were bright.

"Good morning, Graylight," Will addressed the old friend. There was no mention of their meeting earlier that month with Nellie Pretty Feathers.

"Marjorie's sister's Betsy is having a baby. We saw you bring in Mr. Matthews. Our room is not big. Mr. Matthews while he waits out his breakfast might like company."

R.T. nodded.

What would it be like if he and Dixon and Jeanette and Virginia and their children followed the traditions of the Crow, moved in to sleep and eat and smoke and talk and chant with R.T. in his small hospital room? Will imagined Jeanette's chenille and Virginia's long stemmed quilt and bedrolls unrolled by himself and Dixon and all that accompanied the baby on a night away from home.

Will set down the cinnamon rolls Virginia had made on the bedside table. They were tearoom size, sweet and yeasty and still warm. "You boys split these with the nuns," he said. He was about to leave when his father spoke.

"Mr. Graylight here's been smoking his pipe—tells me you've turned into some goddamn saint." He had a twinkle in his blue eyes and looked pleased at having something new to say. "Sounds like you've tacked a piece of Dixon's hide to the barn."

"It sounds like Graylight's telling tales," Will said offhandedly. To himself he said, Graylight's the man who finds water in deserts. "Well, Boss," he said and rested his big hand on his father's bony shoulder, "I've got to catch Meldrum before the devil goes to lunch."

"Tell Virginia she makes the best rolls," R.T. said as he unwound a corner of the rolls. Will left. After he took a bite, and a swallow of milk, he called out after Will who was then down the hall and out of ear shot, "The smartest thing you ever did, Bud, was to marry that woman and move off that godforsaken place."

At week's end, Dr. Roth said that Mr. Matthews was going fast. He could not say when. He told Virginia he was amazed at the change. "The man's not eating," he said. "His blood count is deteriorating. He could get pneumonia." When R.T. came in the Sunday before, Dr. Roth had been skeptical that Mr. Matthews could be as weak as Dixon and Jeanette had said.

Then, two days after Betsy Graylight went home to the reservation with more than her share of grandmothers and grandfathers and cousins and nieces and aunts and half brothers and half sisters and with her newborn papoose bound firmly to her, R.T. shut his eyes and his heart followed suit.

Will came in shortly after his father had died. The nurses had just sent for the doctor. They left Will alone in the room. He picked up his father's wrist and felt for a pulse: it was a reaction he had not had since the war, where it was his job to be sure the dead were dead. In his nightmares he could never reach them. At times, he was one of them. He stood at the side of the bed, his father's rigid wrist between his thumb and forefingers. He looked at The Old Man in profile. He felt he could stand there forever. Will had seen his father set his face to stone before and still seethe with life. But now, that bearing was gone.

Will had little remorse about not reaching the hospital at daybreak. He didn't yearn to have witnessed The Old Man gasp, shudder, cry out, close his eyes, stop breathing. He believed a man accustomed to the solitude of the land, its great spaces, its relentless winds and stillnesses died well if he died alone. It was something a man did best if he did it on his own. Will was grateful that neither one brother nor the other could claim witness to their father's death.

"Well, Boss," Will said, "looks like you got yourself out of here."

Will stopped at the nurses' station and put in the call to Dixon. He left his car at the curb of the hospital and walked the long way home.

He could see his breath. There was deep new snow in the park. He broke a big leafless branch from the willows at the banks of the drained irrigation ditch, and as he walked, he stripped its bark. It felt like marble against his fingers. Like a schoolboy, he poked it at the ice lace edges, stabbed it at the frozen bank until the end frayed. It's going to take the gravediggers a few sticks of dynamite, Will thought to himself. God, The Old Man loved dynamite. He had used it to blow up whole hills to build the spring reservoir. He'd blasted roads through the place. He'd dynamited cottonwood stumps out of his way. At the unshoveled driveway of 42 Broadwater, Will pitched the willow walking stick into the brittle winter lilac bush.

32421116R10186